Kite Strings

Andaleeb Wajid

Cedar books

Published by:

Cedar books

An Imprint of
Pustak Mahal®, Delhi

J-3/16, Daryaganj, New Delhi-110002
☎ 23276539, 23272783, 23272784 • *Fax:* 011-23260518
E-mail: info@pustakmahal.com • *Website:* www.pustakmahal.com

Sales Centre

- 10-B, Netaji Subhash Marg, Daryaganj, New Delhi-110002
  ☎ 23268292, 23268293, 23279900 • *Fax:* 011-23280567
  E-mail: rapidexdelhi@indiatimes.com
- Hind Pustak Bhawan
  6686, Khari Baoli, Delhi-110006
  ☎ 23944314, 23911979

Branch Offices

Bengaluru: ☎ 22234025 • *Telefax:* 22240209
E-mail: pustak@airtelmail.in • pustak@sancharnet.in
Mumbai: ☎ 22010941
E-mail: rapidex@bom5.vsnl.net.in
Patna: ☎ 3294193 • *Telefax:* 0612-2302719
E-mail: rapidexptn@rediffmail.com
Hyderabad: *Telefax:* 040-24737290
E-mail: pustakmahalhyd@yahoo.co.in

ISBN 978-81-223-1083-2

Edition 2009

Printed at : Param Offsetters, Okhla, New Delhi-110020

Dedication

For Abbu, my father, and Amma, my maternal grandmother.

Both of you believed I was special and both of you were the original storytellers of our family.

Acknowledgements

My friends and family have stood by me, believing in my work and my capability and there is no better moment than this to thank them.

My husband Mansoor for his unflinching support, my brother Junaid for being my first critic, Ammi who has been an inspiration to me in so many ways, Ayesha, for listening to all my rants and having faith in me, Kavita, for all the nuggets of wisdom and words of encouragement, my mother-in-law, for all her love and support, and all my friends, who have offered priceless advice and criticism, and my sisters Sidra and Shazu for believing in me. Sowmya, Nusrat, Bijita, Lubna, Christina, Anamika, and all the others who read the book and liked it, thank you once again, and Nusrat, the cover you designed is amazing!

I also want to thank Neha Gupta from Cedar Books for her sheer persistence and belief, as well as all those who have been involved in bringing out this book. Thank you!

Above all, I thank Allah for making this possible and making my dream come true.

Contents

Introduction *** 7

Part 1

Flying High *** 11
Ripples *** 18
The Wait *** 23
Fat in the Fire *** 26
Window to the World *** 29
Questions *** 34
Return of the Chappal *** 37
The Split *** 44

Part 2

Moving on *** 53
Bollywood Masala *** 58
Death *** 63
Zohra Phuppu *** 67
Itch in the Palm *** 73
With or Without Aasia *** 77
Bridging the Worlds *** 81
Ants, Lizards and Mateen *** 85
An Unspoken Agreement *** 88
Chehlum *** 94
Terrace Rendezvous *** 100
First Step Backwards *** 104

Hospital Reunion *** 106
Rewind, rewind *** 110
Friends again? *** 116
Withering Dahlias *** 122
Winning and Losing *** 127
Fated *** 133
Keyed up *** 141
Missing Love *** 145
Painful but True *** 150
Mehendi *** 155
Ahead *** 163

Part 3

Old Houses *** 169
Clues *** 176
Zulekha *** 182
Hopes, Dreams and Reality *** 187
Imtiaz *** 193
Unmade Decisions *** 202
Revelations *** 207
Finally, the Proposal *** 213
Sisters *** 220
Truth *** 227
Beauty and Sorrow *** 232
Mateen *** 238

Part 4

Voices *** 247
School of Horrors *** 251
Coffee House Meeting *** 257
Mrs Dahlia *** 264
Crime and Punishment *** 271
Phone Calls *** 280
Once More, the Terrace *** 289

Introduction

Imagine if your only job in this world was to sit down at a desk, linger over its scratched surface, think, meditate and then just write. Write all day, all week, all month, all year. When I dreamed of being a writer, that was what I thought it would be like. Me writing away endlessly! But reality was far different. Not altogether unpleasant, but not what I expected also. So between juggling with my roles as a wife, and being a mother to a six-year-old, who incidentally is now all of ten years, I managed to finish writing *Kite Strings* in 2005. Since then, it's been an uphill task, but also a learning process, trying to get it published.

Kite Strings is a simple story of a young girl, Mehnaz, growing up and finding her feet in the world. She has a simple desire to be able to do something special, to be someone other than the roles society has defined for her, to be something on her own. Finding one's identity in life, particularly direction, is a universal theme that overrides culture, religion and language and this is what *Kite Strings* tries to portray.

As I wrote *Kite Strings,* I realised that there's quite a bit of me in Mehnaz. Her personality and attitudes seemed to stem from what I felt about life too, though everything else is fiction. Yes, I have been inspired by a few real life events, such as the feud between Mehnaz's father and her uncle.

Such things were common in my home and I think it holds good for all households across the country. Where there are siblings, fights are bound to take place. Some to the extent more than what can possibly be imagined!

As *Kite Strings* is told from the perspective of a young girl, who as I must remind my readers, is bound by a few conventions of her orthodox family, her experiences may seem limited. Nevertheless, it is the only life that she knows and all she wishes is to make it bigger and better.

– Author

Part I

1

Flying High

If I had known that after today, the three of us would never play again, I still wouldn't have been able to do anything. We were on the terrace flying kites and a warm wind buffeted them wildly. Puffs of breeze blowing about quickly only served to undo hair that our mothers had pulled back tightly and held in place with clips. Rehana and I were mere spectators watching Basheer shake and tug at the thread, his head held against the cobalt blue sky, eyes squinted.

I remembered feeling the gritty *manjha* in my hand, the crisp, papery kite with a weight of its own in the sky, the wind crackling the kite, and then the lightness in my hand as I watched the green kite slip away from my hand as another one captured it. After that, Basheer politely refused to let us fly his kites.

The terrace of our house looked out over Vellore and we could see really far, right into the imposing mountains in the distance. Other flat terraces were dotted with children flying kites like Basheer; some were just watching.

Across the terraces, no one spoke. Concentration from the kites wavered for only a little while, before it slid back to the sky with determination. However, for Rehana and I, watching Basheer fly a kite was like watching TV. We continued talking to each other, and would even encourage him enthusiastically. Once, he threw away the spindle and glared at us before walking away because our constant chatter had distracted him. We tried to be silent, but often forgot and it was understood between the two of us that Basheer probably flew kites better when he was alone.

Basheer was a silent boy, around my age but a little younger than me. He was often shy and he stuttered when he spoke to us. But most often he was seen staring at the sky, his brow bunched together in numerous lines, his eyes turning inward into slits as they followed the kites bobbing around the sky.

I once asked him what the big deal was in flying a kite.

"I mean, you just make sure it rises in the air and then you try to make it fly high. What's the point in that?"

He looked at me and curled his lips in a sneer and said, "What would you know, Api?" It was one of the few times he had spoken to me disrespectfully. He was the only one to ever call me Api because Rehana always called me by my name and Mateen, my three-year-old brother had tried calling me that but ended up calling me 'Pee'.

I pestered Basheer to explain what he meant. He shrugged his shoulders in a jerky movement and stumbled over the words. "You have to... you've got to feel the power of putting a kite in the sky and, and... letting it fly without letting it go out of your control."

The logic seemed a bit warped to me. "You want to let it fly, and you still want to hold it in your hands?" He turned away from me, a little irritated and proceeded to ignore me for the rest of the evening.

I looked up and saw his sky blue kite duel with a maroon one. I plucked Rehana's sleeve and we both tried to follow what was happening. The maroon kite was wildly circling ours.

"Yes, Basheer, go on, cut out his kite!"

Basheer ignored us and with deft flicks of his wrist, he moved his kite up and down. My eyes tried to follow the string trying to see which house it led to, but each time I tried to pin it down, it seemed to belong somewhere else. Basheer's fingers had a crisscross pattern of cuts, some of which had dried and some of which bled afresh from the *manjha* on the string. Sweat ran down in a thin stream at his temples as he concentrated on saving his kite. He was desperately trying to manoeuvre it away from that horrid maroon one.

It was over in two minutes. Basheer stamped his foot and flung away the spindle and walked away angrily. Our blue kite danced a bit in the air, and then flipped and fell away from our sight. A whoop followed it. On the same line of houses as ours, a young boy was jumping and waving wildly on his terrace. He must have been fifteen at least.

He was clapping and hooting and my face felt warm and without really thinking of why I was doing it, I slid my foot from my rubber *chappal*, picked it up and flung it hard in his direction. The slipper fell on his terrace and Rehana shook my arm and whispered, "Are you mad?" The boy laughed again. Feeling a strong surge of irritation, I pulled out my other slipper and this time, with a short prayer I swung my arm right behind me and flung it forward. The slipper hit the boy's shoulder and he flinched.

We laughed at him but stopped when we saw him bend down to remove one of his slippers. Rehana and I ran to the door that led to the terrace, and we barely got it open when we heard a thud! Rehana giggled. Another thud and both of us burst out laughing. Dark streaks were spreading across the sky, gently bringing in dusk. It was time to head downstairs, anyway.

I could even hear Ammi calling out for me. Her voice coming from downstairs seemed to emanate from another world and although I detested to leave this one and go down, I suddenly realised that I didn't have any slippers. How was I going to explain that?

Rehana ran across the terrace once more, and was back before I could even guess what she was doing. She held out two well-used slippers. The sole was flat like a *chapati* and it was almost the same colour as my own *chappals*. It would have to do.

I slipped my feet into them. They felt grainy, as though they had been sprinkled with wet sand. Watching my mouth curl in distaste, Rehana glared at me. "Just wear them Mehnaz! You'll be lucky if Taima doesn't notice the difference."

The sole of my *chappals* slapped against the stairs. It was two sizes big. We walked down the darkened stairway, holding each other's hands for comfort, and when we finally reached down, Rehana and I ran to the bathroom to wash our faces and hands. Could guilt show itself on our faces? Would I be able to wash it out, I thought, as I rubbed my face vigorously with the Hamam soap that was kept on the soap dish.

Surprisingly, Ammi had not been curious about where I had been all evening. For once, I didn't hear the litany that I dreaded so much, *"Kahan thi... Kidhar thi... Kya kar rahee thi..."*

The kitchen smelled gloriously of *biryani*. If all the family members assembled in Vellore at the same time, Ammi always cooked *biryani* on one day, at least. Chachi of course could cook quite well too. But *biryani* making was like a race full of obstacles. Obstacles that Ammi cleared with utmost ease. (I had often imagined her saree-clad, holding a huge ladle, jumping over the large barricades.) Of course, Asifa Chachi was so petite and demure that the obstacles just collapsed all over her.

In the hot kitchen, Asifa Chachi stood next to Ammi, trying not to look like an eager pupil when Rehana walked into the kitchen, declaring that she loved my mother's *biryani*. Chachi smiled but I could see the strain as she fought to keep it pasted on her face.

"What's for dessert? Chachi, why don't you make some of that chocolate pudding?" I asked with as much enthusiasm as I could muster. She beamed. "Oh! There's no cocoa powder here," she said, "but when we return to Bangalore, I'll definitely make some for you!" I nodded, thankful that Ammi didn't remind me that it was she who had given Chachi the recipe for the pudding.

Basheer's mother, Zohra Phuppu hardly spoke. At eight o'clock, when Sadiq Chacha asked her where Basheer was, she said that she didn't know and shook her head despondently. When Basheer came back, Abbu and Chacha both questioned him. "*Kyon, mian,* where were you?" Abbu asked officiously.

Basheer stood there with his head down and didn't answer. Abbu's face started turning red, a sure indication of his rising anger. I didn't want Basheer to face Abbu's ire especially on the day he had lost a kite.

"Abbu," I interrupted, "I had sent Basheer to the market to get... to get some things for me," I said, laughing a little nervously.

"Go have your dinner. And if I hear from your mother that you came home late again, I'll skin you." Abbu said to Basheer sharply. Basheer turned around and ran away. Maybe he was going to cry. Abbu was the same man who doted on me, and yet he could inspire such terror in another. It was not a comforting thought.

****

Sometimes Ammi and Chachi took Phuppu with them to Gandhi Road and forced her to buy new clothes. But Phuppu preferred her frayed sarees and Ammi and Chachi stopped taking her along. They would venture out instead to get their blouses stitched, or to see if any new jewellery designs had arrived in the shops.

Abbu and Chacha always brought clothes for Phuppu and Basheer from Bangalore each time. Once, Abbu got really angry when we arrived in Vellore and found Phuppu wearing a faded saree. Ever since then, Phuppu wore the clothes her brothers brought for her, but probably only till we stayed in Vellore. After we returned, I was sure that she wore her old clothes again. Maybe they comforted her, made her believe that everything would be like how it had been, when those very clothes were new.

Rehana and I slept next to her. She had changed drastically since her husband went away. We were not supposed to talk about it, or mention the subject in front of her but we did wonder at times.

I looked at her huddled form. When life was going almost perfect for one person, why was it all wrong for another? My happiness at coming to Vellore dissipated a little each time I saw Zohra Phuppu's sad eyes.

Her mother-in-law was a strange woman. She hurled insults at Phuppu but was also very ingratiating whenever she saw Abbu. Abbu disliked Ammabi (we had to call her that, including Basheer, because the old woman disliked being called Dadi), and tried to ignore her.

In Abbu's absence, Ammabi bossed us a lot. I often answered her back. Ammi never scolded me right away, but after a pause, she would remind me about my manners.

Phuppu got married when I was just four or five years old. But a year later when she gave birth to Basheer, her husband just left them and went away.

Abbu and Chacha were angry and tried to convince her to come to Bangalore but she refused adamantly. She also insisted on taking care of her foul-mouthed mother-in-law. Abbu fixed up the house that he had grown up in, and he settled Phuppu, Basheer, and Ammabi there.

I loved coming here, because this house was 'Vellore' for me. This was where I found life to be an interminable string of events, where there was no homework, and all I did was to play with Rehana. But all this was marred for ever because of Ammabi's presence. The old woman taunted and ridiculed Phuppu, rocking her body slowly, her breath emitting nauseous fumes of snuff and sometimes *Pan Parag*.

"Rehaan," I whispered. She shifted sleepily and squinted. The zero-watt bulb glowed dully, and I could barely distinguish Rehana's outline as she turned towards me.

"What?" she whispered.

"Do you think that boy would have found my *chappals*?"

She half sat up, leaning on her elbows. "Why?" she asked.

"I was just wondering whether his mother would get upset with him when she finds out he's lost his *chappals*."

"Isn't it too late to think about that now?" she whispered, and slapped my arm.

"Ouch! Okay, whatever," I mumbled and shut my eyes.

2

Ripples

I was happy when Aasia first came to our house because I thought she would be my companion and playmate. Then I learnt that she was there to take care of Mateen.

"I need someone to help me out," Ammi said and the subject was closed. An old acquaintance, whom I called Khala whenever I met her, had brought Aasia with her to Bangalore one day. Khala's burka looked faded, and each time she came home, the black colour seemed to have seeped out a little more from the fabric.

Ammi brought tea in an old brown tea cup, which confirmed Khala's social status and as Khala sat on the sofa, her back slightly hunched as she sipped the tea. Aasia sat down on the carpet near her leg and looked around awed.

I tried to see my house through her eyes. The huge ceiling, the big chandelier that rocked gently, the lovely ivory walls, unblemished and clean; it was almost frightening. I felt a little bit of kindness towards her at first, but then I realised this would be her home too.

Aasia – thin, dark, with two oily braids tied right till the curved end with a pink and green ribbon – fascinated and repelled me. She was older than me, but I called her Aasia and she called me Apa. She came from a small town called Dharmapuri in Tamil Nadu. Before Khala left, she turned to Aasia and said, "Now be a good girl. These people will take good care of you. I'll write to your mother and tell her that you have reached safely."

Aasia nodded quietly, her eyes wide and glistening and I wondered how she felt about leaving her mother and coming all the way to Bangalore.

Aasia was quiet and kept out of the way of both my parents. But she loved Mateen like her own baby brother. Each day before I went to school, I would watch her playing with him. She could play the whole day if she liked while I struggled with Maths and Geography; but one day, I saw her in the backyard, scrubbing clothes. One by one, she shook the bright coloured clothes and hung them out on a thick nylon rope, which was fixed to a pole.

One day Ammi was making breakfast and Mateen woke up, so Aasia ran to the room to amuse him. I followed her and when I saw her bend towards the little cot, something fierce surged in me and I pulled Mateen out of her arms.

"He's crying, Apa, and I have to look after him," she protested mildly.

I held Mateen's soft body in my arms and swung him forwards and backwards, a game that made him giggle endlessly. But now he just squirmed in my arms and stretched his arms out towards Aasia and said, "Aashhi!"

I pushed him into her arms. Mateen stopped wriggling and grinned, showing his pink gums and his white baby teeth and although I wanted to remain angry with him, I couldn't.

At breakfast I noticed that Abbu looked pensive, as he spoke to Ammi about something.

"I've told him what I feel about going into business with that man. I just hope he'll listen to me when he comes here this morning."

Ammi nodded and called out to Aasia.

"Fill the jug with water."

Ever since Aasia had arrived, Ammi had stopped asking my help for anything. She never asked me to set the table, or to fill water in the ice-trays. I got up before Aasia could come and was back with the filled jug watching Ammi as she looked at me surprised.

"Doesn't he know what a cheat that man is? Sadiq himself was telling me the other day about how he tricked Raeez *bhai* out of the partnership. And he wants to start a business with that man? Just because he is his wife's brother?" Abbu's deep voice cut into my thoughts and I wondered why Abbu disliked Rehana's Mamu, Afzal so much? I couldn't believe that he could be a cheat and whatever else Abbu liked to call him. He seemed such a nice man because whenever we visited Rehana's house, he would rush out and bring us big Cadbury bars, not the small ones that Ammi always bought for me. Rehana and I would have a competition to see who would eat slowest and naturally I always lost.

Afzal Mamu also taught us plenty of new card games and tricks, and I displayed my newly acquired skills one Sunday afternoon when Abbu and Ammi were looking bored. But with a sense of growing discomfort, I realised that Abbu's eyes had become small and his face, red and feeling as if I had got onto a hurtling train that was destined to crash somewhere, I continued. When I finally picked out the correct card and showed it to them hesitantly, Abbu leaned forward and took it out of my hands.

"Who taught this to you?" he asked quietly. My mouth was dry as I replied, "Afzal Mamu." He leaned back and turned to look at Ammi who looked embarrassed. "You know how I feel about that man. What were you doing when she was learning cheap tricks from him?" he roared. The cards that I was arranging slipped and scattered near his feet. Ammi had tears in her eyes but she looked at me and they flashed with anger. "Go to your room and do your homework!"

Later, in my room, I heard the sound of Chacha's Fiat stopping near our house. I pushed open the window to see if Rehana had come with Chacha. The compound wall of our house blocked much of my view of our street, but still I could see the top of his car. The white Fiat stood solidly at the pavement. I heard only one door shut which meant no Rehana.

I got engrossed in a book that I had borrowed from the school library. When I shut it finally, I saw that it was nearly lunchtime and I didn't feel like having lunch, but Ammi would never hear of it! I often wondered how long Ammi was going to control how much I ate, and what I ate.

If I didn't want to eat rice for lunch, Ammi wouldn't let me make a simple sandwich. I was still eating food, wasn't I? According to her, we simply had to follow her cardinal rules about rice for lunch and *rotis* for dinner. Why couldn't it at least be the other way around?

When I went out for lunch that day, the house seemed unnaturally quiet, fully and forcefully bringing out the feeling that I inhabited a separate world and visited this one occasionally. In the living room, everyone sat silently and only Mateen played with his toy cars noisily.

Abbu got up wearily and Ammi followed him, looking worried. "I'm not having lunch today," Abbu said and went to his room. Ammi was quiet. Did that mean I had to be as old as Abbu for Ammi to stop telling me about having lunch and dinner and breakfast?

Why hadn't Chacha stayed back for lunch? After lunch, I checked in on Abbu. He was sitting up, with his head thrown back on the pillow. His eyes were closed. I went and sat near him. Sometimes just this much was enough. He made me feel so safe, but a happy-sad feeling also tingled through me.

He opened his eyes and saw me. Smiling a little, he reached out behind him and handed me a small flat bottle of liquid balm. I opened it and tipped the bottle against my fingers to coat them with the cool liquid. Then I rubbed my fingers on his forehead and he shut his eyes.

There was a line in the middle of his forehead. It was like a crease, like his skin had been folded there. I wondered if I could straighten it out. Maybe I should use more of the liquid. With harder pressure on his forehead, Abbu screwed his eyes and winced. “What are you trying to do?” he asked. He would laugh if I told him. “Trying to get rid of your headache,” I said. He smiled. “Why didn’t Sadiq Chacha stay back for lunch?” I asked suddenly. The smile went away.

Maybe I should have realised that this was probably the beginning of something big and unpleasant, but it didn’t occur to me. I was only thirteen.

3

The Wait

I often don't admit to myself that I'm a mediocre. Admitting it would make it seem ominous and true. In school I was an average student, one who had to struggle that little bit extra to get things right. I did make the effort, but sometimes out of sheer laziness, I didn't bother.

Report-card time made me extremely anxious. I didn't know my own capability and it was a torture to see Ammi, *burka*-clad, standing at the teacher's desk, listening to the comments quietly. When Ammi walked back, I looked at her face eagerly for any sign. She raised her eyebrows at me and gestured me to come out of the classroom.

"Did... did I pass?" I asked her, my chest tight with worry. "Of course, you did. What did you expect?" she asked surprised. "But your teacher says that you need to improve and work harder."

I had passed! I was in the eighth standard! I felt quite grown up and important now. At home, I quickly dialled the number of Abbu's shop and smiled to myself when I heard him pick up. "Abbu! I passed!" I glowed when I heard his praise. After all, he was one of the biggest reasons I actually made an effort to study during the final exams.

Abbu gave a lot of importance to education. He was not formally educated and he knew very little English. Ammi had been educated in an Urdu school and she shied from conversing in English. Abbu wanted me to excel in studies and most importantly in English. When he wasn't tired, he would make me read out some sections from the newspaper. Earlier, I would stumble through the words and sentences. But now, whenever I looked up from the paper, I would see a smile on his face and his eyes would shine.

Mateen had woken up from his nap. He tugged at Aasia to carry him ignoring my efforts to pick him up. How could he like Aasia more than me? I was his Api.

When she had first come, she had looked at all my books and had asked me shyly if I could teach her to read and write. Of course, I replied importantly. In the evenings, she would sit patiently with a notebook that she had managed to acquire from somewhere, and a small pencil stub. Each time I emerged from my room, she would look at me expectantly. I kept putting it off for later.

"I'll start as soon as I finish my homework."

"We'll get started as soon as this cartoon gets over."

"I'm playing with Mateen now, later."

Later. The word was so large. So much promise, so much hope. None of it fulfilled. Later. I never got around to later. One rainy Saturday, when I was sitting in the kitchen helping Ammi by picking out stones from the rice, I saw the notebook. Aasia was with Mateen, lulling him to sleep. I flipped open a page, and stared. The pages were covered with exquisite *mehendi* designs.

Long, intense, flowing lines, lovingly ran across the length of the palm that she had drawn in first. Arches, curves, and paisley shapes filled the palm in different but captivating ways. "What's that?" Ammi asked as she started beating an egg vigorously with a fork for Mateen's omelette. I blinked.

"Ammi?" I asked. She was now chopping tomatoes for the chicken curry. "Why do we need Aasia?"

Ammi whirled around. "What have you got against the poor girl? What has she ever done to you?" she asked, frowning at me. I looked away.

"Mateen likes her more than he likes me, and I'm his sister, not she!"

Ammi smiled. "Aasia helps around a lot in the house," she said. "She takes care of Mateen when I have to cook. You're not at home all day to help me out. And anyway, we'll get her married one day, so she will be going. You, however, are the daughter of this house."

I knew I should have felt happy on hearing this. But a small doubt crept in anyway. "So she's going to stay here till she gets married?" I asked. That wouldn't be for a long time.

Ammi didn't reply. I think she had already tuned me out. She had switched on the mixer to puree the tomatoes, and the loud whirr of the machine drowned out my question. Ammi had sent Aasia out to buy something from a shop. Ammi usually ordered everything once in a month from the nearby provision store. But when she ran out of things now and then, she sent Aasia to get them, though she didn't like to. She insisted that Aasia wear Ammi's old *burka* and go, although I was quite sure I couldn't find anyone more modest than her. Definitely she was more modest than me.

I had got my first period last year. After that everything changed at home. First was this *dupatta*. This awful *dupatta* that trailed everywhere with me! Ammi insisted I had to wear it all the time. Not like before, when I wore it if we went out somewhere. The *dupatta* was for covering my chest, and I thought Ammi should be grateful that I wore it at home. But her insistence that I cover my shoulders and my head suffocated me. I was still getting used to it while Aasia looked like she had been born with it covering her head and her arms and her back, so modestly. I realised Ammi was probably happy that at least one of us was listening to her, though I had no doubt that Aasia would drape herself even if she was not instructed by Ammi.

From the kitchen window I could see Aasia walking home slowly, head bent and fist around a small plastic bag.

❖❖❖

4

Fat in the Fire

Fouzia Phuppu was a contradiction. Her sweet, fair face looked young and her skin was smooth. But she was not angelic. She was my father's other sister, but she differed so much in looks and temperament that I often wondered how she came to be related to us so closely. She was not very tall, but she was very, very fat. She always wore *salwar kameez*. I had never seen her dressed in a saree like Ammi or Asifa Chachi so we could never really see the rolls of fat that slithered around her belly.

When Rehana and I were small, we thought that Fouzia Phuppu would become thin if we pushed a pin into her. Once, in Vellore, she was taking a nap after lunch, sprawled on the *divan* in the hall. Rehana and I crept up to her slowly, safety pin in hand. With lips pursed tightly, I remember pushing the needle into the thick fabric of her *kurta* and standing back in case she exploded. She chose to wake up that moment.

Rehana and I quickly ran away disappointed. But the pin hadn't reached her skin and it hung limply from her *kurta*. Phuppu shut her eyes again and turned over, and let out a yowl. The pin had gone in! Phuppu braced her palms on the small *divan* and got up. The *divan* creaked. She fumbled about in the front of her *kurta* and yanked out a safety pin. She looked at it puzzled. We had made the mistake of hanging around to see what would happen and she looked at us, her eyes narrowed.

"Shaitan bachche!" she thundered. Her face was red as she lunged forward to get out of the *divan* but it collapsed, and she fell with it. Instead of trying to help her, we ran away from the spot.

We didn't want those fat fingers twisting our ears tightly! I have a feeling that she still holds that grudge against me.

Waiting for Phuppu's weekly visit was an endurance test. She lived in Bangalore, in a small house above a hardware shop, in the squelchy City Market area. Every other Saturday morning she and her daughter Farha visited us. Breakfast would barely be over and she would be standing at the door, finger fused with the doorbell, until someone opened the door.

Farha was about my age, but there was nothing about her that I liked much. I could never team up with her, like I did with Rehana. Farha hardly ever left my room once she entered. She would sit at my desk and look through the drawers, perusing my books with interest although she had never even heard of Agatha Christie. I hated entertaining her, so sometimes before she could invite herself to my room, I left her with Aasia and disappeared to my room with a book.

Phuppu loved to sit at the dining table and look at the remains of our breakfast with great interest. "Oh, you made *keema paratha* today. Is there any left? Farha, come have some of this *paratha* that your Mami has made." I would look at my mother's expressionless face as she delayed her lunch preparations and made some more breakfast for these two.

Abbu thought her husband to be a wastrel and a freeloader. I felt quite bad for her whenever Abbu sat with Phuppu, asking her about the errant ways of her husband. She would sit on the sofa, twisting the edge of her *dupatta* miserably, answering Abbu in quiet whispers.

But it was when she sat cross-legged on the kitchen floor on a mat, pretending to be doing something useful for Ammi like peeling garlic or cleaning the wheat that her true colours emerged as she indulged in her favourite pastime. "Last week Asifa made such horrible *dal*. I really think you should teach her how to cook. Poor Sadiq has lost so much weight because of her cooking."

Ammi continued with her work, pretending not to hear because if she even made a simple comment, Phuppu would surely add a lot of *mirch* and *masala* to it and tell the embellished version to Asifa Chachi with a lot of relish. Phuppu had done it many times before, creating a rift between my mother and Rehana's, which had been resolved only when Ammi and Chachi had got the facts straight.

After lunch, Phuppu took a nap in my room. Every now and then, I popped in to see if she was awake. But she and Farha would be sleeping, stretched out inelegantly on my bed. They would get up at five in the evening and then she and Farha liked to make a huge mess of my bathroom as they washed up and made *wuzu* for *Asr namaz*. I had a feeling Farha simply liked to spray water from the faucet all over my mirror and walls. How else could the whole bathroom be so wet after she left?

After reading *namaz* in my room, Phuppu would sit down to comb her hair. Each Saturday, I thought of hiding my personal things away from my dresser so she wouldn't use it, but every time I forgot. I knew that Ammi wouldn't like me to be rude to her, so I watched her use my hair brush on her hair as well as on Farha's with distaste. That hair brush often went into scalding hot water after they left.

She would leave the house reluctantly at seven. Ammi and I would watch her leave, pushing aside the curtains from the hall, and without consciously realising it, we both would let out a huge sigh. Finally, now our house was our own.

5

Window to the World

My first term exams started in a month and my class teacher had called Ammi to express her dismay that I still hadn't mastered basic algebra while the rest of the class had moved on to quadratic equations. Ammi nodded silently while Ms Lobo showed her my class workbook, explaining rapidly to her that I badly needed help. She kept pressing the book in Ammi's hands until she took it. Ammi grimaced when she saw the number of red marks with which Ms Lobo had graced the pages.

On the way back, she looked thoughtful. I wished Ms Lobo hadn't admonished me in front of her. After consulting Abbu, she announced that they were going to send me to tuition classes to improve my Maths. Oh no! I hated the very thought of going and sitting in someone's house, with hordes of other children.

Three years ago I had taken tuitions for Kannada at Ms Nalini's house. Ms Nalini was a nightie wearing middle-aged lady who took tuitions in her house for every subject and for all classes. Naturally, I found myself sitting with gangly ninth standard boys who liked to pull the braids of the girls and snigger at them, and giggly seventh and eighth standard girls who sweated badly. Not to forget the little ones right from first standard who had been sent to tuitions by their enthusiastic mothers. I was not going through that again.

Ammi was adamant. I had to go, she said, and she had found me a teacher already. This woman lived down the road, and I had to go to her at four-thirty each day. She would teach me

Maths until six. I wondered if Abbu would listen to me. He seemed preoccupied with an account book and looked up confused, when I spoke.

"Abbu, I don't want to go for these tuitions. I promise I'll study harder on my own," I said fervently. He shook his head. "I'm sorry, *beta,* but you have to listen to your mother. She knows what she's doing," he said and his eyes fell back to his book of accounts.

I had to leave for school in fifteen minutes and there seemed to be no way to convince Abbu any longer. Abbu punched a few numbers on the calculator and checked the entry in the account book. Frowning, he reached for the telephone by his bedside.

Ammi was calling me for breakfast and when I left the room, I heard him speak to Sadiq Chacha on the phone. The tone of his voice was harsh and I wished I could stay back to listen to their conversation properly.

That evening, Ammi accompanied me to the tuition teacher's house. From the next day, I would go there on my own. Ammi wore her *burka,* wrapped up Mateen's ears in a heavy woollen scarf although it was only early August, and carefully locked the house. Aasia hovered nearby ready to take Mateen in her arms.

Rose Lane was rather narrow and there were hardly any cars there. It was quite safe to play outside but Ammi hardly let me step out on the road also. Ammi, Aasia and Mateen seemed to be enjoying the walk, but I frowned in dread of the coming one and a half hour. I carried my Maths textbook and a notebook.

We emerged from the lane and turned left. The park was just a little further, and I longed to sit on the quiet benches, watching bright gulmohur flowers scatter gently on the ground. But we walked a little further to reach a dull green house with an unkempt garden. Ammi opened the creaking gate and we walked in cautiously. A dog came bounding from inside. We all jumped. Panic, fear, disgust, and a myriad other emotions swept across Ammi's face, finally settling down to a worried grimace. I felt triumphant. Would Ammi send me to a house to study where dogs roamed about freely?

She strengthened her resolve and shooed the dog away. The door opened and a small, diminutive woman stepped out. We all stared. She was wearing a frock! The kind that had frilly puffed sleeves and more frills at the collar! She was almost the same shade of pink as her frock.

"Oh hello, dear! Are you the young lady who needs coaching in English?"

I shook my head.

"My English is quite good, thank you. I need coaching in Maths."

The woman had stepped out, and I saw that she was quite old, nearly sixty. A pair of glasses were perched on her head and she leaned back to look at me, although I stood far from her. Ammi looked nervous. I enjoyed her anxiety and just as soon felt bad about it. Ammi wasn't fluent in English, and whatever little she knew, she wasn't going to practise it in front of this woman who sounded like she had just stepped out of British Airways.

Mateen who had been in Aasia's arms, twisted himself and got down. He ran along the length of the garden, stopping short when he saw the dog.

"Yoohoo! Chumly! Come back to mother!" she called out in a singsong voice. The dog bounded back to her and stood in front of her, thumping its thick bushy tail on the ground. We all stared in horror and fascination.

Ammi knew she was going to verbally thrash Mrs Farrokh, who had suggested this woman as a prospective tuition teacher. I wished Ammi would physically thrash the woman too. Mrs Farrokh was our local version of Fouzia Phuppu, corpulent, heavy-breasted, and breathless most of the time. She met Ammi occasionally in the park.

"Well, dear, why are you standing out there looking so confused? Do come in," she said graciously. I moved a step forward. Ammi nudged me. "One minute, please," I said and excused myself.

"What is it, Ammi? She's calling us inside," I whispered.

Ammi looked hesitant. "I don't know if she's the right person to teach you."

I rolled my eyes. "Just because she has a dog, and she's not fully Indian?"

Ammi nodded unhappily.

"Let's go in and see what she has to say," I said, and she agreed reluctantly. I felt something surge inside me. For the first time in my life, I had overruled my mother. It felt good but scary. Ammi was supposed to know all the answers and be confident all the time. When she faltered, it seemed like things were more wrong than they actually were.

The house was cool, dark, and smelled slightly musty. Ammi sat on the sofa, right at the edge, holding Mateen. Aasia stood in the corner, twisting her *dupatta*. I sat down and made myself comfortable.

"Well, dear, what exactly is your problem?" she addressed the question to me.

"My mother feels that I need help in Maths," I said, glancing at Ammi, who was seated next to me. She was looking around the house. Anything to avoid looking at the woman.

"That shouldn't be such a problem," the old lady said, smiling once more. I looked at her face. Her eyes were set deep in her puffy face, and her nose was very small. When she smiled, her eyes crinkled up. I realised that I liked her on sight.

"But do you know ICSE Maths?" I asked her sceptically.

"My dear girl, I taught at Baldwin's for thirty years, so I know what I'm talking about," she said. I raised my eyebrows. Baldwin's! She had taught in my school for so long?

Ammi got up abruptly. "Let's go."

"We'll come later and fix up everything," I said to the tuition teacher and she nodded.

At home, Ammi refused to send me there. But I wanted to. For once Abbu was on my side. He told both of us that if I wanted to study there I could, but that I would continue there only if I showed some improvement in my marks. I agreed. Life suddenly seemed to open up in so many differing possibilities and I wanted to explore each one of them.

6

Questions

One morning, I saw Basheer sitting at the dining table, quietly eating his breakfast. He hadn't seen or heard me yet as I crept up behind him, and thumped him loudly on the back. He jumped up startled; and I laughed. "What, Basheer? When did you come? Who else is here with you?"

He blushed and I realised that he hadn't seen me in my school uniform before. Maybe seeing my wobbly knees had made him tongue-tied. He didn't answer my question but instead he looked down quietly. Ammi came out of the kitchen just then, her face pulled into a frown.

Abbu came out of the room, tucking his shirt into his pants and straightening his sleeves. "Finished?" he asked loudly. Basheer got up respectfully.

Abbu picked up the car keys and went out without saying anything, expecting Basheer to follow him. He didn't even turn and look at me as he left after Abbu.

"Basheer ran away from home. Yesterday morning. Only last night your Zohra Phuppu mustered enough courage to call up your father. He's been looking everywhere for that ungrateful boy," Ammi explained, walking into the kitchen.

Basheer had run away from home? Like something out of a movie? "Why, Ammi? Isn't he happy there?" I asked. Ammi looked at me as if that thought had never occurred to her and neither should it have to me. "Sit down and have your breakfast. Then go to school," she said curtly. "I have to see to Mateen."

I sat down at the table, quietly pondering over this new development. Imagine, actually running away from home! It was scary and exciting at the same time. If ever the time comes to leave my house, I knew I'd be very unhappy. But I would also look forward to see and experience the world outside this house. For a moment I envied Basheer as I tore my *aloo paratha,* dipped it in Ammi's pungent tomato chutney, and stuffed it in my mouth. I knew he loved his mother, but Ammabi alone was enough to drive anyone away from home.

I called up Rehana that evening. Cradling the phone between my neck and ear, I fished out a bar of chocolate from the pocket of my jeans. My last pair of jeans. "No more jeans, no more skirts. You're almost as tall as I am," Ammi had said apprehensively.

Chachi answered the phone. I asked for Rehana, wondering how Rehana always managed to make small talk with Ammi, while I didn't know how to chat like that with Chachi or any adult. When Rehana got on the line, we spoke for a while about school and she asked about Mateen. That was when I told her about Basheer. She was very surprised. Neither she nor her parents had any idea of it. She was sure that her mother didn't know.

"Ammi would have told me," she insisted stubbornly. "Why did he run away? One minute, Ammi wants to speak to you." Before I could say anything, I could hear Asifa Chachi's soft voice. "What's this I'm hearing, Mehnaz? Basheer had run away?"

For some reason, I knew Ammi would be angry with me as I answered Chachi's questions. But I didn't have any answers at all, especially to the question as to why they had not been informed about it.

I finally kept the phone down and finished my chocolate in peace. Later, when I was finishing my homework, I heard the phone ring once more. I stepped out cautiously but Ammi had already picked it up. It was Sadiq Chacha.

I heard Ammi explaining the situation to him. "I know, Sadiq. He's your nephew too. But your brother was in a big hurry this morning."

She listened for a while, and then once again tried to explain. Finally, she asked the question I dreaded. "How did you hear about this?" Before I could hop back into my room, she looked up at me and glared hard. I sat at my desk, my heart pounding heavily. I didn't know that a simple phone call was going to cause so many problems.

Ammi didn't come to my room as I had expected. When I finally ventured out for dinner, she was quiet. It took me about ten minutes to realise that she was giving me the silent treatment. If I ever became a mother, I had to remember that this method of punishment was by far the best and most effective way to treat errant children.

I sat down for dinner. "Ammi, I'm sorry, for whatever it is I've done. Please talk to me," I pleaded. Silence followed. "Please?" I repeated.

Her full anger exploded. "Why did you tell them about Basheer?"

"What's wrong if I did? They are also a part of our family," I said, defending myself. Sometimes Ammi's anger was so unreasonable that I'm sure she didn't quite understand it herself.

"You know that man Afzal? He's always there in your Chachi's house. Now he'll go and tell this to all the people, and everywhere we go, people will ask us why Basheer ran away. That's why. But I don't think you would understand that."

She looked at me, and I looked back at her angrily. This was another of Afzal Mamu's faults, I suppose. That he couldn't keep his mouth shut. Well, who could? I thought hotly. "Your father is coming back tomorrow. Just pray he doesn't get angry when he hears about this," she said.

I couldn't understand this two-fold logic that the grown-ups had. One that applied to them – they didn't want to be answerable to anyone – and the other that applied to us – we had to answer them every single time.

❖❖❖

7

Return of the Chappal

The journey to Vellore was always tiring but something in the humid, still air, made me drowsy. Aasia looked miserable. Maybe she had been hoping to pass her town on the way. But Dharmapuri was not on the Bangalore-Chennai highway through which we travelled to reach Vellore. She sat by the window in the car and kept quiet all the time.

The house was cool and dim when we entered. The air still reverberated with the sound of the *azan* from different *masjids*. One by one, they all ended. It was the time for *Zohr namaz*.

We washed up and Zohra Phuppu made tea for Abbu and Ammi. I watched her carefully, noting if there were any changes in her appearance. But the same face stared out from under her saree *pallu,* which was tightly tucked behind her ears. She smiled at me. Maybe Zohra Phuppu knew what was happening around her, but she wasn't really aware of it. As though she didn't really care what happened.

It was all because of that husband of hers. She seemed to have lost the will to live ever since he had left. How could one man's absence reduce a woman to nothing? I looked at Ammi. She was so devoted to Abbu. If he ever went away like that, would she too become like her? Circumstances had a way of changing priorities, but I knew Ammi was a stronger person in comparison to Phuppu.

But if something like this happened to me, I was sure I wouldn't wither away like Zohra Phuppu. I would live for myself. I wouldn't allow any man to have so much control over my life.

Basheer wasn't at home. I asked Phuppu if he was at school. She shook her head. "He has stopped going to school. He says he doesn't want to study," she said. My father looked up sharply and almost growled, "When did this happen? Why didn't you tell me?"

"It was a-after you brought him back from B-Bangalore, Bhaijan," she said, "He told me that if I told you, he would run away again."

Abbu's face reddened.

After lunch I slept. It was dark when I got up. Had Basheer returned? Raised voices came from outside the room. I dragged out my *dupatta* from under the pillowcase where it had got entangled. Draping it around my shoulders, I stepped out of the room with a heavy feeling.

"Since when has this been going on?" I heard Abbu's voice. Basheer was in big trouble. But the voice that replied was not Basheer's. A slightly old man stood in front of Abbu. The man wore a crochet *topi* on his head, a pair of trousers, and a *kurta*. He was much shorter than Abbu. I stood facing Abbu's thick back and yet I could feel the vibration of his anger.

"And now you say that Sadiq has been taking money from this shop for nearly six months. Why didn't you tell me before?"

This man was responsible for managing Abbu's business in Vellore, I assumed. He wiped his forehead with his palms and answered after a moment, "He said he'll tell you. I thought you knew about this."

"Okay, you go now. I'll talk to Sadiq myself."

The man left, looking very relieved. When Abbu used to get angry, he no longer differentiated between those with whom he was angry and those he loved dearly, including me. So I walked past him very cautiously when he stopped me. "Do you know where Basheer is?" he asked. I shook my head.

The house in Vellore had an open *aangan* and a patch of sky could be seen from there. I stood just outside the *aangan* and looked at the crows whirling around the roof. I wanted to go up to the terrace, but it was no fun without Rehana and Basheer.

Just a couple of years back, things had been different. Basheer would shyly take Rehana and me on a trip around Vellore. Ammi didn't mind so much then and she was often occupied with Mateen and she seemed to be satisfied that I was with my cousins.

Basheer liked to take us to some of the smaller *gallis*. We would walk along the gutter-lined streets, watching goats wandering around among the piled-up rubbish, and small children playing on the steps of their houses. The houses stood quietly next to each other, huge pillars standing sentinel before the entrances.

Once, Basheer took us to the shop from where he bought his kites. Rehana and I walked behind him, hand in hand, wondering why he was looking so excited. The shop was more of a shack, and had kites of all hues arranged haphazardly on the walls. A man was sitting cross-legged on the floor and whittling the bamboo sticks that would form the spine of the kite. His *lungi* was hitched up to his thighs, like most of the men we saw on the road in Vellore, lifted up and tied around the waist with a knot. He was surrounded with bamboo sticks and coloured paper.

Rehana and I watched Basheer as he considered each kite carefully before deciding to buy a dark blue kite, which was rather large. He took out some coins, carefully counted them, and gave them to the shopkeeper.

I didn't have the chance to see Basheer fly the blue kite. When we reached home, he had run upstairs, but Ammi hadn't allowed me to go. I fretted and wished Ammi was the kind of mother who would give into a tantrum, but she simply wasn't. Rehana remained downstairs with me and we watched TV. Basheer finally came down that evening, looking tired but happy.

In the kitchen Ammi and Aasia were peeling garlic, while Zohra Phuppu was cooking something over the stove and Ammabi had gone to visit someone. Mateen was still sleeping.

I asked Ammi if I could go up to the terrace for a while.

"Why?"

"I'm bored! There's nothing to do here!"

"Okay, but get back before the *Maghrib azan* starts."

I walked upstairs, feeling sedate and quite bored. What one enjoyed most seemed to have changed so much when the people you enjoyed it with were not there. I opened the door to the terrace and stepped out. It had cooled down since we had arrived, and my *dupatta* flapped gently around me.

I stood there for quite some time watching the sky darken, and with it, the number of kites dotting the sky reduced. I whirled around and ran to the other side to see if I could spot that boy at whom I had thrown the slipper but I couldn't remember which house it had been.

At home, I knew something important happening. It had to do with Abbu and Sadiq Chacha. I hoped they would resolve it soon. Deep inside, there was some amount of dread for what the coming days could bring. Since we had last met in Vellore, I hadn't seen Rehana and I had spoken to her just once or twice over the phone. Although I had friends at school, none were as special to me as she was.

I stood at the railing, watching the mountains in the distance, when I heard a shout. My mind still hadn't focused yet when there was another shout. It was from the terrace some three or four houses away. It was that boy! He was waving at me madly with his *chappal*. I looked at him, amazed.

I turned to run back to the house when I heard another shout, *"Aye, darpok!"* Swallowing hard, I turned back. I was no coward. Folding my arms in front of my chest, I shouted out, "What?", even though my heart was beating madly. I felt a little breathless and scared, facing him without Rehana by my side.

He was grinning as he put his hand on the parapet and climbed over it. He was crazy. "You'll fall!" I called out. He scratched his neck briefly and shook his head. And before I could say anything else, he jumped across his terrace to the next one.

The terraces were not far apart, but if he had missed, he would surely have broken an arm or a leg.

"What..." the words remained stuck in my throat, as I watched him jumping from that terrace to the next one, until he was standing on the terrace of the house next to ours. I got a proper look at him while he tried to regain his breath. He was tall, with wheatish complexion and very dark eyes. His hair was flying in all directions and he almost looked comical, but I didn't laugh. Now that he was right in front of me, I didn't know what I could possibly speak to him about, so I turned around to go downstairs.

"Hey! Wait a minute!"

I stopped and turned back. He was leaning against the parapet and had an arm outstretched rather dramatically. When I faced him again, he bent down and removed his slippers and handed them to me.

"I don't want your silly slippers."

The sound of his laughter seemed to break away at some chink of metal around my heart, and I felt like smiling.

"They're yours, remember?"

I felt my face flush.

"Uhh... yes, yes... I don't have yours, so you can keep them."

"Well, I don't want mine. Just wanted to give you yours back."

I really didn't want them back. Especially now that he had worn them for so long, who wanted them?

"Keep them. I really don't want them back." My face felt hot although the sun had gone down by now.

"I've been hoping to see you again."

"Why?" I asked, feeling scared.

"I've been scanning the terraces whenever I'm in Vellore, but you were never there. I really wanted to return your slippers to you."

I leaned over the parapet to take the slippers. Somehow I knew Ammi wouldn't be happy if I told her about this. Naturally I wasn't going to. I glanced down and saw Basheer walking up the road, head bent. Abbu was still angry and I had to warn Basheer. I quickly snatched the slippers and ran away.

The boy was still standing on the other terrace. Confident that I would never see him again, I waved wildly. His eyes widened and he grinned once more and waved back. I ran downstairs.

Basheer was already inside the house. Before I could catch up with him, he was in the hall right before Abbu. The *Maghrib azan* started and echoes of different *azans* rang out from different *masjids*. He refused to look up and meet Abbu's eyes, but with his head downcast, he listened as Abbu berated him. I tried to edge myself into one of the rooms.

"Mehnaz! Where were you all this while? I called out for you at least ten times."

"I was on the terrace. Ammi said I could go up and be back before *Maghrib*."

He found nothing to argue with that and nodded at me. The focus of his ire shifted once more to Basheer. Abbu heaved his large body out of the chair and got up, pulling out a white crocheted skullcap from his *kurta* pocket and adjusted it over his head. He was going for *namaz*. Basheer walked behind him slowly and I felt a pang for him. Regret, compassion, understanding, I don't know what it was.

In the room I found that Ammabi had returned from her visit and she had been looking forward to talk about it with someone. Ammi had excused herself, saying that she had to read *namaz*. Phuppu had retreated to the kitchen, and Ammabi's rather reluctant audience was comprised of Aasia and Mateen.

Ammabi lifted her eye glasses and looked at me. I tried not to look at her, but it was hard to ignore someone who rocked back and forth uninterrupted. I had left my *chappals* at the bottom of the stairs and now, I relived the encounter wishing I could talk about it with someone. He had actually jumped over terraces just so he could return my *chappals* to me!

In the background of my thoughts, Ammabi's voice crept in, hard and edged with the crusty *paan masala* that she had taken to popping into her mouth every few minutes these days. "And when I told him that he should have taken his *chappal* out and hit his good-for-nothing wife with it... he laughed and said that I had some of the best ideas he had heard."

I blinked.

8

The Split

Abbu returned to Vellore many times without us. Business, he said. But I really had no idea what Abbu actually did. It was mandatory at school to fill out forms every year with information about ourselves and our families. Whenever I came across the box marked 'Father's occupation', I would muse, wondering what to write. How I wished I could have written doctor or architect, or maybe lawyer, but each year I would write in neat block letters 'BUSINESSMAN'.

"What business?" Ms Caroline, my previous class teacher, had asked, almost looking interested. My answer was almost the same, a shrug and a brief, "I don't really know." Ms Caroline looked at me dubiously. Her expression was fixed in my mind. Soon I began to view my father's business dubiously too. What if he was actually a smuggler or something? How would my teacher react if I wrote that down as my father's occupation?

Well, business it always was. What a small word, I thought. Business. So many things could be included in it. I only knew that Chacha and Abbu were in it together. They also had a shop somewhere in City Market. What they sold I had no idea. Whenever Abbu and Chacha discussed business, any children present were sent out of the room. We were not allowed to stand and listen.

What did they sell in their shop? I had heard Abbu talking about hinges and drawers, but I was too ignorant then to realise that they were doing the only business that most Lababin Muslim men knew well – hardware. Whenever Rehana and I met, we would be so engrossed in thinking up new games that mundane things like business never concerned us.

Sometime before Ramzan started, Ammi and I had gone to Commercial Street to do some shopping. We stepped inside one of the shops which sold mounds of glitzy fabric and Ammi had asked the shopkeeper to cut out the required length. I was bored and looked outside the glass window and watched people on the road, men trying to manoeuvre cars into tiny parking spaces, women walking hurriedly and children being lugged around impatiently by their parents.

Two women caught my attention and I stared at them as they crossed the road. They were both wearing *burkas,* and carrying a couple of plastic shopping bags. When one of them turned, I saw that it was Asifa Chachi.

Excited to spot them, I couldn't explain anything to Ammi and I ran outside the shop and called out to Chachi. The other woman was probably some relative of hers whom we didn't know. Both of them turned around and I stopped, startled when I realised that the other *burka*-clad person was Rehana.

Ammi had asked me to start wearing a *burka* a few days ago but I ignored it, feeling a little uneasy about covering myself in its black depths. Abbu had said that I could wait for a few more years before wearing one and for some reason, it had cheered me immensely.

Ammi had followed me outside after paying the shopkeeper and looked at me curiously because after calling out to Chachi, I hadn't spoken a word to them. I was still trying to understand that it was Rehana standing next to Chachi, looking like a miniature version of her mother, with a handbag slung on her shoulders too.

Ammi and Chachi had only exchanged *salaams*. For some reason, we were all standing there, each waiting for the other to speak and the people milling around us almost knocked Chachi over at one time.

"Let's go and have a *pani puri!*" I suggested brightly. I loved the *chaats* and *pani puris* that some of the restaurants sold in the bylanes of Commercial Street and I felt that whatever awkwardness there was, for whatever reason, would soon disintegrate when we crammed our mouths with the dripping *puris*.

Rehana smiled at me and I smiled back at her in relief, but Ammi and Chachi looked at me like I was demented. Or maybe they realised my presence over there, just then and suddenly, in a flurry of movement, Chachi grabbed a startled Rehana's hand and she said, *"Khudahafiz"* and turned around and left.

Ammi and I stood there, Ammi looking thoughtful, and I, more confused than ever. I was still pondering over Chachi's unusual behaviour when we reached home. Abbu had gone to Vellore the previous day and was returning home tonight. I wished someone would explain to me what was happening but Abbu seemed to be the last person I could ask.

That night when Abbu returned, I wondered if I should ask what was going on. But the frown on his forehead cut deeply. His face was dark and closed when he walked in that night. After washing up, he sat down in the living room, his expression not softening for even an instant. What could have happened?

He reached over and took the phone from the side table. Placing it precariously on his lap, he punched in a few numbers.

"Hello. Tell Sadiq to come and meet me tomorrow." He banged the receiver into the cradle.

That night I slept with a heavy heart. I knew there would be a major confrontation tomorrow, the outcome already making me very nervous. I pulled up my blanket and twisted it around myself.

In the morning, I saw Abbu in the living room, sitting on the same sofa. It seemed as though he had sat there all night, in the same position. But his head was back on the headrest and he was asleep. I touched his cheek and he opened his eyes. He looked at me, almost smiled, and then he frowned. He got up slowly and walked to his room. Half an hour later he was dressed to go outside but he didn't go anywhere. He refused Ammi's offer of breakfast and waited for Sadiq Chacha.

At half past ten, Sadiq Chacha came, his face was serious and he didn't smile when I held the door open. He walked up to the living room when he saw Abbu. He murmured a greeting to which Abbu didn't reply. He sat down on the same seat, which I had now termed the hot seat. Everyone sat there whenever they had to answer to Abbu, whether it was Ammi, me, Fouzia Phuppu, or now Sadiq Chacha. He shifted a little, trying to get comfortable and I came and stood behind him.

"Mehnaz, get some tea for us and after that I want you to go to your room."

Feeling annoyed I walked into the kitchen. I wanted to listen!

Ammi pressed the tray into my hands. She had made tea the moment she heard Sadiq Chacha's car. I took the tray and walked back outside. Chacha and Abbu were still sitting stiffly, without speaking. Abbu waited for me to keep the tray on the centre-table and he shook his head slightly, indicating that I should leave.

I walked back slowly to my room but didn't go inside. They had started talking now. I couldn't hear anything at first. When I looked across the hall, I saw Ammi standing at the door of the kitchen, twisting her *pallu* and swallowing nervously. All of a sudden, their voices were raised.

"You don't want me to do anything on my own. All my life you want me to be dependent on you. Well, no more!"

"Sadiq!"

"I'm not fifteen anymore, Bhai. I'm not going to listen to your raised voice and get scared. I can't see why you're so prejudiced against Afzal. He's a good man."

Afzal Mamu. The charismatic and friendly man who I used to adore... he was responsible for this fight?

"I've already gone into business with him. I would have liked to do it with your blessings, but just because you don't like it doesn't stop me anymore."

"And to finance your new business, you've been taking money from our shop in Vellore?" Abbu shouted back.

Sadiq Chacha was quiet but I sensed that he wanted to say a lot of things to Abbu. "Sadiq, you didn't even tell me about it. What did you think, I wouldn't know? You could have asked me at least, right?" Abbu reasoned quietly relying upon Chacha's silence, thinking that he was relenting. But he was wrong. Abbu's gentler voice seemed to have spurred on Chacha's anger and he started shouting.

"Why should I ask you anything? I'm as much of a partner in the business as you are! I am tired of you telling me how to do everything."

There was silence once more and I imagined Abbu and Chacha glaring at each other, breathing heavily. The thought brought a sense of such deep despair in my heart and I lifted my hands to shut my ears when I heard Abbu shout again.

"Then get the hell out of my house. Never show me your face again. And when that rat Afzal tricks you out of every *paisa* you have, don't come whimpering to me."

I ran to my room and locked the door. Where was Mateen? I wanted to hug his small warm body and reassure myself that everything would be all right. I leaned against the door and shut my eyes.

They kept shouting and in the midst of it all, I could hear Mateen crying. He was probably frightened. I wanted to seek him out, but to go outside would mean facing them. Their voices – cold, poison-tipped – I couldn't bear to hear anymore.

Abbu was kicking Chacha out of the house. We were never to see him again. I rummaged through my desk until I found my Walkman and shakily plugged it in my ears. I turned up the volume as high as I could tolerate. It was a cassette of Amitabh Bachchan hits. *"Chhookar mere mann ko kiya tune kya ishara."*

The song that normally revived my spirits just made my head ache now. But it blocked their voices. I didn't want their resentment and anger to sear my heart. I didn't want to hate Chacha.

A door slammed loudly and the windows vibrated with the violence. I removed the earphones slowly. I think it was at that precise moment that the feud between Abbu and Chacha started. I curled up on my bed and cried, wishing Mateen was beside me. I cried myself to sleep.

When I got up, my face felt swollen. I looked at the time. It was 2.30 p.m. Way past the lunch time. Why hadn't Ammi woken me up? I winced when I remembered what had happened. I splashed cold water on my face in the bathroom and rubbed my eyes vigorously.

Ammi was in the dining room trying to make Mateen eat.

"How many times do I have to call out for you? Why do you shut yourself up in your room all the time?" she looked at me angrily.

In the living room, the tray was still there. The tea in the cups was untouched. A thick brown skin had formed over the cold liquid. My back prickled. Ammi was just trying to act normal. She was much more upset than she was showing, and I knew it now. Ammi couldn't stand to see a thing out of its place. Cups of tea – whether drunk or not – should have been returned to the kitchen long back.

"Aasia!" I called. Aasia came from the kitchen, looking worried.

"Couldn't you take the tray to the kitchen? Do we have to tell you everything?"

"Apa asked me to leave it here." But she took the tray and went away.

Abbu was in the bedroom. He was sitting on the bed, his head propped up on the pillow, his eyes shut. He wasn't asleep. But I was scared of him now. He opened his eyes and smiled at me weakly, beckoning me to come inside. I walked in nervously. Like hundreds of other times, he gave me the liquid balm to rub on his forehead. I took it from him and stared at the line in the middle of his forehead. It was a groove now. Etched forever. On his head, on our lives. No matter how much I rubbed it, it was there to stay.

Part 2

9

Moving on

I am seventeen now and my opinions are my own, not influenced by the limited perspective of my parents. But if I could make them a little more understanding about some things, I would have done it gladly. Especially family feuds.

Even so, my own strong feelings over it had subsided over the last year. No one could possibly worry about trivial matters such as family feuds when faced with something as huge as the ICSE exam. The exam had become my sole purpose of existence and I obliterated everything else from my mind as I studied.

Mrs Dahlia, my old tuition teacher was also responsible for some of the change in me. Her attitude in the beginning had surprised me very much. Our lengthy discussions had always been mostly about her family, never mine. I had been quite thrilled to hear of her children's exploits, or about her husband who had been a pilot during some important period in history, I'm not sure which.

But she had noticed that I was subdued during those first weeks after the split. I tried really hard to concentrate on school and studies and it was what Abbu wanted me to do. But it wasn't easy. Abbu wanted us to forget that Chacha or his family even existed. Even if we met them outside anywhere, we were instructed to look through them and not even say *'salaam'*. It was unfair and childish. I couldn't meet Rehana, or even talk to her on the phone.

Looking back now, severing ties with Rehana may have helped me more than I had realised. At least now I had a real life, with real friends, and I had some good times with them instead of waiting for that elusive phone call from Rehana. I don't know why I had made her my exclusive friend and never interacted with other girls in my class. I thought it wouldn't be fair to her!

Still, I was finding it difficult to study with the feud drama simmering in our homes. With just a little gentle prodding from Mrs Dahlia I told her everything, haltingly. She listened quietly, nodding her head and saying 'I understand' every now and then. After she had heard me out, she went into the kitchen and brought me a big plate of biscuits.

"Here, have some of these."

She didn't say anything while I ate. The biscuits were crumbly and buttery, and in my lousy mood I forgot that Ammi had told me not to eat anything in Mrs Dahlia's house.

"Family feuds are something that will happen in every family, however big or small. There's not much you can do about them except hope that with time, the differences between your uncle and your father will wear down. That's all."

"But can't I do anything? I mean, can't I or anyone bring them together?"

She shook her head. "Believe me, there are plenty who will try and others who will try to widen this rift too for their own purposes. You are just a child, you can't do anything. In fact, no one can unless they themselves want to. They have to put aside their differences and their egos and only then can your family be one again."

I felt something in me grow dark and heavy.

"You mean there isn't going to be any solution to this unless they decide themselves? But that might never happen!"

She patted my hand. "I know. Believe me, you can't do anything about this. But why do you want to involve yourself in it? This won't affect you unless you let it. And you are such a bright child! Why worry about something that grown-ups have done?"

I wanted to believe her that I could exclude this episode from my life, but I knew it was quite impossible. At least I could try and I did. Every time Abbu started his tirades against Chacha, I got up and walked away, sometimes dragging Mateen with me. I didn't want both of us to be prejudiced against Chacha. Since it was Abbu's policy not to let us hear about business-related things, he didn't really notice.

I sighed and looked around the room. The table beside my bed was covered with sparkling gift-wrapping paper that rustled under the fan. It had been a week since my birthday and I still hadn't cleared the mess. Abbu had proudly presented me with four new sets of clothes for me to wear to the college. I grimaced when I saw the full-sleeved *salwar kameez,* all four of which had suffocating Chinese collars. I hadn't worn any of them yet because I was planning to take them to the tailor to see if he could make something even remotely fashionable out of them.

Ammi didn't believe in birthdays, she thought that the whole cake cutting and making-a-big-deal about a birthday was a Christian concept. "What's there to celebrate? You're growing older! One year less of your life which Allah has ordained for you! And you want to celebrate that?"

I had no answer to that, but I ignored her pointed ignorance of my birthday because Abbu had gifted me and so had Mateen. He had done a painting of a pot with a droopy flower. He was learning painting in school and he had decided that his lop-sided picture would be his gift to me. I was very touched.

Mrs Dahlia had presented me with a hard-bound edition of Jane Austen's *Pride and Prejudice.* I was awed by the book. I turned the heavy cream coloured pages and sniffed the crisp scent of the book wondering at how Mrs Dahlia got on. She didn't have other students and she didn't go out to work. Her children were all in England. Maybe they sent her money now and then. But surely it was not enough. If they did, then surely her house would have been in a much better condition.

Whenever I thought of Mrs Dahlia, I felt very protective. She no longer taught me as I had taken Arts in college much to my father's disapproval. But I still visited her every other day. We spoke of many things now that we weren't bound together by numbers.

I called out to Aasia who came and stood behind me.

"Clear this mess... I have to go out now."

I looked at my watch. I had only half an hour to get ready. My friends were coming home and together we were going to a movie. It had taken me nearly five days to convince Ammi, to plead with her, to let me go. She couldn't understand the concept of friends because she didn't have any. Abbu had agreed reluctantly but he had made me promise that I wouldn't go anywhere other than the movie hall. Ammi had insisted that I wear my *burka.* At that point I had burst into tears. Finally, Abbu had said that I could go without my *burka.*

As I pulled out my *salwar kameez,* I saw my *burka* lying in the corner of my cupboard. I shuddered. I would be the laughing stock if I wore it and went. Aasia had finished cleaning up and was leaving the room. Aasia lumbered out of the room slowly and I watched her retreating back with a measure of irritation.

I carefully draped my *dupatta* over my head and walked out, looking almost modest. Ammi didn't say a word. These days she had started giving me the silent treatment almost every other day. But now I tried not to let it affect me much.

Abbu was sitting in the hall reading the paper, and Mateen was playing with his cars on the carpet. Abbu looked up but didn't say anything. I didn't know how it had happened but I could sense my relationship with Abbu had changed. He no longer regarded me as a child like Ammi still did. The new respect I saw in his eyes (was it because I was in college now?) made me a little uncomfortable. I smiled at him and adjusted the strap of my handbag firmly on my shoulder. The bell rang and I looked up. They were here.

10

Bollywood Masala

Despite all her show of indifference, I could see Ammi peeping out from the window as I got into the auto. I waved at her and turned around to my excited friends. I settled myself comfortably in the corner. We chatted all the way to the cinema hall.

Once there, I stared in awe at the crowd. "Will we get a ticket?" I asked Sahana. Going to the movies was a completely new experience for me. Any movies I had seen were all watched on video at home. My parents might have taken me to a theatre when I was small but this feeling of anticipation, a breath of independence, had been missing then.

I immediately compared the feeling to what I felt when Abbu had taken us to the beach in Madras. I could see the great blue expanse of the ocean, smell the tart, salty breeze, and I wanted to be there immediately. I resented the fifteen minutes it took to walk down to the beach. I felt deprived. And here, in front of this white building with people jostling in the queue, I felt the same.

As we paid the *auto wallah,* I mentally urged Sahana and Jyoti to walk faster, fearful that they would laugh if I actually asked them to. We stood in the queue and Sahana seemed quite unperturbed that the movie started in exactly twenty minutes and we were still without a ticket. She was staring at a couple a little ahead of us.

The girl must have been my age or so and the boy a little older. They were standing with their arms around each other's waists and she had her head on his shoulder. We watched fascinated as he brushed a few strands of hair from her face tenderly. I didn't know I had sighed.

Sahana looked at me amused. She prodded me with her elbow. Feeling my face flush, I grinned. Jyoti shook her head.

"You two will always find some guy to ogle at, won't you?"

"I wasn't ogling at him!"

The queue inched forward and I looked at my watch again. Fifteen minutes. The two of them couldn't keep their hands off each other. I saw the girl holding his palm and draw circles on it with her fingers. Thank god, Abbu wasn't here. Nowadays it was embarrassing to watch TV with him because he always complained about the short clothes worn by the film heroines or about the increased intimacy between the hero and the heroine.

His tirade, which I had heard one thousand and thirty five times, was always the same. *"Kitne behaya ho gaye hain ye log! Kya kya dekhne ko milta hai."* I could hardly imagine how he would react if he saw the young couple.

They were at the counter now. Two men who had bought the tickets and were walking inside looked back at them and one of them leered, *"Laila-Majnu ko corner ki seat dena, bhaiyya. Film boring hogi to in ko dekh lenge hum."*

The other slapped his friend's back and they walked in laughing. I saw the boy look at them angrily but he looked embarrassed also. They bought the tickets and went inside hand in hand.

When we finally entered the darkened auditorium, I was dismayed. The movie had started. Sahana and Jyoti nudged me forward as I continued staring at the screen.

"Sit down and we'll watch better," Jyoti whispered. Feeling quite foolish I hurried up to our seats and sat down. I was almost glad I wasn't sitting between them I thought because they kept whispering comments to each other.

I felt a bit left out, but soon I concentrated on the movie and was extremely engrossed in the plot. It was a regular Hindi film with a lot of songs, dances, and fight sequences. During the intermission I smiled at them.

"Typical Hindi movie, no?"

Sahana made a face. "You know what's more interesting?' she whispered, leaning towards me. "It's those two behind us."

I didn't turn around, but I felt my face grow hot.

"Oh, leave those two alone."

Sahana smirked, and reached out for the popcorn that Jyoti had brought back. I tried not to think about the couple seated behind us. Although I too was curious about what they were up to, I didn't want others to make snide remarks about them. It was a bit ridiculous, since I had also felt a bit of righteous indignation towards them.

After a lot of fights during which the villains were bashed up, mothers were reunited with lost sons, heroines smiled coyly at heroes, the movie was over and the lights came on. I got up feeling strangely depressed. Today was a milestone of sorts. I had defied Ammi and gone out with my friends (something she claims she had never done when she was my age) but I felt quite cheated. Maybe, I had been hoping my friends too would be excited, but going to the movies wasn't something that they got unduly excited about.

Maybe the next time would be better. Sahana crumpled the popcorn packet and threw it in the dustbin as we emerged into the bright, dusty afternoon.

What had started out as a promising day finally ended in the worst way possible. When my friends dropped me back home, I saw that we had been invaded once more by Fouzia Phuppu. She sat in the hall like a fat warrior, hands crossed in front of her chest, eyes gleaming. Ammi sat next to her looking angry and uncomfortable.

"*Wah!* So you send your daughter, who I think should have got married last year itself, you send her out to see a movie with her friends, and that too without a *burka!*"

I stopped and felt the blood rush to my face, my neck, and my ears.

"Shabana, you should see how Asifa has brought up Rehana. I am proud to call her my niece. Wherever she goes, she wears a *burka* and she also wears a veil over her face. She is the perfect daughter apart from my own Farha."

Ammi was getting angry. Though I wanted to lash out at Phuppu, I knew it wouldn't be wise. I slid my feet out of my sandals and walked quietly to my room. Whatever would happen, Ammi would handle it. I wish Abbu had been at home. Phuppu wouldn't have dared to say anything in front of him.

When I changed, Aasia came into my room to ask if I wanted to have lunch. I shook my head. Lunch would mean that I would have to sit outside and eat under Phuppu's acerbic glare.

"I can get something for you here if you want."

I was annoyed with her for being so considerate. Hunger won over my annoyance however and I nodded my head.

I didn't step out of my room at all that day and that angered Phuppu further. She lumbered into my room and sat at the edge of my bed. I was propped up on my pillow reading a novel, and I continued reading.

"What are you reading?"

"A novel."

She got up with one of her sudden movements that always surprised me.

"Never have I been so insulted in my life!" She stormed out. I heard her leaving the house after saying something to Ammi.

Ammi came in, her face furious. "Isn't it enough that you have no respect for me, but you have to show disrespect for her too?"

I got up, anger pounding through me.

"What do you mean I have no respect for you? Of course, I respect you. Just don't ask me to respect her."

At this, Ammi's face tightened. She spoke softly but furiously. "You don't know how things work in our house. What will you know when you are cooped up inside this room for ever? You make a mistake and I get blamed for it because I have brought you up. Your father should have never brought us to Bangalore. If we had been in Vellore, you would have been married by now. Still, there must be some truth in what Fouzia Apa said. If Rehana can be demure even though she was brought up here, I don't know what I did wrong with you. If you have any consideration for me, any respect at all, don't ever do what you did today."

I felt tears pricking my eyes.

"But what did I do?"

"I told you not to go for that movie, yet you went. I told you to wear a *burka,* but you didn't. What do you think everyone will think of me when they hear about what you've done?"

I cried at the unfairness of Ammi's accusations. For Sahana and Jyoti, going to a movie was just a change in their routine. But for me, it was like I had committed the biggest crime ever.

11

Death

When Abbu came home that evening, he sat down on the sofa wearily. He looked old and tired, and the thought made me nervous. Parents were supposed to be invincible. They couldn't just die like that, could they?

When I was in the ninth standard, a girl in my class lost her father. I couldn't understand how she continued to live, how she faced each day without the reassuring presence of her father. I knew that if anything were to happen to my father, I would die myself. I pushed the thought away and went up to him. As always when he saw me, his face lit up.

"How was your movie?"

I sat down beside him. "The movie was good. But when I got back home, Fouzia Phuppu was here and she said a lot of horrible things to me."

"What did your Phuppu say?" He seemed amused when I related the whole incident to him. "Your Phuppu is just an old busybody. Just ignore whatever she says."

I beamed at him. "But Ammi also scolded me." Ammi was in the kitchen making dinner and would not take it too kindly if she saw me influencing Abbu's opinion before she had laid the matter before him.

Abbu nodded. "Your mother is right. Why don't you listen to her now and then? Just to keep her happy." I nodded slowly wondering why such a simple thing was so difficult.

After dinner, Ammi started the topic but Abbu cut her off and started telling her about Sadiq Chacha's latest exploits. He winked at me but when he looked at Ammi, the humour had vanished from his face. His face hardened noticeably every time he spoke about Sadiq Chacha. I listened to Abbu call Chacha all kinds of names. I finished dinner quickly and dragged Mateen with me to my room where we both played Ludo for a while.

I heard the phone ring. Ammi picked it up.

"Ya Allah!" I heard Abbu cry out. I scrambled out, terrified. What had happened?

Abbu was crumpled on the floor, the receiver dangling from the cradle. "Zohra! Zohra!" he cried. Heart pounding loudly, I ran to him. He hugged me hard, crying. Ammi was sitting next to him and crying too. Basheer had called from Vellore. Zohra Phuppu was dead.

We had to leave for Vellore that instant. In all the confusion, I suddenly remembered Sadiq Chacha. Had Basheer called there? We had to let them know so I brought up the matter hesitantly. Abbu looked at me stonily and I didn't wait for a reply, quickly dialling the number.

It rang and rang but no one picked up. We had to leave now. I swiftly packed my clothes and Mateen's and then went to Ammi's room. She was sitting on the bed and crying, and she hadn't even taken out any clothes yet. Abbu was checking the car, whether there was enough oil and water, although I didn't know how he could be so practical at this time. I quickly opened Ammi's cupboard and pulled out a few saris and blouses and stuffed them inside a bag. Abbu's clothes also went into a bag, and then I wore my *burka*. Ammi was still crying. Phuppu had been like her own sister. I pulled out Ammi's *burka* from the cupboard and pressed it into her hands. She wiped her face with her palms, put on the *burka* and we rushed out. Aasia too carried her belongings in a small bag. Ammi's hands shook so badly that she couldn't lock the house properly. Twice the keys fell from her hands and sniffling, she picked them up and finally locked the house.

Only when we were in the car did I remember that I hadn't called my friends to tell them I wouldn't be coming to college. It was February, and final exams were just a month away. I didn't know how many days we would be in Vellore. But looking at Abbu's tear-ravaged face, I kept quiet.

Trips to Vellore were always meticulously planned by Ammi. She took care of everything, preparing *keema samosas* and other dry snacks, which we could eat on the way without making a mess. Sometimes she would even make *biryani* to eat at some place cool and shady on the scenic highway where Abbu stopped the car. We passed a lot of hamlets on the way, dipping into Andhra Pradesh before venturing into Tamil Nadu. Travelling to Vellore was always like a picnic.

But now she was unable to think for even a minute. She couldn't even remember to take a bottle of water for the journey. I was in charge and I hated it. I quickly filled a couple of plastic bottles with water and grabbed some biscuit packets for Mateen from the cupboard. By the time we left, it was nearly ten at night. Ammi sat in front with Abbu, while Mateen sat wedged between me and Aasia. I closed my eyes and tried to think about what had happened. How did she die? Was she ill? I hadn't the courage to ask Abbu.

What would happen to Basheer? I wished Abbu would bring him back to live with us. Then another horrible thought came. Would Ammabi also come and live with us? Oh god, no! Please don't let that happen I prayed fervently.

I opened my eyes and saw Bangalore rushing past. Shops were closed and dim lights inside houses showed people having dinner or watching TV. I leaned my forehead against the cool glass of the window, feeling wretched. When life came to a horrible stop for us, how could it go on normally for everyone else? Sahana and Jyoti were probably fast asleep by now.

Abbu seemed to be focused on getting us to Vellore safely and quickly. Ammi was now calm. She spoke with Abbu softly, realising that he needed to stay awake while he drove. I curled up on my side wishing I had brought a shawl, for the night was very cool. Mateen was already asleep, leaning against Aasia who was also sleeping. I dragged him upright and pulled him close to me and tried to sleep.

When we neared Vellore, I awoke. I enquired about the time from Abbu . "Three o'clock," he said curtly. I shifted my position trying not to disturb Mateen, who was sleeping peacefully. I fidgeted a bit with my *burka*. What was acceptable in Bangalore was not acceptable over here. There, Ammi didn't mind so much if I didn't wear my *burka* to college, although she had suggested it. But here, it was different. My *burka* was supposed to be my second skin.

After the big fight, Abbu had reduced our Vellore trips drastically. Although he, himself went there every month, to give Zohra Phuppu some money, and every other week to see how his business was faring. He had just stopped taking us there. We went to Vellore during Eid, which had been a very distressful experience in the past few years. So the anticipation about going to Vellore was slowly replaced by indifference. Now I almost dreaded going there. I hadn't seen Rehana in a long while. The last time I saw her was during Bakrid, and she had avoided me as much as her father had avoided mine. I had been terribly hurt.

Although now I pretended indifference, sometimes I remembered the old days. How happy we had been together as a family. And now we had to ward off all the uncomfortable situations that arose out of the feud. During Eid, when we were forced to live together, I would watch amused – and even scared – at the way Abbu and Chacha ignored each other.

We were now just ten minutes away from Vellore. I woke up Mateen gently. He got up and rubbed his eyes wearily. Outside it was still dark. As we entered Gandhi Road, I sat up straight. Suddenly I realised that Zohra Phuppu was dead.

❖❖❖

12

Zohra Phuppu

The house was cold. Ammabi was sitting on a mat on the ground. In front of her, on the *divan,* Zohra Phuppu's corpse was laid out, the feet facing towards Mecca. Ammi flung whatever was in her hand, and she dropped down near Zohra Phuppu. Abbu cried, his head in his hands, his shoulders shaking. When he looked up, I could see his face had contorted, making him look ugly and a little mad.

I had read somewhere that grief can sometimes numb you. Now I knew it was true. As I sat looking at her, at the people who came pouring in, there was a strange sensation all over my arms and back. It was prickly at first and then there was nothing, almost as if something cold had been poured over me that had slowly congealed and refused to let anything enter.

I expected Ammabi to perform some kind of theatrics for my father, making him feel that she was all alone in the world, and so we would have to take her in. But even the thought of Ammabi living with us didn't evoke any feelings.

But she wept quietly, and didn't utter a word. She had to be acting. The worst would come soon. But nothing happened. Only then did I realise that Ammabi thrived on Phuppu's presence. She needed someone to taunt, someone who was her own and yet not her blood.

Histrionics were of course supplied by Fouzia Phuppu about whom I had forgotten completely. She wailed and she cried. "Zohra! Where are you, Zohra? Why did you leave us?" she cried out loudly, every ten minutes. My Abbu and Sadiq Chacha kept a reasonable distance from each other even in their grief.

Phuppu had been suffering from typhoid fever for a few days. When Abbu had visited last, he had taken her to a doctor and bought medicines for her. Sadiq Chacha too claimed to have bought medicines for her. Yet she had died. Basheer was nowhere to be found and I couldn't begin to fathom his pain.

The crying reached a crescendo when it was decided that it was time for Phuppu's bath, her last *ghusl*. They took her away to another room, where they prepared her for the burial. There were passionate outbursts from Abbu as he shook his head, wiping his face, and Ammi looked like she had lost everything she had ever loved.

They brought her back on a wooden bier. Her face was covered with the white *kafan* and she was wrapped tightly in it. We all gathered near her to see her for one last time. Mateen's face turned white with fear, and I wanted to take him along with me and go away to some other place. But Ammi had dragged me too to the spot and we stared at Phuppu's peaceful face. After some time, the men asked us to move aside and took her body away.

When they had left, amid the loud cries of women, some of the numbness evaporated. I turned to the nearest person and clutched her arm, hugging her, crying. When I opened my eyes, I saw it was Rehana. She too was crying. Forgotten were the cold stares as we clung to each other and cried for our beautiful Phuppu, who had allowed her life to be wasted away, inch by inch.

That evening I sat in Phuppu's room reading the *Quran*. Rehana came up to me, wiping her eyes.

"Just see this!" She handed me a plastic box. Strips of medicine lay neatly arranged in layers in the box. Not even one of them had been opened. Hatred for the man, who had reduced her self-worth to such an extent rushed through me, but at the moment I focused on Rehana who was saying something. We were once again tentatively trying to become friends. No matter how much I protested, that the feud that has kept her away from me didn't make much difference to me, I knew it wasn't true.

Basheer hadn't turned up at all, which made everyone worry immensely. Abbu had taken his absence lightly. Grief had made the boy stay away, he said, and was sure that he would be back. But Abbu was wrong. Basheer had disappeared. A day later, Abbu sent a few people to search for Basheer in every possible place in Vellore. Someone had seen him boarding a bus for Madras. But how could one search for a young boy in such a big city?

Guilt ate away Abbu. He had let down his sister twice, apparently. Once when he had failed to see how ill she had been, and now when he couldn't locate her son. Chacha's family had left after two days and so had Fouzia Phuppu. With Rehana gone, I was once more left to myself. We had become friends, but I had a strong feeling that when we returned to Bangalore, we would revert to the feud attitude once more.

Ammi had taken over the household temporarily. I had heard Ammi and Abbu talking about how they had asked Ammabi to come and live with us but she refused. Although I was thankful, I wondered how she would manage to live alone.

Ammi didn't seem to care where I was or what I was doing. I went to the terrace hoping that Imtiaz would be there. In the past few years, he had jumped over the terraces quite a number of times and I had become acquainted with him, rather reluctantly.

Aasia was there, pulling the stiffly dried clothes from the line. I ignored her as she bundled the clothes in one arm and put all the clothespins into an old aluminium plate placed nearby especially for the purpose.

She held the bundle of clothes in the crook of her arm and stared out into the *galli*. We stood there in silence, watching the evening descend, hearing the shouts on the terraces retreating into silence, the kites dotting the sky slowly being reeled back inside and stored safely for the next day's sport. A little later, I moved to the other wall and watched the sky darkening gently around the mountains. Aasia finally went downstairs and I watched her leaving gratefully.

Imtiaz's terrace was empty. I felt a crushing sense of disappointment because I wanted to talk to him. I contemplated on going back downstairs and turned away. Then, on an impulse I turned back. Imtiaz was on his terrace, waving at me and my heart actually leaped.

Feeling foolish, I quickly scanned the other terraces to see if anyone else was around. No one I knew was watching. No one who would find it inappropriate that I was waving to a boy. So I waved back at him. It was all the invitation he needed. Once again, I watched fascinated as he bounded across the terraces and soon he was on the terrace immediately next to ours.

"Hi!"

"Sorry about your Phuppu."

"Do you know Basheer well?"

Had their acquaintance moved beyond the occasional kite fight on the terrace? He clicked his tongue and nodded.

"What an idiot he is! Running away the day his mother died."

"How can you say such a thing?"

"I... I...Well, I can't imagine why he would want to run away like this!"

"If you can't imagine, then don't pass judgement on him at least!"

"I wasn't! I just said..."

"I won't talk to you if you talk in that tone again."

He looked amused but when he saw that I was serious, he scratched his head absently.

"Sorry."

"How come we keep meeting like this here? Almost every time I'm in Vellore, and if I come to the terrace, I meet you."

"You really think that's a coincidence?"

For a moment, just for a moment, I forgot Zohra Phuppu, Basheer and the problems of my family. He looked at me steadily. I looked away and grasped the parapet wall tightly.

"What do you mean?" I asked, the question sounding sharper than I had intended.

"Every time you come to Vellore, a friend of mine who works in Gandhi Road spots your car and lets me know. And I'm on the terrace, hoping you'll come."

His words rang in my ears. I felt my throat tighten.

"Who works in Gandhi Road?" I managed to ask.

"My friend Suresh works in Gandhi Road. In that gold shop there, Sundaram Jewellers."

I nodded, but didn't know what to say.

"Mehnaz, what happened?"

I still couldn't speak. There was worry in his eyes. He took a deep breath and started speaking.

"Look, I don't know why you're looking so strange now, but I just wanted to tell you that I really like you. Is there anything wrong with that? I can't explain it, but every time Suresh calls me up and tells me he has spotted your father's car, my heart swells up in anticipation. Of seeing you... of talking to you!"

The breeze had grown sharp. It stung my arms and I wrapped my *dupatta* around myself like a shawl. He was looking at me expectantly.

"I have only this pair of *chappals* with me here in Vellore. Don't tell me you want these also?"

He looked confused so I grinned at him and he smiled back hesitantly. I didn't have to say anything, did I? All he said was that he liked me. Well, so did I but I wasn't going to tell him that.

But he was still looking at me expectantly. I raised my eyebrows exaggeratedly and huddled into my *dupatta*.

"It's getting cold. I think I'll go downstairs. Take care. Bye!" I said and turned around. He caught hold of my arm and spun me around abruptly. He released my arm when he saw that I was getting angry.

"Will you come to the terrace tomorrow?"

I shook my head. "We're leaving tomorrow morning."

When he didn't say anything to that, I felt obliged to add something at least. "I'll be coming for Phuppu's *chehlum*. Maybe I'll see you then." When he smiled, I smiled back relieved.

13

Itch in the Palm

I missed Phuppu. It was hard to accept that she was gone forever and there was always the question of Basheer nagging me. Why had he left us and gone? While we were still in Vellore, Abbu had gone to Madras to search for him but he had come back unsuccessful.

I went to Mrs Dahlia, who comforted me with thick slices of home-baked chocolate cake.

"Will anything ever be normal again?" I asked her feeling misery wash over me.

She leaned back on her faded sofa and smiled. "Life overpowers death, my dear. The pain of all loss, no matter how horrid, will eventually grow less and less because, you see, life takes over."

Perhaps her pop psychological analysis was right. I was preparing furiously for exams while Mateen was also engrossed in school. Abbu had started going to the shop after a couple of days and Ammi... if she stopped what she was doing, we would all come to a standstill.

When I wasn't thinking about Phuppu or about my father's clash with his brother or about Basheer, I often thought of Imtiaz. I liked to relive the entire incident slowly, playing it back in my mind, like my own personal movie. I tried to recall the other times I had met him, and tried to infuse this special feeling in those moments too. But I couldn't remember much about what had happened then.

My exams were to begin a week after Phuppu's *chehlum,* the fortieth day after her death. I was worried, but I also wished the days to pass faster so that I could meet Imtiaz again. I wanted to see if what I was feeling was just my imagination or if it really existed. Sahana and Jyoti thought that the *chappal*-throwing incident was just too funny and I laughed with them, but I started feeling indignant when I realised they were still laughing at me.

"Stop it!" I whispered furiously in class. They looked at me and nodded, but their faces told me that they still thought the incident was very funny. I vowed not to tell them anything further about Imtiaz. But at lunch time, as we sat in the college canteen eating crisp *masala dosas,* they both promised that they wouldn't laugh.

"What's he like?" asked Sahana hesitantly. I glared at her but she looked solemn. I shot a look at Jyoti, who was scooping up some potatoes with her dosa and she nodded.

I felt a strange heat warming my cheeks as I spoke of Imtiaz. "He's not bad to look at. He's tall and he has a very nice smile." Jyoti looked at Sahana and they both started giggling again. I turned away from them and finished my *dosa* alone.

That evening Asifa Chachi and Rehana came home. I walked towards them quickly when suddenly Aasia beckoned me from the kitchen. I went in feeling curious. Why was she calling me? Where was Ammi? I walked into the kitchen and saw Aasia making tea.

"What?"

She didn't look at me. She was concentrating on pouring tea into cups.

"Your mother asked me to tell you that nothing has changed between Bhaijaan and Rehana Apa's father. She just wanted me to warn you of that."

She had finished straining the tea and arranged the cups on a cream coloured tray and biscuits from a plastic jar onto a plate.

As she did all these things, I realised the extent to which I hated her. Who did she think she was? She looked so important, as if she was Ammi's daughter and I was just a child. Relaying Ammi's messages to me like I was a dim-witted fool. That too, personal messages about my family.

She covered her head with her *dupatta,* getting ready to take the tea tray out. "Give me the tray," I said harshly. She looked at me and then shook her head. Feeling furious, I tried to wrest the tray from her but she had a strong grasp. "Aasia, give me the tray," I said as calmly as I could, even though I could feel my nostrils flare with anger.

The teacups shook as I pulled the tray from her. She looked at me angrily. I kept the tray on the marble counter and slapped her hard. Some of my anger dissipated when my hands stung. Feeling a bit satisfied and a lot more apprehensive, I took up the tray. She had turned towards the sink and was crying. I felt remorseful. But how could I apologise to Aasia?

Ammi sat stiffly with Chachi and Rehana. She hadn't asked them to remove their *burkas,* and I didn't think it was right of me to ask. Ammi looked at me warningly. The incident about Aasia immediately forgotten, I smiled at them and said *salaam.* They greeted me in return. There was a cellophane-wrapped *mithai* box on the centre table.

I served them tea and tried to draw them into a conversation. Rehana finally spoke.

"Mehnaz, I passed my tenth exams."

"I'm so happy for you Rehana!" I said feeling genuinely glad. So the *mithai* was for that. After that, both of us were silent once more. My attempts to strike a conversation were met with a strained silence.

I looked at Rehana. Her head was bent and she looked down modestly. The scarf that she wore with her *burka* was wound around her head tightly. Not one stray strand of hair peeped out. She was wearing black gloves. I looked at her feet. Black socks, too. Since when had Rehana become so religious?

She made me uncomfortable now. I realised that we had no common ground to speak about. Ammi had asked Rehana what she planned to do further.

"Ammi wants me to stay at home and help her, but Abbu wants me to do my PUC at least," she said softly.

What do you want? I wanted to voice my thoughts and ask her but I knew that Ammi would think it improper or some such thing.

"So what will you do now?" Ammi asked. Rehana looked at me and then at Ammi. I noticed for the first time what beautiful eyes she had. Maybe I noticed it now because it was the only part of her face that was uncovered. Large kohl-lined fluid eyes that held a hint of vulnerability.

"I will probably do as Abbu says." She looked down at her glove-covered hands. I leaned back on the sofa, trying to repress the urge to ask her the numerous questions that were buzzing in my head.

They got up after a while to leave. Ammi didn't say anything. She too got up silently. I got up and told them they should drop by some other time. They didn't reply. Why did Rehana have to change so much? Why did she have to grow up so soon?

She didn't even say good-bye.

14

With or Without Aasia

Ammi took us shopping the next day. She asked me to get ready and when I emerged from my room ten minutes later, she was ready with Aasia. Mateen too stood waiting. Why was Aasia coming along? Obviously she had told Ammi that I had slapped her. I kept waiting for some indication from Ammi. But instead she was taking me shopping.

"Wear your *burka*. We're going to Shivajinagar." I went back to my room sulkily. When we were outside the house, I looked at her face. It seemed calm. I was going to act normal.

"Why are we going to Shivajinagar? You know that I don't like to buy my clothes from there."

She didn't reply as we got inside an auto. It was a rather tight squeeze. Mateen had to be wedged uncomfortably between Ammi and me. Aasia was at the other end, next to Ammi.

Ammi was talking to Aasia and ignoring me completely. So this was her new punishment, I thought. Well, I wasn't going to bother myself too much about it. Aasia answered Ammi's questions quietly, almost sullenly.

What did Ammi want to buy in Shivajianagar? Aasia looked around, trying to take in everything all at once but without looking too awestruck. When her gaze fell on the display section of a shop, she walked forward hesitantly. The pasty white mannequin was dressed in a gaudy green *ghaghra choli*. The outfit was embellished with sequins all over, glinting in the dull afternoon sun. She leaned forward, resting her palms gently on the glass of the display window.

We went inside the shop. I looked around, trying hard to conceal my distaste. If ever Sahana and Jyoti found out I actually came here, they would never stop laughing at me! I sat down on a patched-up stool near the long counter. Ammi, Aasia and Mateen too sat down. A man stood behind the counter and smiled at Mateen. Ammi pointed towards something in a corner and the man pulled it out obligingly. He shook it open. It was a saree, pink with golden sequins. The tiny golden nubs flashed enticingly in the fully lit interior of the shop. The horror on my face was evident as Ammi looked at me and then at the man. She bought the horrid pink saree, a yellow *ghaghra choli,* a blue *salwar kameez,* and glittering *red dupatta,* which I personally thought was the worst.

As we stepped out of the shop, I could bear it no longer. "Ammi, why are you doing this? Why are you buying clothes that you know I will never wear?"

Ammi looked at me quietly. "Mehnaz, they are not for you. They are for Aasia."

"Why?" I asked her. I knew I sounded childish and recalcitrant.

Ammi shifted her weight from one foot to the other, bunching the handles of the three plastic bags that she was holding. "Didn't I tell you? I'm thinking of getting Aasia married," she said.

When we got home, I was very quiet. I didn't know what to make of Ammi's announcement. We had visited two more shops and the number of bags had increased from three to seven. We bought a pair of glittering slippers, saree petticoats, and some modest underwear. Ammi didn't say a word after that. I followed her quietly. I looked at Aasia now and then. She seemed calm. So, Ammi had told her already, or she would be as shocked as I was. I knew I should be happy. After all, I had been waiting for this day for so many years. I imagined the house without Aasia's annoying presence. Ammi would then turn to me for any assistance. I would then become indispensable to her.

During dinner, I sat down as usual with Abbu and Mateen. Ammi and Aasia ate afterwards, after cooking all the *rotis*. But Ammi called me to the kitchen. Reluctantly I got up and went inside. The exhaust fan was on but the smoke from the *tawa* ran high up to the ceiling. Ammi was rolling out a *roti*.

She pointed to the *tawa* and asked me to cook the *roti*. Why? Where was Aasia? I looked around and saw her at the sink washing dishes.

"It's time you too learnt that the kitchen is a part of your own house, Mehnaz," Ammi said, rolling out another *roti* deftly, "When Aasia gets married, you will have to do at least half of the things she does now. Though I doubt how you will, with your nose buried inside a book all the time."

I flashed a look at Aasia's back. Did Ammi have to lecture me in front of her? I opened my mouth to protest and then kept quiet. This is what I got for temporarily relieving the itch in my palm by slapping Aasia. But it had been worth it, now that I was going to get rid of her permanently.

"Turn the *roti* now. It's burning on one side," Ammi issued orders curtly. She was like an army general, I thought as I dabbed oil on the cooked *roti*. When I finally went outside, Abbu and Mateen had finished eating. I sat down with Ammi. We ate in silence. The only sounds which filled the room were those from the TV.

"Your Phuppu was right," Ammi said breaking the silence. "Asifa has brought up Rehana better than I have brought you up. Rehana looks so demure and I'm sure she doesn't get into silly spats with the servants."

I swallowed hard, trying to get the *roti* down. But it was difficult to do that with tears blocking my throat.

"I should have been stricter with you. I should have taught you how to manage the house and other important things. Rehana would manage beautifully if she were to get married tomorrow. And you... I would be ashamed to call you my daughter."

Ammi ate calmly as she said these horrible things to me. Did she really mean it? Or was she just angry about the slapping incident? My throat was blocked now. I hastily reached for a glass of water. Tears burned my eyes. I couldn't speak or defend myself because I knew I would start bawling if I did. I tried to finish my meal as calmly as I could, even though all I wanted to do was run to my room and cry. Ammi got up abruptly.

"Has anything I said affected you at all?" she asked, picking up her plate. I broke my *roti* into bits and forced myself to eat it. She cleared the table efficiently. Once she had finished, she came out of the kitchen, wiping her hands on her saree *pallu*. I was still at the table eating.

"Stop dreaming and hurry up," she said and went to the hall. Aasia too walked to the hall and sat down at her usual place. They all sat there watching TV.

The dining hall was dimly lit because Abbu liked the effect. I got up slowly with my plate in my hand. Ammi had switched off the kitchen lights already. I walked in the dark and kept my plate in the sink. I washed my hands at the kitchen sink and rushed to my room blindly.

I shut myself in the bathroom and stood staring at my face in the mirror watching my face contort and twist, as finally the tears came rushing out. I couldn't stop crying. I cried till my chest hurt and then I stumbled onto my bed. Self-pity can make you do a lot of things. Mine dulled my senses enough so I could sleep that night.

15

Bridging the Worlds

In the morning, things seemed different. Although nothing had changed much, I could sense a shift. When I got up, it was a bright and cool day.

So Aasia was finally getting married. She would be gone in a few weeks' time. I tried to remember the day when she had first arrived. I couldn't remember much, except that I didn't feel so strongly against her then. What had happened between then and now that I have come to hate her so much? Was it because I feared she would take my place in the house? That was absurd.

But Mateen cared for her. And Ammi depended on her. I shook my head and stared at the ceiling. They didn't love her like they loved me. Why had I let my resentment get so out of my hand that it had turned into full-fledged hatred? She had left her family to come and work for us. Not once, had I asked her about her family. How they were? How she felt about living so far from them? I could have befriended her if I had really tried. Instead, I had antagonised her and now hurt her.

I was getting late for college. After ten minutes when I was slipping into my *kurta,* I thought of what Ammi had said. Did she really regret that I was her daughter and not Rehana?

Rehana was perfect and I was miles away from being that. Even then, I couldn't bring myself to hate her. I resented Ammi who had those expectations from me.

Aasia looked glum. I watched her as she set the table for breakfast. Although she said nothing, I had a feeling that maybe she wasn't happy about getting married. Abbu sat down on his chair at the head of the table with a grunt. Mateen was already eating as his school bus arrived early.

I munched on the toast and remembered that I hadn't picked up my history book. I ran back to my room and got it. I was stuffing it into my bag when I saw Aasia watching me. How different our lives were! Although I was just a little younger than her, my life revolved around college and friends. For Aasia, the house and the kitchen was her world. She knew nothing of sitting in the canteen and sipping hot coffee, or of bunking classes to go for a dance programme in the auditorium. There were so many things that she would never experience.

Abbu was waiting for me in the car. He was silent. As the car edged slowly forward in the morning traffic, I looked out of the window. It was indeed a beautiful day. "Mehnaz, your mother wants to get Aasia married," he said. I turned to look at him. He looked ahead, concentrating on the traffic. His face looked a little puffy to me now. His eyes looked tired and dark circles framed his eyes. He seemed to have let go of himself after Phuppu's death. His hands gripped the steering wheel tightly. What was I expected to say?

"Well, what do you think?" he asked. I looked out of the window again. It was odd. Abbu treated me more and more as an adult. He asked my opinion on various issues and we sometimes even discussed politics. I felt strange but happy that my ideas were being respected and considered as being worthy. But the more Abbu treated me as an adult, the more I got diminished in Ammi's eyes. She regarded everything I did, as a waste of time. I realised that Aasia probably knew more about Ammi than I did. All I ever saw her was in anger.

I tried to think of how to answer Abbu's question. Should I tell him that this was what I had wanted all along?

"Well, she had to be married some time anyway."

He looked at me before his head whipped around to look at the road again. "Your mother told me, you hate Aasia so much that you slapped her. Is that true?"

I looked at my hands. That day, it had felt so good. But the repercussions of that one slap were tagging behind me, making my life cumbersome. Would Abbu understand how I felt about her, when I myself couldn't pinpoint the reason why she irked me so much?

"It was a mistake, Abbu." The car stopped at a signal. All around us other vehicles too waited. Abbu looked at me and I was forced to meet his gaze.

"Why?" he asked softly. "When I have not lifted my hand and hit anyone I employ, not even once, no matter how much I have been provoked, then why did you do so?"

I had been wrong. Things were no different from last night. I was still being blamed. But trying to put that maddening thought aside, I looked at Abbu and whispered, "I'm sorry, Abbu."

"Did you say that to her?" he asked, starting the car once more. Other cars zoomed ahead of us, while we moved on slowly. I shook my head.

"I want you to apologise to her before she gets married," he said curtly and then we spoke no more. Looking ahead, I could see the arched gates of the college and I sighed. I already felt free.

The car came to a stop outside the college gates and I picked up my bag. Abbu wasn't looking at me. I couldn't leave without trying to make things between us, at least a little better. "Okay, Abbu, I'll do that."

A cool morning breeze rifled through my clothes and I shivered. A few girls sat on the stone steps leading to one of the college buildings. Someone was relating a joke and the others listened seriously before erupting into loud laughter. Ammi didn't let me laugh like that. She said it was rude and was not the way how good girls or women should laugh. What did their mothers tell them? From the second peal of laughter, I surmised that their mothers probably had more important things on their minds.

I walked into the class and saw that Sahana had saved a place for me near the window. I smiled gratefully. As much as possible, I chose to sit near the window. While the lecture progressed I would often surreptitiously glance outside and daydream. When at times I fretted that things that had happened were not to my liking, I was just glad to remember the times spent looking out of the windows. I was even thankful that I had the opportunity to step, out of the house. Mrs Cherian walked in, holding the attendance register. I nudged Sahana and asked her where Jyoti was and she shrugged. I studied her profile as she looked at Mrs Cherian. Although we were close friends, I often felt that a wide chasm existed between us. One, that I desperately struggled to cross, one that she never knew even existed.

16

Ants, Lizards and Mateen

Ammi had decided to send Aasia back to her town after Phuppu's *chehlum*. Ammi had been hoping that she might get a good proposal for her when we were in Vellore. Abbu and Ammi were going to provide her with clothes, some jewellery and money so her wedding would progress smoothly. Aasia looked more depressed as each day neared.

The days smoothened into weeks, and soon there were only three more days left for the *chehlum*. I looked at the calendar above my desk. It fluttered slightly. I had marked each day with a tiny cross, hardly visible. But now that it was actually here, I felt ashamed about it.

I went back to my books. The first exam was of Hindi Literature, my nemesis. I stared at the lengthy novel that I had to read and shuddered. One look at the clock and I shut the book, feeling a little relieved, a little alarmed. Ammi had allotted me the new duty of making tea every afternoon.

Aasia was peeling the garlic and as I took out the saucepan imperiously and poured milk in it, I could feel her stare piercing my back. Ignoring her, I set about making tea. Where there was resentment from my side only at first, now there was full-fledged animosity from her too. I could have befriended her. But now it was too late, I thought as I watched the milk erupt into tiny bubbles at the surface. I sprinkled tea leaves generously and turned around to see her. Her head was bent as she forced open each clove of the garlic by pressing them down on the hard ground. "Where's your tea cup?" I asked her.

Dusting her *salwar* she got up slowly and washed her steel glass and gave it to me. I poured tea into our cups and hers meticulously.

I lifted my gaze and met her eyes. There was a pleading look in them that made her look like a beggar. She clutched my hand suddenly and the tray turned up slightly. The cups slid down on one side and a little tea sloshed out. “The tea’s getting cold,” I said. But she didn’t let go of my hand.

Expelling a deep breath, I removed her hand firmly from mine.

Ammi was curled up on one of the sofas in the hall, reading something. It was strange, and I wondered, how I never knew that Ammi liked to read Urdu novels. Maybe, now that I was spending more time outside my room, I was noticing all this. I watched her face as she read avidly, her eyes scanning the lines swiftly.

Mateen came running out of his room. I looked at him, feeling a little awed that he was almost as tall as me. Abbu and Ammi had even allotted him a room of his own now. Our house had two guest rooms, one of which Abbu had given to him. Abbu had painted it a bright yellow and had curtains fitted on the windows. Carpenters had been called and Mateen’s bed and desk were built to his liking.

At times, the barest twinge of jealousy would enter my mind but I refused to acknowledge, that I could possibly be jealous of Mateen. He was like my own child. And whatever Abbu gave him, he deserved it. There had never been any sibling rivalry between us.

“Api! Come and see this, please, you have to, please!” he said, grabbing my arm. Before I could get up from the sofa, he had dragged me up.

“Hold it, Mateen. You’ll pull my arm right out,” I said as I tried to wriggle my arm from his small but powerful grasp.

He took me to his room. The faint smell of paint still lingered in the room. Bright apple-green curtains fluttered at the windows. Cartoon posters with cute and witty blurbs stared out from the walls. Mateen had gone to his bathroom which was open, and I could hear his voice calling me in, sounding slightly muffled. "Api! Come!"

Intrigued, I walked into the bathroom and found him staring in fascination at a dead lizard on the ground that was covered with ants. How was it that in the movies the heroine could scream so effortlessly? I opened my mouth but only a hoarse shout came out. I called for Ammi. I ran out and sat on his bed, closing my eyes tightly but my mind immediately presented me with the gruesome picture.

"AMMI!"

She looked annoyed because I was shouting so much, then walked into the bathroom and screamed with ease.

Ammi and I both have an inveterate fear of lizards. She rushed out screaming again. Finally, Aasia had to come with her broom and sweetp it up. I averted my eyes when she came out of the bathroom holding the dust pan. Mateen had found everything so funny that he clutched his stomach and laughed to his content. Resting my head in my shaky hands, I stared at my little brother. His eyes glinted with mischief. The cute cherub of a few years ago had now metamorphosed into a little *shaitan*.

Despite having seen him from the time he was a baby, there were times when I felt I didn't know Mateen at all.

17

An Unspoken Agreement

I was shocked when Abbu said that he wouldn't drive down to Vellore.

"We're going by train," he announced at dinner that night. Ammi, who had been pouring out water for him, looked at him, alarmed. She set the jug on the table splashing some water on me.

"Why? Aren't you well?" she asked, looking worried. We always went to Vellore by car. Always. What had happened to Abbu now that he decided to go by train? I waited for his answer. He looked weary.

"I booked the tickets a week ago. We have to leave in the afternoon by the Brindavan Express."

When Ammi persisted, Abbu huffed impatiently. "We're not going by car because I'm too tired to drive. What do you want? That we all meet with some accident and die or land up in some hospital?"

Ammi didn't say a word. Her head was bent as she forced herself to eat, but I noticed a tear slowly rolling down her cheek. Vicious pleasure grabbed hold of me suddenly for a moment, reminding me of my own crying fit some days back.

We had to take two autos to Cantonment Station. Ammi, Aasia, Mateen in one, Abbu and me in the other. Abbu was quiet in the auto. I didn't want to provoke him unnecessarily, so I didn't speak to him. Whatever it was that was annoying him would soon disappear, or he would tell us about it on his own.

The train journey was a refreshing experience for me. I watched the clouds merge together and diffuse into shapeless forms. The mountains in the distance rolled by endlessly, green paddy undulated in the wind, and I felt that it was all so romantic. Sipping the watery coffee that Abbu bought for all of us from the railways vendor, I looked outside the grilled window. The train stopped at numerous stations like, Bangarpet, Kuppam and Jolarpettai, unfamiliar and new names as we never passed by them on the road.

The train neared Katpadi Junction where we had to get down. Outside, the sky was darkening rapidly and a cool breeze ruffled my hair. Abbu got up and hauled out the luggage from under the seat and Ammi looked harried as she tried to determine if we had missed anything. The train screeched to a halt and I held on to Mateen's hand tightly. We both lurched forward but didn't fall.

We stepped outside Katpadi station and Abbu hailed an auto. The autos here were larger, I realised, because we all fitted in one auto. We all were compressed together but managed till we reached Vellore.

As we passed Gandhi Road, I wondered how Imtiaz would know I was here. When the auto stopped, I got out and looked at our house. There was no more anticipation of coming here, no joy.

Rehana and her family had arrived in the morning by bus. Sadiq Chacha had stopped driving out to Vellore from many years and always came by bus or train. He sat in the hall, his shoulders hunched forward, looking down. Fouzia Phuppu and Farha were arriving that night. I kept my bag on the floor and looked around. The house was the same but not as clean as earlier times. Piles of dust had accumulated in the corners. Cobwebs dangled precariously from the ceiling, and the fan was darkened with grime.

Asifa Chachi and Rehana had occupied one room. They had heard us come but they didn't emerge. As I saw Ammi and Aasia haul our luggage into the other room, I wondered how it was going to be. We were all here, but we didn't exist for each other. How would we manage dinner? Ammabi sat in the hall, rolling prayer beads between her fingers. Phuppu's death had changed everything because I actually felt sorry for Ammabi.

Mateen was in the bathroom, and so while waiting for my turn I sat down next to her. She looked at me, all the while rocking back and forth. I asked her how she was but she only mumbled something.

Mateen came out of the bathroom, but before I could rush in, Abbu went inside. I went to the kitchen where Ammi was making tea for Abbu. The blackened walls, the Sumeet mixie that Abbu had given Phuppu a few years ago stared back at me. Zohra Phuppu who had ruled her kitchen gently with resigned affection, had been so excited on seeing it, making me realise how easy it was to please some people.

Would Imtiaz be on the terrace? It was quite late and usually all the terraces were deserted at this time. Maybe I could meet him tomorrow.

When I finally emerged from the bathroom, I saw before me, Abbu and Chacha seated stiffly on the far ends of the sofa. They both looked away from each other. Abbu was sipping tea. On the table in front of them, another cup of tea sat, cooling. Ammi had made tea for both of them, of course.

I went inside, which was to be our room and wiped my face with my towel. Mateen didn't know – and didn't care – that the other room was not ours to explore. He ran in there before anyone could stop him. Ammi bit her lower lip anxiously. Abbu hadn't noticed. He had been very preoccupied with ignoring Chacha.

Mateen came out after a while and decided to drag me in there. "Come, Rehana didi is in there. Chachi also. Come!"

I freed my hand from his grasp and sat down in the hall next to Ammabi. Abbu and Chacha looked like two overgrown children who had decided not to talk to each other. Maybe it was watching them together, realising how similar they looked that made me do the comparison. Or maybe, it was because they looked like harmless but miffed children. For the first time in my life, I dared to intervene in the matters of the adults.

Clearing my throat, I spoke fast. "Abbu, Chacha, please forget all this nonsense and become brothers again. It's not too late to say sorry to each other. You can still work things out if you want. Please don't continue like this."

Abbu glared at me until I feared his eyeballs would pop out. Ammi yanked me up from the *divan* and shook me. "Mehnaz!" she said and dragged me to the room. I turned around and saw Chacha getting up hurriedly and walking to his room. He shut the door resolutely. Abbu's face was red, his fingers curled into a fist.

Ammi flung me on the bed and raised her hand to slap me. I flinched, and she stopped herself.

"Mehnaz! What did you think you were doing?"

I sat quietly for the next half an hour listening wearily to Ammi as she told me succinctly that I had no business interfering in what my Abbu and Chacha did. How dare I advise them?

Ammi and Aasia made dinner, while I stayed in the room, studying. I was sick at heart. I wanted to talk to someone. Rehana, my friend to whom I used to tell everything was right across the room, but I couldn't approach her. Not just because she was locked up with her parents, but because she was no longer the same girl with whom I could share all my confidences.

Fouzia Phuppu arrived by a late bus. I didn't come out to greet her as she ambled up the hall slowly. Farha had put on a lot of weight too, I realised. Not surprising, I thought. Maybe soon we wouldn't be able to distinguish whose bulk it was, mother's or daughter's.

Phuppu removed her *burka* and sat down in the hall, her face all red. Silently, she saw that the rooms had already been divided and conquered. What remained to be occupied was the hall, and there too, the *divan* had been usurped by Ammabi. She flashed a resentful glance at me when I came out to have dinner. Rehana's family hadn't come out.

We had dinner in silence, the *rotis* once again getting stuck in my throat. Abbu didn't say much. I looked at the closed door. Weren't they going to have dinner? Maybe they were waiting for us to finish so they could come out and eat. If I wasn't feeling so much like a martyr, I would have laughed.

But it was true. Once dinner was over, Ammi herded us into our room. Fouzia Phuppu looked offended, but Ammi for once ignored her. Abbu too came in to sleep. Aasia as always would sleep in the kitchen. This was the same bed where Rehana, Phuppu and I slept whenever we were in Vellore. And now to see Mateen's and Abbu's curled forms on the bed looked odd. There was place for one more person to squeeze in. That was me. Ammi slept on a mat on the floor.

I could hear Fouzia Phuppu grumbling as she spread out a mat for her daughter and herself. My ears slowly became accustomed to Abbu's soft snores and Mateen's gentle breathing. I had been correct. The door to the opposite room opened softy. I heard light footsteps moving towards the kitchen. I could also hear Fouzia Phuppu's ingratiating voice talking to Chachi. Probably complaining about my mother. Chachi was rolling out *rotis*. I heard the stove being switched on. I got up and kneeled on the bed. If I just peeped out, I could see Rehana.

Yes, there she was, bringing in a jug of water. Even if she tried to look in, she wouldn't be able to see me because it was pitch dark inside. No gloves, I saw, and hopefully no socks too. But she had covered her head with her *dupatta*. It was ten o'clock in the night.

I lowered myself back on the bed gently and closed my eyes. I was feeling sleepy. Drowsily, I wondered how things were going to be like tomorrow. We couldn't possibly hold Phuppu's *chehlum* with this unspoken agreement of keeping out of each other's way. I shifted uncomfortably and turned away from Mateen.

18

Chehlum

Ammi woke me up at five, the next morning. The whole household was asleep and I staggered outside sleepily. On the *divan,* Ammabi lay curled into one side, facing the wall. On the floor, Fouzia Phuppu and Farha lay on two mats, stretched out inelegantly. Dawn had not yet broken, and it was dark and quiet.

I shivered a little. In the kitchen, Aasia too was stretched out, her covers flung far away. Ammi woke her up and together the three of us started the preparations for Phuppu's *chehlum.* It was definitely the most tiring day of my life.

A professional cook came and occupied our kitchen briefly, issuing curt orders to his assistant who peeled onions with alarming rapidity. He then proceeded to cook huge quantities of *biryani* for the *fatiha.* Ammi and Aasia sat down on their haunches after he had left, and distributed the hot *biryani* into plastic packets, dishing out the steaming rice with dinner plates instead of the usual large spoon. Once that was done, they turned to the *daalcha* that the cook had made, a gravy made with *dals,* meat, brinjals and potatoes, and divided it into the packets. I had watched them for some time, wondering if I should join and help. Ammi looked tired but she was still mustering enough energy to complete the task before the actual *fatiha* began. When all the packets were done, Ammi kept them in a huge plastic basket, the kind that we used to carry lunch to school in, only this one was about five times larger. Abbu hefted the bag and ordering Mateen to come with him, they went to the *masjid* where they gave away the food to the poor.

Abbu had invited everyone he knew and everything went well. Except for the fact that Chacha's family stayed inside. It was amazing but I still hadn't seen Rehana. At ten in the morning, when Aasia and I were in a frenzy of cleaning up the house and helping Ammi, Asifa Chachi opened the door of her room. She stepped out quietly and without looking at us walked softly into the kitchen. I looked up from my corner where I had been swiping at cobwebs with a huge broom.

I was getting really annoyed with their behaviour. If they had come for the *chehlum,* it was only right that they too should help. Instead, they were sitting inside resting while we slogged. And that could be said in double measure of Fouzia Phuppu and her darling daughter. Both of them were asleep on our bed, in our room. They got up for breakfast, then for lunch, and went back to sleep.

Chachi returned from the kitchen, holding a tray. It had two covered plates and two cups of tea. She went in, looking straight ahead, and the door closed behind her. Aasia was scrubbing the floor in one corner and chose that very moment to look up. She caught me looking at the closed door and then she smiled slightly. I didn't smile back. Dusting cobwebs was back-breaking work.

The same pattern was repeated at lunch. A tray went inside while we stared at the closed door in silence. Later in the day, when other people had started coming, I saw Rehana sitting with a couple of women, talking to them softly. She seemed very comfortable with everyone, smiling, saying *salaam* while I looked on feeling like an intruder. They were safe, now that others were here and there could be no confrontation, no messy emotional outbursts. Chachi and Rehana seemed to have blossomed under the gaze of strangers.

Phuppu's death had changed too many things. What had always been there could now disappear for ever. Abbu had been talking of letting out this house, after persuading Ammabi to come live with us. I listened to the news, feeling more and more depressed. First the feud, then Phuppu's death, now Abbu was thinking of letting total strangers live in our house.

I was very tired. I sat in a corner of the hall, no longer wishing to be an active participant of this event. I wanted to be on the sidelines, an observer. There were three women who sat next to me, talking in hushed tones. They spoke about water scarcity, about the price of onions and tomatoes. One woman said that she wished she had removed the drying clothes from the terrace.

Mentioning the terrace was enough to evoke Imtiaz in my mind. I blocked myself from the conversation around me, and mentally moved to the terrace. But Aasia came and softly asked me to join her in the kitchen. I got up and my back throbbed with the effort of the work I had put in today. Ammi had told Aasia to make tea while I was to serve it to everyone. Cups that were arranged neatly on trays disappeared into the waiting hands of many people. I had to collect the empty cups and take them back to the kitchen, where Aasia prepared more tea for those who hadn't yet been served.

A twinge of pain worked its way down my back as I bent down to offer tea. As I approached Rehana and Chachi, I felt nervous. Rehana took a cup, looked at me for barely a second, and went back to talking. I froze in that bent position. It was only when I heard someone else asking for tea that I turned around.

I walked back to the kitchen, my throat feeling dry. Those beautiful kohl-lined eyes were blank. There was no recognition in them, nor was there any acknowledgement of my existence. I might have been a waiter. Not the girl with whom Rehana had shared many confidences. Not the girl with whom she had thrown slippers at a laughing boy. I had hoped that after Phuppu's death we would grow a little close at least. But I hadn't known that Rehana would see things differently. Who was right? Her father or mine? I closed my eyes and tried to blink away the headache that was searing my temples. When had it started mattering to her?

I sat on the kitchen stool and told Aasia that she could go and serve tea while I made it. She said there was no need for more tea.

The house was small. Adequate for us, but not for a huge gathering. Abbu had seated the men outside. He and Chacha were gracious but reluctant hosts. When the *hazrath* finally came for the *fatiha,* the women were divided into two groups, as they had to occupy the two rooms, while the men sat down in the hall for the prayer.

Everyone was in a hurry to get inside. I found myself jostled into Rehana's room. She was seated on the bed with Chachi and a group of others. There was silence when the *hazrath* started the *fatiha.* Ammi and Aasia were in the kitchen and I wished I was there with them.

The Arabic verses were soothing in their familiarity, the deep baritone of the *hazrath's* voice very stirring. I stood at the door, which was slightly ajar, inhaling the cloying fragrance of the *agarbattis* that were lit in the hall. My eyes felt itchy and I swallowed.

Vague questions about Basheer crowded my mind and I clutched the door handle tightly, hoping to find some comfort in its scratched and rusted surface.

I hadn't thought of Phuppu's *chehlum* as a picnic, but I hadn't expected it to be so emotionally draining either. After the *fatiha,* everyone sat down to dinner but I stayed away from it, choosing to sit in one of the slowly emptying rooms. I watched women don their *burkas,* the *biryani masala* smell, still clinging to their hands even though they had washed them in the washbasin. Some people laughed and there were few sombre faces about, but there were others who recounted what a good woman Zohra had been. Gloom and despair added and multiplied and I refused to eat when Aasia came to call me. Ammi had been too busy to notice and not for the first time I was glad that I had escaped her eagle eyes.

When once again there was silence in the house, I crept into my corner of the bed and curled up. I felt very cold and I didn't know when I had fallen asleep. When I awoke, it was quiet, still and dark. I shivered, trying to wrest my bed covers from Mateen and I feebly realised that they were his covers I was trying to pull. There seemed to be no strength in my arms and I cried softly in frustration. I called out to Ammi and she stirred. I knew she was more tired than I was but I was feeling so cold. Oh god! So cold! Ammi finally got up and looked at me, annoyed. She touched my arm and flinched. I gasped when she turned on the light and tried to turn my head away. She woke up Abbu and I thought I heard the word 'fever'. My eyes hurt and so did every muscle in my body. I finally pulled Mateen's covers over my head and fell into a deep sleep.

When I woke up the next day, it was late afternoon. Chacha and his family had left in the morning. Fouzia Phuppu and Farha were leaving after lunch, obviously. I turned around and my forehead touched a cool cloth. Ammi had probably used it to cool my forehead in the night.

"When are we leaving?" I asked her when she came to check my temperature. She didn't say anything. Sitting down on the bed beside me, she smiled. "How are you feeling now?" she asked me. "Your father has decided to return only when you're feeling better."

I didn't want to stay here any longer. When the people who had made this house special had changed so irrevocably, why do I care about what Abbu does with it? I wanted to get back to Bangalore, to my house, to college. Oh god! My exams!

"Ammi! My exams start in four days! We have to leave today!" I told her frantically. I had so much to study! Ammi looked thoughtful. "We'll leave early tomorrow morning, okay? By then, you'll be feeling much better."

By evening, I was feeling better, although a slight headache persisted. Would Ammi let me go up to the terrace? I wanted to meet Imtiaz, I thought desperately. If I asked her, she would refuse outright. But without asking her, she was likely to find out, and what would I explain to her then?

I watched the clock tick away to five o'clock. At five-thirty, I was in extremely low spirits. Ammi came into the room, looking worried.

"Your father has gone out, Mehnaz. I was hoping to take Aasia to my Farzana *Khala's* house. *Khala* had told me that she had heard of a good proposal for Aasia. But she wanted to see her first. I have to take her with me. Mateen also wants to come. How will you stay alone?" she asked.

"Ammabi is there, so why are you worried? Go on," I told her calmly. Ammi looked unsure. "Come on, Ammi. If we leave tomorrow morning, then you won't be able to take her na? Go on, I'll be all right."

Ammi left in around fifteen minutes. It took me another fifteen minutes to splash my face with water and get into my white chikan *kurta*. I looked in on Ammabi who was sleeping in the room that had been occupied by Rehana's family.

Taking a deep breath, I walked upstairs and pushed open the door to the terrace.

19

Terrace Rendezvous

There was a strong wind which blew outside, and my *dupatta* flapped around wildly. Although it wasn't dark yet, I could see a few stars dotting the sky. I looked around nervously. Most of the terraces were empty. The children had gone back inside acutely reminding me that I was no longer one of them, and somehow lending an air of danger to what I was doing.

I walked quietly with measured steps to that part of the terrace where I could see his house. I didn't look up until I approached the railing. My excitement at being on the terrace was no longer strange. It was an excitement that I had lived with these past weeks, reliving it, anticipating it. There was a loud thump. I looked up startled.

Imtiaz was on our terrace. He had jumped on our terrace! Our terrace! The word echoed in my head until I could think no more. What did he think he was doing? He was crouched on the terrace. He slowly got up, dusting his knees and hands. I stepped back. How could he have become taller in a few weeks?

Words refused to form into coherent sentences. He smiled and some of my uncertainty slowly evaporated. This was Imtiaz. But...

"Hi!" I said shakily. I looked around at the other terrace. There was no one around, but what if someone saw me talking to him? Would they tell Abbu? Would I get into trouble?

Since it was getting dark, even if someone came on another terrace they might not see me if I was sitting down. So

I sat down cross-legged. He looked at me, startled. Then he followed my example and sat down too. My white *kameez* would be disgracefully brown, I thought as I stared at the dust on the terrace floor.

"Why did you come to my terrace?"

He looked serious. Looking down again he spoke softly.

"I've been waiting for so many days, Mehnaz. So many days."

I felt happy, yet in a foolish sort of way.

"When I saw you come on the terrace I couldn't help myself. I intended to come only to the last terrace like always but when I saw that you hadn't even seen me, I just took my chance and jumped on to yours."

I ran my finger in the dust, wondering what to say. "Did you wait for me yesterday?" I asked.

He smiled. "Actually, I've been waiting the whole week. I didn't know when exactly your Phuppu's *chehlum* was. But I didn't want to miss out on you."

I smiled widely and then looked at him shyly. Neither of us spoke and I was finding it difficult to meet his stare. His eyes had a searching look in them, as if he was looking intently for some answers to the questions I didn't even know. Ignoring it, I started speaking about Rehana, about how much she had changed. Before I knew it, I was telling him about Chacha and Abbu's silly feud. He listened quietly. I poured out to him my foolishness of yesterday. My juvenile attempts to bring back together what was severed for ever. He didn't say anything. Instead he just took my hands in his.

Was it possible for one's heart to stop beating for just a second even though one was still alive? Because it felt that way. My hands in his. I stared at our entwined hands, not attentive to what he was saying even as he said it. He had done it just to comfort me. I was distressed about my father, and he was... he was... what was he saying? I hadn't heard a word of it.

I slowly withdrew my hands from his and looked at him. Yes, he had done it solely to comfort me. But could something as simple be so dangerous? I suddenly realised that I was aware of him in so many different ways. His proximity was doing strange things to me and I wanted to go back downstairs. But I didn't want him to know that. And I still wanted to talk to him.

I looked at the slowly darkening sky. It was rather beautiful. He looked up too.

"Have you ever noticed how beautiful the night sky is in Vellore?" I shook my head. He was looking at me again. I felt breathless although I hadn't run at all.

"I have to tell you something."

I bit my lower lip nervously. I got up. I knew I had to go. I shouldn't be here on this terrace talking to him. Even though I had known him for three or four years, he was still technically a stranger to me.

"Imtiaz, Ammi will be coming. I have to go." I got up and dusted the back of my *kameez*. He was still sitting.

"But you can't... you can't just go like that," he protested, looking confused.

"I have to. Actually, I had a fever last night and Ammi will be mad if she finds out I've been sitting upstairs in the cold wind for so long. Okay then, bye."

"Wait!" he called out loudly. I stopped and turned around slowly. "Why are you running away from me? Are you scared or something?" I didn't answer and he sighed. "How can you be scared of me?" he asked.

"Why did you change things then?" I asked him feeling unsure of what I meant.

"What? What things did I change?"

"What was between us was good. But now, I can't understand you. You seem so different. And it scares me. I'm not even sure of what I'm saying to you," I said and turned around to go.

"No, wait. I didn't change anything. It's been there from the beginning. Maybe you realised what it was just now," he said softly, his hand resting lightly on my shoulders.

I turned around to look at him. If Jyoti or Sahana were here, they would have called it a 'filmi' moment. I wriggled out of his grasp. This was getting too complicated. I took a deep breath.

"Look, Imtiaz, I have to go now. We're leaving tomorrow morning and I have no idea when I will be back in Vellore."

"But you haven't even heard what I have to say to you," he protested.

"Don't. Don't say it. Let things be as they are for now, please?" I pleaded and ran towards the door.

I turned around to see him. His hands were crossed in front of his chest. I had put off what he had been trying to say but the next time I was in Vellore, maybe I would be ready to listen to him.

My hands moved of their own volition, into a half-hearted wave but he didn't wave back.

20

First Step Backwards

Can we really demarcate any particular day as the worst or the best day of our lives? Something is bound to come up that will measure up more or maybe less. But in the throbbing and alive present, some days slowly seep into our memory and remain etched there, as a reminder, as a yardstick to measure our future joys and sorrows.

The shrill sound of the phone cleaved through the silent morning, startling me as I hurried to pick it up. Abbu was just leaving for his shop and Ammi was seeing him off at the door. It was a public holiday and Mateen didn't have school while I didn't have classes at college either.

"Mehnaz," a soft voice spoke, the gentle cadence a mere memory and my pulse quickened. "Rehana?" I asked.

I hadn't heard from her in the three years since Phuppu's death. And after the way she had behaved there, I hadn't wanted to talk to her either.

"Mehnaz, are your parents at home? Can you tell them to please come to Manipal Hospital?"

Alarmed, I asked her, "What happened? Who is in hospital?"

Rehana seemed to take a shaky breath as she said, "My mother. She's getting operated in some time and I'm so scared," she ended weakly. I had a feeling she was crying.

Luckily, I was able to stop Abbu just as he was, getting on his scooter and told him about what had happened. I looked at his helmet clad face trying to see if there was any indication of what we were going to do.

He unstrapped the buckle and removed the helmet, muttering to himself, "Why doesn't she call her Afzal Mamu?" He knew that no one was going to reply to his question so he started walking back to the house, Ammi and me following him hurriedly. I had been focused on Abbu's reaction and I hadn't noticed that Ammi had paled when I spoke about Chachi being in hospital.

We reached the hospital some time later and then, once inside we tried to locate Rehana. There she was, the lone solitary figure near the operation theatre, clad in her *burka,* but there was no veil this time, and as we walked closer, I saw that she was not wearing gloves or socks either. We stopped a few feet away from her, and I realised my heart was beating madly on an uneven tempo.

Rehana saw us and then walked up her steps gaining speed slowly. As she reached us, I couldn't control myself and stepped forward to take her trembling hand. Abbu awkwardly patted her head and she embraced him, her head resting against his chest.

She stepped back and stared at us, and I tried to gauge what she was thinking. She held her hand at her chest, as if all her frustrations had channelled into a deep pain somewhere there, and she burst out crying. Ammi somehow pulled Rehana to herself, so that now she was leaning against Ammi's *burka* and crying. People were staring at her, but the tears kept coming along with the loud sobs.

Still in Ammi's embrace, she looked down and opened her eyes, which seemed to slowly move along taking in the footwear around her. Mateen's sneakers, my flat slippers, Abbu's leather *chappals*. A pair of shoe-clad feet stopped near us and Rehana's head snapped up. She looked into her father's face.

❖❖❖

21

Hospital Reunion

Sometimes death can bring together two estranged families. Since that hadn't happened at Zohra Phuppu's death, I had given up hope of any reconciliation. But now, staring at Sadiq Chacha's pale face, I felt afraid for Rehana.

She struggled out of Ammi's embrace and faced her father. Would he ask them to leave?

They both seemed to be waiting for each other to speak. It seemed like they were going to wait for ever. Everyone looked uncomfortable and before I could change my mind, I stepped forward and spoke, "I think this is enough. If both of you can't find it in you to forgive each other, then at least try and forget what happened. The past isn't important now. The present and the future are."

Rehana looked shocked. Different expressions flitted across the faces that surrounded us. Mateen looked uncomfortable as he traced a pattern on the cool marble floor with the tip of his sneakers, pretending that he wasn't with this group of emotionally charged people. Ammi's eyes flashed angrily but only Abbu and Chacha looked at each other.

Finally, Abbu spoke gruffly. "She's right. I think we should leave that in the past and move ahead." Chacha didn't say anything. I urged him mentally to take that one step forward and forget all that had happened. The doctor with whom he had been consulting before came and stood near them. They were taking Asifa Chachi for the operation.

The whole group surged forward as one family and we rushed towards the operation theatre. As the nurses wheeled out her mother, lying on the stretcher, looking pale and nervous, Rehana's eyes flooded with tears once again. Not knowing what else to do to help her, I clutched her hand and she looked at me, surprised and grateful, through a haze of tears.

The doctor told them not to worry and soon they took Chachi inside and shut the big doors. Rehana looked as if she would collapse right there, crying, when she spotted Abbu and Chacha looking at each other again.

Abbu had already made the first move. Chacha had to just move one inch forward and maybe... maybe the hurt and the pain that had solidified slowly, encasing their hearts, would slowly melt away. Chacha shook his head and embraced Abbu with tears in his eyes. Rehana's fingers tightened around her hand and I realised that all of us were crying.

Abbu and Chacha still looked a bit awkward as they sat side by side and discussed Chachi's condition. From the little bit I could glean from them, Chachi was having a hysterectomy because of a weak uterus that had been causing her a lot of problems. Rehana was muttering soft *duas* under her breath and looking down at the floor, as if she didn't want to meet my eyes. Much later, the doctor stepped out, reassuring them that Chachi was all right, but very weak. They would bring her out in an hour. Chacha collapsed back on the hard chair and Abbu patted his hand. Everyone had been so worried.

Lunchtime had come and gone and no one had felt hungry except for Mateen who looked distinctly uncomfortable. Ammi seemed to notice it too. "Mehnaz, you take Rehana and Mateen back home," she said. "Have something to eat and come back."

Rehana shook her head. "I'm not going anywhere until I see my mother."

She turned to ask me about my college and I leaned back a bit to see Ammi's expression. Even I had stopped defying her these days, simply because I was tired of it. Ammi had crossed her arms and was staring into space.

"Final year," I answered. "It's almost over. So which college did you finally join?"

Rehana shook her head. "After my PUC, I didn't join any college but Abbu wanted me to do so."

"Then?" I prompted curiously.

Rehana seemed at a loss for words. "Actually, Ammi hasn't been keeping well from quite some time and I've had to manage the house and everything. After PUC, I thought of doing a correspondence course but Abbu wanted to me to join a big college, like yours."

"Well, then why didn't you?" I asked her.

"I thought I'll skip this year and join later, because by then Ammi will also be feeling better na?"

I sat quietly for some time, wondering if I would have been able to do something like that too. Did I have it in me?

"I think you are amazing," I said.

After a brief silence, she asked, "What will you do after college?"

"I don't know. What else, I'll probably get married." I replied, wishing I could have said anything else other than the bitter truth.

These bits and pieces stitched together, however haphazardly, made the fabric of our lives. But there was no more time to discuss it. The operation theatre's doors swung open and two nurses wheeled out Chachi on the stretcher, a drip bottle swaying on the stand. She was still unconscious. We all hurried to take a look at her.

Rehana stood by her father's side. He looked old, tired and worn out. She rubbed her palm against his absently.

They had taken her mother to the ICU from where they would shift her to a room once she regained consciousness. Once again, with Chachi out of their sight, they were left facing each other awkwardly. Abbu cleared his throat. "Maybe you should go home and rest a bit, Sadiq. You're not looking so well. I think you were up all last night too."

Chacha shook his head. "I can't leave her and go," he said simply.

Abbu refused to listen to Rehana when she protested that she too wanted to stay, and he insisted we go home for lunch. She finally agreed, probably because she didn't want to upset the delicate equilibrium that had sprung up between our families.

22

Rewind, rewind

I couldn't believe that Rehana was sitting with me in the auto. Had things really been sorted out between our families now? Was everything going to be okay? Would it be like before? How could anything be like before? Despite the way Sadiq Chacha and Abbu had met, I felt that it was coloured by painful memories, which both of them had decided to put away for the time being.

Rehana looked ill herself. I was amazed that she was the one fully managing her house now. She hadn't changed much since the last time I saw her at Phuppu's *chehlum*. At least the way she looked. Inside, she seemed to have become a different person altogether.

The house was dim and cool and I switched on the hall lights and then feeling a little self-conscious, asked Rehana to sit down but she didn't. The last time she had come was after she had passed her exams. I removed my *burka* and threw it on my bed. Rehana had followed me inside, looking pale. I didn't know what I was expected to do. There were so many memories between us, but I was afraid that the common thread that had bound us together had frayed and worn out.

She hadn't spoken a word since the time we reached home. I touched her shoulder and shook her a bit and she seemed to snap out of something. I made her sit down on the bed and ran to the kitchen. I quickly made some tea and took it back to her. Mateen had disappeared into his room already. Sometimes I felt that giving him his own room wasn't such a good idea after all because he always seemed to shut himself inside. She took the teacup from me and I could see that her hands were shaking as she sipped it quietly.

Finally she spoke. "Thank you so much for coming today."

Feeling a bit foolish, I chided her, "What are you thanking me for? If the situation was reversed, wouldn't you have come?"

She looked at me thoughtfully. "I honestly don't know. After Phuppu's *chehlum,* I was afraid to talk to you again. I'm so sorry for that day. I'll never forgive myself." Tears rolled down her face and then she broke down, her chest heaving as she cried.

Oh god! What was I supposed to do? Ammi should have been here. She would have handled this situation with ease. Tentatively, I put my hand out and stroked her shoulder. She immediately started crying louder, with more desperation. Feeling like crying myself, I told her, "It's okay. Don't cry. These things happen." I was letting her off so easily. All these years I had imagined a situation, a face-off between Rehana and me. I wanted to throw all the hurt and unspoken accusations at her face. I wanted to be contemptuous and hard-hearted towards her. I had been sure I wouldn't listen to anything she had to say.

But here I was telling her that everything was going to be all right.

"I was so scared today, Mehnaz," she said, her voice falling to a whisper. "If your family hadn't been there, I think I would have run away to some other place. All these days, I've had to be so strong. Ever since we knew that she would be getting operated, I've lived in fear of her death. And today I really thought she was going to die. I was so glad you came when I called."

What could I say that wouldn't sound trite or clichéd? She was sobbing quietly now, her hair mussed up, face streaked with tears. All that responsibility, and she had taken it up so stoically. I still found it amazing. Imagine running the house entirely! The thought simply baffled me.

Which reminded me, I still had to cook lunch. Patting her on the shoulder, I got up. There were so many more hours for the day to get over, and already I was wishing for the night. I wanted to curl up under my blanket and sleep away everything.

Right now, the kitchen beckoned me and I went wearily. After nearly an hour, lunch was ready. I had to clean up the kitchen before Ammi came and started her lecture about not being orderly enough. I went to my room and saw Rehana sitting by the window staring outside. She looked at me and smiled. She had washed her face and was looking a little brighter. Her eyes were bright from unshed tears.

"I want to call up to the hospital."

In the hall I picked up the yellow pages and got the hospital number from there. When we got through, they called Chacha on the phone. The tears in her eyes spilled over and at that moment, I knew I couldn't keep feeling resentful about that one day, three years ago. I realised with horror that it made me no different from Abbu and Chacha with their petty squabbles.

As she got up from the sofa, I hugged her hard. She looked surprised. "Abbu said that Ammi is okay now. She even spoke to them. They will take her out of the ICU tomorrow."

"That's good news," I said, letting her go. She stepped back, feeling uncomfortable. I called out to Mateen. He came from his room and sat down for lunch with us. I was going to make Rehana feel better, I decided. Things could once again become like how they were before. We could once again be a happy family. With such cheerful thoughts I insisted Rehana eat properly and afterwards Abbu came to take Rehana to the hospital. I wanted to go with her, but Abbu thought it would be better if I stayed at home. Anyway, Chachi was still in the ICU and they weren't letting many people in. It was nearly 5.00 p.m. My parents and Sadiq Chacha had eaten some *bhajjis* and *vadas* at the hospital canteen.

Pulling out my diary from the drawer in my desk, I turned a fresh page. After penning down my thoughts, I sat back and let the breeze from the fan rustle the pages. I had started writing this diary last year, but I tried to include all the significant things that had happened to me before.

On one of the pages, Imtiaz's name swam before my eyes. I shut the diary. Thinking about him did all kinds of funny things to my insides. After Phuppu's *chehlum,* we had left Vellore the next day and there was no indication of our return. My mind was thoroughly muddled when I left, wondering what Imtiaz had wanted to say. It was exciting and yet unnerving.

Sahana and Jyoti thought that I was the biggest dud they knew when I told them how I hadn't even listened to him. Thinking and rethinking about that incident romanticised Imtiaz more than ever in my mind.

Some months later, Abbu had taken us to Vellore for a weekend. This was the first time in many years that Aasia wasn't there with us in Vellore. She had been married a few months after Phuppu's *chehlum*. I didn't know how she was, although we did hear about her from the old aunt who had brought her to work here. The aunt visited us during *Ramzan* every year to collect the *zakath* money and saree that Ammi gave her. From her, each year we heard something about Aasia. She had two children now, both boys. She would have been extremely happy if only her husband kept to his job properly. Ammi always pressed a hundred rupee note into the old aunt's hand for Aasia.

Without Aasia, Ammi reluctantly came to be dependent on me for small chores. Earlier, in Vellore, I would never have entered the kitchen unless it was to get water for myself or for Abbu. But during that weekend visit, Ammi had me working away too. Dusting cobwebs, wiping the table, and sweeping the rooms, I did everything through a haze of slight resentment and laziness. At the end of it, I was so tired, yet I summoned the energy to wash up. Ammi and Mateen had decided to take a nap, so I rushed to the terrace.

I knew Imtiaz wouldn't be there. There had been no way of letting him know of my arrival. The sunny, empty terrace seemed like a yawning chasm, one that had swallowed Imtiaz temporarily.

But when I went up again a couple of hours later, he was there. I couldn't contain myself when I saw him, and jumping a little, I waved at him. But he hadn't seen me, and after a few minutes I wanted to throw a *chappal* at him again. When he did look at me, I stopped jumping and looked at him unsure. I decided I was going to pretend that things were like before.

He bounded across the terraces but this time he didn't jump onto ours. I was relieved and also disappointed and our conversation was strained. He too had decided that he wasn't going to bring up that day. I wished I had listened to him then, because if I wanted to know more, I was going to have to bring it up myself. He wasn't saying much and his arms were folded across his chest. He turned around to leave and I called out to him. He stopped and looked back.

"Don't go yet," I said without thinking. He waited for me to say something more. But I didn't know what I could say without sounding foolish or naïve. I stood there staring at him. Soon it became uncomfortable. Standing with him under the darkening sky, I could smell rain in the air. Tiny drops bounced on my bare head, but I didn't move.

The rain was warm as it seeped into my cotton *salwar*. My back was getting wet, but I kept looking at him waiting for him to speak. Something that would put this whole situation in perspective, that would make me understand his intentions. Or just anything. Instead of this disconcerting silence.

Ten minutes had passed and we were still staring at each other, not saying a word, getting drenched in the rain. The rain now fell heavily, beating down on us in a steady rhythm. I was feeling cold now and Ammi would get suspicious, I worried. Just then someone called out his name. Startled, he turned back and saw someone standing on his terrace, beckoning him.

"Oh god! Someone saw me standing here talking to you!" I said as I started walking away to the door that led downstairs.

"Mehnaz! That's okay! He's just a friend!" Imtiaz called out. I turned, my wet *dupatta* slapping against my body uncomfortably. Then he smiled at me. Feeling elated, I smiled back and ran downstairs.

How was it possible that Ammi had not called out to me yet? Could she still be sleeping? I peeped into Zohra Phuppu's old bedroom and saw that she was. Mateen was up, playing with banging toy cars on the ground, making so much noise, and yet Ammi hadn't woken up.

I changed swiftly, praying that Ammi's hawk eyes wouldn't spot why I was wearing a different *salwar* now. Lately I noticed that Ammi often missed out a few things that she would have immediately spotted when I was ten years old. Was it a good sign or bad? The rain had started slowing down, yet the muted sound of the raindrops hitting the roof lent an air of calm. I rubbed my hair vigorously with my towel, and only then did I discover Ammabi staring at me from her *divan*.

23

Friends again?

Asifa Chachi was coming to our house to recuperate after being discharged from the hospital. When adults decided on something, they immediately put it into action. Once they had decided that they didn't exist for each other. And it had stayed that way for many years. And now, it seemed like all those years had collapsed and the bitterness that had flooded their hearts was never there. I knew I should be happy. I was, but at the same time it seemed strange.

Anyhow, Rehana had been staying in our house ever since Chachi's operation. We were sharing my room and although that had been something I would have loved a few years ago, now, I couldn't bring myself to explain what exactly I felt having her with me all the time. She always got up before me and opened the curtains, letting the morning sun stream in. And then, switching off the fan, she would finish her ablutions, read *Fajr namaz* and then the *Quran* loudly.

I woke up every day to the sound of her reading the Arabic verses soulfully. I wanted just five more minutes to sleep and then I had to get up for college. But her voice droned into my ears anyway and I opened my crinkly eyes to see her rocking rhythmically. Her face was all I could see under the *dupatta* that she pulled behind her ears tightly and wrapped once around her head so that not a single strand of her hair could be seen.

I was in college when Asifa Chachi came home. Ammi had prepared the guest room for them so Rehana could stay with her mother. I couldn't seem to wait for that day. I got ready for college and went out for breakfast. Rehana was already in the kitchen, helping Ammi. I should be helping Ammi, but I had college while she didn't.

The first day that Rehana stayed with us, she stared at me, unable to take her eyes off me while I dressed. I was just dabbing on a neutral shade of lipstick. Her eyes grew round when she saw me spray a little perfume on my wrists.

"Mehnaz! Taima allows you to do all this?"

And this was Rehana who was also brought up in Bangalore like me. Which world did she occupy? I shook my head. Of course, Ammi hated it. I always wore very little and drastically subdued make-up to avoid her lectures. What really staggered her was that I went to college alone and without a *burka*. As I walked out of the house, I saw Ammi and Rehana staring at me from the window.

They should have been mother and daughter, my mind blurted out before I could realise it. The insecurities that had ebbed away when Aasia had left were now slowly edging back. But this was Rehana. My own cousin, who was more like a sister to me. I waved at them, and Ammi responded with a small, diminutive shake of her hand. Rehana waved back and smiled, and in that one instant she was once again the old Rehana. I hailed an auto and got in. Turning back, I looked at the window. Both weren't there.

I thought of my day and the things it was filled with. Lectures, attendance, notes, marks, teachers, friends, canteen, *samosas*... and I thought of their day. What was it like? Already my mind was seeing them together as they carried on with the million things that seemed to be done in a house. Only once I had managed the house for a day when Ammi was ill. By evening, my back was aching, my legs felt wobbly, and I felt like an absolute martyr. I snapped at Mateen, got irritated with Abbu when he didn't come down for dinner, and behaved badly with everyone. I felt that because I had done all that work at home, I was entitled to it.

Only when I went to sleep did I realise that Ammi had been doing all this for years. Indeed, she hadn't done anything else at all. It wasn't that she never complained. She did, but in a more matter-of-fact way that this was her life, and why couldn't I help her more. I however had carried on like I had done a huge favour for everyone.

Rehana was so much like her. They seemed to even talk the same language of ginger-garlic paste, the cost of sugar and lazy servants. Even if I wanted to, I could never carry on a conversation with my mother like her.

The day was cool, and the sky was dull white, tinged with grey. I walked inside college and immediately felt at home. The noise, the babble of excited girls, the bikes, the laughter... this was my world. I spotted Sahana sitting under her favourite tree, reading a book. Jyoti hadn't come yet. We discussed the history project that was due in another week's time. She told me about the college festival that was approaching soon and we discussed all the exciting possibilities.

My mind had tuned out Ammi and Rehana completely until Jyoti joined us and asked me how my aunt was. "She's fine," I replied. "She'll be coming home today." We talked a little more about the strange turn that life had taken suddenly. The bell rang and we got up complaining good-naturedly. This was my life. But I couldn't be a student for ever, evading the responsibilities that waited me back home. This was my last year in college and the thought saddened me immensely. I wanted to hold every moment tight, clasp it to my chest and not let it squirm away from me.

It was September already. Just a few more months. What would I be doing next September? Fouzia Phuppu had been haranguing Abbu and Ammi for nearly three years now, insisting that they should get me married. Every time I heard her tell Abbu or Ammi in that nasal voice of hers that because of me they couldn't get Rehana or Farha married, I panicked. Get them married, I had challenged her once when Abbu wasn't there. Ammi looked at me, her eyes narrowed as she sipped her tea.

Fouzia Phuppu clutched her hands together and held them to her bosom dramatically. "Shabana Bhabhi, this girl amazes me more and more. I find it hard to believe that she is your daughter." I wanted to smother Fouzia Phuppu with that insufferable orange *dupatta* of hers. "Look how she talks! How can we get them married before you? What will people say? This is just not done!" she said, shaking her head resolutely.

Will Abbu finally listen to Fouzia Phuppu and get me married? The thought was so painful that Jyoti prodded me in the ribs. "What's the funny face for?" she whispered. I shook my head. I instinctively knew she wouldn't understand.

As for Imtiaz, I couldn't let that go and pretend that nothing had happened. But the truth was that nothing had happened between us after that. I felt wistful and slightly melancholy on rainy days because they reminded me of that day on the terrace. That had been the last time I had seen him. Each time we went to Vellore, I had rushed to the terrace, only to find it silent, empty and accusing.

There were times when I thought of Basheer. We never found him after that, and although the pain that Zohra Phuppu's death had brought us had lost some of its edge, Basheer's absence still cut into our lives sharply. What was he doing? Where was he? Would we never see him again?

At home, Sadiq Chacha was sitting in the hall when I walked in from college. My heart clenched for a moment, like a fist around a balloon, and then I tried to relax. The feud was over, remember? I had to remind myself of it constantly.

Chacha had been so energetic and young back then, and now his hair had thinned and he seemed pale. Chachi's illness also had him worried I supposed. But where was that Afzal Mamu, the man who had been the cause of the feud? Why hadn't he come to the aid of his only sister? How come Rehana had turned to us? I wanted to ask her but was not comfortable about broaching the topic as it seemed inappropriate somehow.

I went and sat in Chachi's room for a while. She was looking better at home than she had at the hospital. Her cheeks looked fresh, and although her eyes had deep circles beneath them, there was a sparkle to them. I spoke to her, trying to cull out a common topic for us to speak without getting awkward. The rift had cleaved our family and with it, I had got used to a life without them.

Chachi asked me about college and I spoke about it enthusiastically. This was something unrelated to the unpleasantness of the past, something I could talk about without being anxious about what Ammi would say if she knew I had spoken about it.

"Mehnaz, you must convince Rehana to join your college, beta," she said. I looked at her surprised. Chachi continued, "That girl grew up too soon. Before I knew it, she was on par with me with everything in the house. She needs to get out in the world and see some of it at least before she gets married. Once that happens, all she will see is the house and nothing else."

The words twisted my heart, making me feel breathless. House... home... it looked like this was all there was to it. I tried to shut the thought out for the present and listened to her.

"She's my only child and I don't want her to lose out on anything. Especially something as important as her education. She's adamant about staying at home. Says she'll do a correspondence course. What can be wrong with her?" she mused.

Who would want to miss out on all that college life offered and opt to stay at home? "Chachi, she feels that you need her at home, with you. She feels that you won't be able to manage without her," I pointed out. Chachi smiled at that and shook her head. "The child we bring up with so much trouble, grows up and tells us that we aren't capable of looking after ourselves."

I didn't know what to say to that. I had never given so much consideration to Ammi. "Do you know that when she was born, there was no one in the house to help me out? No one. My parents had died just a year before she was born, and I had to take care of her, and manage the house. I did it single-handedly."

I thought of Ammi. Bringing up children must be real hard work. Ammi too had done it alone. Ammi's father had died a few months after she got married, and her mother, my Naani, lived in their old ancestral house in Vellore. For some reason, she hadn't been able to come to Bangalore for my birth. Naani died the year I was born. Ammi too had to take care of me and manage the house. And when Mateen was born... I knew now why she had needed Aasia.

Chachi continued talking. "I'm already feeling much better now these days. Try and talk to her about it." I nodded. Chachi had closed her eyes and was drifting off to sleep. I got up from the chair. As I left the room, I saw Rehana standing near the kitchen wall, holding a tray with a bowl. She had heard us talking. Feeling uneasy, I recalled that we hadn't said anything that should upset her. But it had.

24

Withering Dahlias

Chachi and Rehana stayed with us for a week before returning to their house. The house seemed hollow, as if somebody had scooped out all the vital contents and stashed them away. It took some time for us to get used to being only four. I had approached Rehana and told her about Chachi's ideas about her joining college. She listened to all I had to say and then shook her head.

She knew what she wanted and I envied the clarity of mind she possessed. I had no idea what I wanted from life, or whether I would be happy with what I would get. But she seemed to have formulated all her wants and her longings into a tangible entity. Her house. I gave up after that. Soon after, Rehana received a proposal of marriage from a reputed family originally from Vellore but now settled in Bangalore. I heard Abbu and Ammi talking about it one night over dinner.

Ammi was saying, "She has been getting proposals since people saw her at Zohra's *chehlum*. But of course she was too young then."

"She still is young," Abbu said a bit gruffly.

Ammi agreed. "It's up to Sadiq and Asifa totally. If they like everything, if those people like Rehana, then what's there to stop them?" Her voice faltered and I realised what was approaching. Yet I stayed outside their door, listening with a sense of growing alarm. "What about Mehnaz? Isn't she the one who should be getting married first? What will everyone say when they hear of it? How will I explain to everyone why we still haven't got our daughter married?"

I strained my ears to hear Abbu's reply when I heard Mateen clearing his throat behind me. He looked at me with censure in his eyes.

"Are you listening to Abbu and Ammi talk?" he asked.

"Mateen, it's not like that... but why are you standing here?"

"It's bad manners to listen at doors. You told me so yourself!"

"I wasn't listening. I was just passing by. Have you finished your homework?" I whispered furiously.

He went away. I had to know what they were saying about me. I couldn't wait until the day Ammi decided that it was time to inform me about my fate. Why couldn't I just barge in and demand that they discuss my future openly?

When I listened at the door again I realised that Abbu and Ammi were no longer discussing me.

Feeling annoyed with Mateen for interrupting, I suddenly thought of Mrs Dahlia. I had to tell her about all these new developments in my life, even about Imtiaz. She was my sounding board and she always presented me with an objective picture of my own life, where I could see things clearly, with a fresher perspective unhampered by emotions and thoughts.

I had met her last about six months back. Ammi always looked at me with a little revulsion when I spoke of Mrs Dahlia, especially when I returned from her house. She would insist that I change my clothes and wash my hands before I ate anything. She always looked closely to see if she could spot any dog hair on my clothes or body although I never petted Mrs Dahlia's dog. But it sometimes slept on the same sofa that Mrs Dahlia asked me to sit in, and a few stray strands would be entangled in my clothes. The first time Ammi found one on my *salwar,* her face had tightened as though someone had turned a screw inside somewhere. She made me take a bath, although I had just taken one and gone out.

I decided to visit Mrs Dahlia without telling Ammi about it. Stepping outside the house, I quickly walked towards Mrs Dahlia's house. I looked at the trees that swayed gently in the wind, at the leaves that rustled and fell to the ground in a heap. The weather was so unpredictable in Bangalore but I hadn't felt like carrying an umbrella. But a look at the darkening sky above me made me a bit nervous. I quickened my steps and turned into the lane where Mrs Dahlia lived.

The two houses that flanked her house had disappeared. On one side, there was a half-finished apartment complex, and on the other side a completed apartment. When had this happened? Between the buildings, Mrs Dahlia's house looked timid, pathetic and shrunk. Her garden was overgrown and the grass reached above my ankles, tickling my legs as I waded through it to reach her front door.

I rang the grimy doorbell and waited. It took longer than usual for her to open the door. When she did, I was shocked to see her face. She looked haggard and a grimace had now replaced the smiles she always had for me. I immediately offered her my arm and led her back inside the house. She hobbled back with me and sat down on the sofa. I felt guilty. I should have visited her more often, should have dropped by every week at least. How could I have neglected her so?

"How are you Mehnaz?" she asked, her voice wavering. I didn't answer. What had happened? Six months ago, she had looked all right to me, although a bit tired. But in those six months, years had fled, leaving their ghastly marks on her being.

"What happened to you?" I whispered. The air was still in the house and I felt the mustiness more pronounced than ever.

She laughed softly. "So many things happened. What can I say?"

A deep sadness, dull and aching, lodged itself within me. It was hard to control the tears that pricked my eyes. She looked at the picture frames that she had kept on a chest of drawers. Those pictures had always fascinated me as a child. I would stare at them while waiting for Mrs Dahlia to correct my Maths problems, or while waiting for her to emerge from the kitchen with some delicious biscuits or a cake that she would bake specially for me. My surprise would always be doubled when sometimes I saw that a new picture had appeared. I was drawn by the excitement of exploring the new picture, touching the frame, and trying to discover what the picture represented. Her children sent her photographs of themselves and of their children too, and Mrs Dahlia would select the best of the lot and get them framed.

"My son died," she said, expelling her breath forcefully. I stared at her. "I hadn't seen him for the last fifteen years."

I sat silently as she spoke to me about her son. Where was her little dog? He usually came and sat quietly by her feet. I didn't want to interrupt her. For once, I didn't tell her about my troubles, my fears and apprehensions. She would have listened to me, but I now realised how selfish I had been all these years. I had drawn at the well of her sympathy while not once caring to see how it had fared all these years. We were silent for some time.

I got up to go. She looked at me surprised. "Going so soon?" she asked.

I nodded. "Ammi doesn't know that I'm here. She'll get worried," I said. Angry, your mother will get angry. I read the thought in Mrs Dahlia's eyes. I sat down beside her again. She looked so very old. Gone were the floral dresses that she used to wear. Now she wore a faded blue nightie that showed the splotches in her neck and arms. She shivered in the cold and I looked at her helplessly.

"Can I get you a shawl?" I asked her. She shook her head.

"You go on to your house. Your mother won't like it if you get back home late."

I left her house feeling despondent. Fat raindrops fell on my head and by the time I reached home, a slow drizzle had given way to a steady downpour. I hoped that Abbu was at home. He usually felt charitable towards Mrs Dahlia and Ammi's anger would be a little tempered in his presence.

Fearfully, I rang the doorbell and waited. The door opened and Ammi stood there. I walked in, attempting to appear casual and nonchalant, but she held my arm and turned me around to face her. I looked at her and cringed. Only Ammi possessed the power to make me feel like a ten-year-old again. A very scared and bewildered ten-year-old.

"So where were you?" she asked, her voice calm. I took a deep breath. She was my mother. And I was almost twenty-one, an adult. I shouldn't have to be scared of her. Feeling slightly comforted by the thought, although wishing Abbu were there, I told her that I had been to Mrs Dahlia's house. Ammi didn't say anything. She looked at me and walked away. I should have known that the silent treatment was in store for me. But honestly, this time I didn't deserve it. As I didn't, most of the other times too.

25

Winning and Losing

When talk of a marriage begins, somehow things snowball into something beyond our control. Before the month was over, we heard that people would be coming to see Rehana. This was a mere formality as they had already seen and liked her. Ammi was still not talking to me. One Sunday, Mateen informed me seriously that Ammi said I should wear something respectable, and not my handloom *salwars,* which were so chic for college. We were going to Rehana's house.

Respectable, I muttered. What does she know? I went through my wardrobe and picked out a light-pink *salwar* that had deeper pink embroidery on it and very light *zari* work in silver. It wasn't flashy but was subtle and spoke of good taste. As I combed my hair, I wondered how Rehana was feeling.

I had wanted to call and ask her but then felt reluctant. She had grown up too soon and I wasn't comfortable with her anymore.

Ammi favoured Rehana so much more than me that it used to hurt sometimes. She always compared me to her and no matter what I did, I fell short of her expectations. I wrapped the *hijab* around me, feeling like a martyr. No one appreciated me.

We drove to Rehana's house in silence. As we neared her house, I wondered how much their house had changed. Ammi had visited them often to see Chachi after the operation, but I hadn't been able to. I was setting foot in this house after many years.

Abbu stopped the car outside Chacha's house and Mateen opened the gates so he could park the car inside. Ammi and I got down, the silence between us was heavy. When we went inside, the first person I saw was Fouzia Phuppu sitting with Farha, feeding her milk *pedas*. Looking at Farha I remembered my childhood preoccupation with Fouzia Phuppu and pins. Now I wanted to see if both could be deflated.

Asifa Chachi looked tired as she sat at the dining table and instructed a small servant girl to wipe the centre table with more Colin. The little girl sprayed more of the blue liquid on the glass table and scrubbed it vigorously.

Chachi started getting up to welcome us when Ammi stopped her.

"You sit right where you are, Asifa. No need to get up for us," Ammi said. Chachi smiled. I looked at them, wishing the years we had spent apart would vanish and leave us with only the good memories.

Ammi sat down with Chachi and asked her if anything had to be done. "No, no, everything is done. Rehana's Abbu got the *mithai* and *samosas*. We just have to arrange everything. This little girl here is a big help. I don't know how I managed without her."

Mateen had switched on the TV and was lost in a cartoon show. I sat down on the sofa, as far as permissible from Fouzia Phuppu and Farha.

The little girl wore a yellow *salwar kurta* and had a thin whisper of a cloth wound around her neck to pass off as a *dupatta*. I watched her as she wiped the sofa legs and other crevices, which would be difficult for Chachi to even think of reaching.

"Asifa," Ammi said, her voice barely a whisper. I leaned back to hear her better. She was probably talking softly because she didn't want to include Fouzia Phuppu in the conversation.

"What's the hurry, Asifa? Why are you getting Rehana married when she is so young?" Ammi asked.

I knew the real reason for her worry. Me.

"And just when you had such a big operation. You should be under rest, not tiring yourself with all this excitement. This could have waited for a year at least."

Chachi sighed and flicked a dust cloth lightly over the dining table. When she didn't say anything, Ammi pressed closer and said, "Aren't you going to even let her study?"

When I finished tenth standard, Ammi had grumbled and agreed to let me do PUC. When that was done, she insisted that I stay at home and learn how to manage the house. Abbu had stuck to his decision that he would see me graduate with a degree. And here I was in my final year.

"What can I say? She doesn't want to study further. We hadn't thought about getting her married. It was just that we received this proposal and they seem to be nice people. Might as well get this done when we're both alive and well," Chachi ended with a weak laugh.

Ammi was frowning. Obviously she felt that this was something that she and Abbu should be considering too.

I got up decisively, and went upstairs to Rehana's room and knocked on the door.

"Who's there?" I heard her call out, her voice sounding muffled.

I opened the door and went in. Just how did she manage to keep her room so orderly? Every small thing had a place designated for it. Even if it was moved, there was a big likelihood that it would return to the very same place.

She was dressed in a sea-green *ghaghra,* its material wispy and chiffon-like as it floated around her. She didn't smile at me.

"What's wrong?" I asked. She looked surprised at my directness. Shaking her head, she sat down in front of the mirror and combed her long waist-length hair. I stood behind her, so she could see me in the mirror.

"Shall I remove the tangles?" I asked her. She nodded and handed me the comb. I lifted her soft hair and ran the comb through sections of it gently. "What's the matter, Rehaan?" I asked, reverting to the name I used to call her, all those years ago. "You can tell me," I assured her.

"I don't know why Abbu and Ammi are in such a hurry to get me married."

The thought had occurred to me plenty of times, especially in the car as we had driven to her house.

"I don't know how it will turn out. I'm scared."

I didn't know what to say. I continued running the comb through her hair as this gave me something to do. The door opened and Farha ambled into the room like an elephant. She sat down on the bed with a thump and the bed creaked. Rehana remained silent. Obviously she didn't want to say anything in front of her. I understood her reluctance and continued combing her hair. When I had finished, she took the comb from me, ran its tip across the parting in her head and straightened it. Then bunching her hair behind her, she swiftly braided it.

Chachi walked in slowly, holding a metal box in her hand, followed by Ammi. She sat on the bed and grimaced in pain. We looked at her, concerned, but she didn't say anything. I shot a glance at Rehana, who looked white.

"Ammi, are you all right?"

"Of course, I am," Chachi said, and opened the box with a little effort and arranged the jewellery that Rehana was to wear on a large handkerchief. Ammi helped Rehana put on the big necklace. For one silly moment, I felt that it should be me sitting there and Ammi should be draping that necklace around my neck. But Ammi would have just handed over the necklace and ask me to wear it. This tenderness was reserved for only Mateen and Rehana.

The doorbell rang, and everyone looked up. "Oh god, they're here!" Asifa Chachi said, trying to get up. Ammi stopped her. "Fouzia Apa is already downstairs. She'll receive them. You come down slowly. No need to hurry. I'll come and supervise everything in the kitchen. You just sit in the hall and talk to the women."

Ammi looked so confident and self-assured that Chachi looked at her gratefully, her eyes watery. "I don't know how I would have managed if our husbands were not on speaking terms again," she said. "Fouzia Apa is hardly any help," she added in a whisper, as Farha was sitting with us. Soon Ammi and Chachi left the room, telling Rehana that they would come for her soon.

Rehana looked at me, her beautiful eyes looking big and sad. I adjusted the *dupatta* around her head. It used to be a childhood game we had played when we were four or five years old. We covered our heads with a *dupatta* and let it hang in front of our face like a veil, while we sat coyly like brides. The other person would lift the veil and say, "Ooh! What a beautiful bride!" and we would end up giggling.

But this was happening for real now. Rehana was going to be a bride soon, and then it would be my turn. There had been an invisible competition between us from the time we were born. Although we weren't of the same age, it was inevitable that we were compared at every turn of life. Who got more marks in class? Who got a better rank? Who learnt Kannada first? I was winning it all. Suddenly, the focus of the competition moved to who could make the better *dal?* Who knew how to make breakfast without burning it? Who learnt embroidery and tailoring? And now it was always Rehana who was the winner.

There was a tap on the door and Ammi stepped in. “Come,” she said softly. Rehana got up gracefully, the *ghaghra* swirling around her toes. She lowered her head and I adjusted the veil of the *dupatta* so that it covered her face. Ammi took hold of her hand and took her downstairs. She didn’t even look at me.

I didn’t envy Rehana but all along, I had fervently believed that I had won the biggest round of them all – completing my education. But it wasn’t being acknowledged or appreciated because it didn’t compare with Rehana’s achievement – getting married. With sudden insight I realised why Ammi was so annoyed that Rehana was getting married. I had lost the biggest round.

26

Fated

There was silence in the room except for the sound of a *samosa* crunching noisily. Fouzia Phuppu peeped into the room and grinned slyly.

"Everything is going well. Looks like Rehana will be getting married soon. Then it's my little darling's turn," she said, looking at her daughter indulgently.

"Ammi!" Farha protested, inspecting her *samosa* intently.

I waited till Fouzia Phuppu left the room and then I stepped out.

"Mehnaz Apa! Don't go," Farha called out. "We're not supposed to leave the room!"

I scowled and shifted the chiffon *dupatta* back on my shoulder. Rehana was downstairs in front of all those strange women and I was not allowed to go there or to be with her just because I wasn't yet married and Ammi didn't want anyone to ask her any questions.

It was good in a way. I didn't want any nosy women looking at me and then suddenly realising that I would be the perfect choice for their son or nephew or whoever. Like how it had happened with Rehana. But being cloistered inside made me restless.

Rehana's house had four bedrooms – two rooms, a kitchen, and a hall on the ground floor, and two rooms on the first floor and a terrace on the second floor. When I was small and we used to come here often, Ammi used to warn me not to go to the terrace as the walls were very low. Even now as I climbed each step, I remembered Ammi's warning, but I continued upstairs and opened the door to the terrace. Stepping out in the crisp evening air, I walked up to the parapet wall. Sadiq Chacha had added to its height some time over the years so it wasn't dangerously low now. I stood there for a while, breathing in the glorious scents of the lovely trees that surrounded me and closed my eyes.

I don't know how long I stood there when I heard voices behind me. "And this is the terrace of the house." "Come upstairs, it's okay." It was my mother's voice. She was clearly leading someone upstairs. Feeling like a ten-year-old, I looked around for a place to hide. The door opened and Ammi stood there with two *burka*-clad women. Ammi stared at me. Oh great. First I had gone to Mrs Dahlia's house when Ammi didn't like me going there. And she gave me the silent treatment for it. Now she had asked me to stay inside Rehana's room, and here I was out on the terrace. She would probably kick me out of the house.

I hoped my face didn't look as scared as I felt and I realised that my *dupatta* wasn't even covering my head respectably. I tried to wrap it around but the wind whipped it out of my hands. My pink chiffon *dupatta* floated down Rehana's house.

The women looked at me curiously. I felt exposed without my *dupatta,* almost naked. I resisted the urge to cover my chest with my hands. Now that would have looked even more ridiculous. Ammi didn't say anything. She didn't say that I was her wayward daughter who never listened to her and how I often got into such foolish situations. Ignoring me, she continued showing the terrace to the two women, who seemed more interested in me, and then took them downstairs. There was a hard glint in her eyes when she turned and looked at me before closing the door.

After the women left the terrace I waited for some time and then ran downstairs to Rehana's room. Rehana had been brought back upstairs.

"Where's your *dupatta?*" she asked. I saw that Farha was no longer in the room. She had probably headed for the kitchen.

I recounted the whole incident to Rehana and she giggled. I glared at her and she looked contrite and then fell silent. Remembering the reason why we were there, I asked her "How did it go?"

"Okay," she said. "You know how it is, na?"

I didn't know how it was. I didn't want to know. But first I wanted to retrieve my *dupatta* somehow. Would Mateen be able to help me? I went to the window and looked down. Our car stood inside Rehana's house. There was Sadiq Chacha's old Fiat, which he still used. Chacha and Abbu may not have spoken to each other for years but they seemed to have arrived at some sort of unspoken agreement. Neither of them had changed their cars in years.

I often urged Abbu to sell the old Maruti we had and buy a new model. For some reason, Abbu refused. It wasn't like we didn't have the money. But he seemed to have lost his interest in worldly possessions. Likewise, Chacha too hadn't traded in his Fiat for a new model.

A maroon Maruti Esteem stood outside the gate. That was the car in which the women had come probably. Our ragged looking cars stood faithfully in the afternoon heat and my *dupatta* was nowhere near them.

I saw two *burka*-clad women leave the house. Ammi would be coming upstairs soon and I felt my mouth turn dry, wondering what was in store for me.

When the door opened, my heart shrank when I saw Ammi standing there, holding my muddied *dupatta*. My throat felt tight with worry. She flung it at me and left without a word. Maybe she was going to publicly disown me. Feeling wretched, I picked it up and saw that it had tyre marks on it. It was ruined. I had to apologise to Ammi. But why, a voice inside me hammered. Why should I apologise? But if I didn't, there was no saying where the situation would lead. What if one of the women who had seen me on the terrace had taken a sudden liking to me? What if they sent a proposal to Ammi and she agreed? Anything was possible given Ammi's present state of mind. If I had to salvage the situation, I had to stuff that voice down, smother it, and apologise to Ammi. It had to be now, before she let her mind dwell on the whole thing and turn it into something worse than it was.

Wearing a *dupatta* I had borrowed from Rehana, I went downstairs cautiously. Abbu, Mateen, and Sadiq Chacha had sat in one of the rooms when the women had come to see Rehana. I looked inside to see Abbu and Chacha deep in conversation. Mateen was asleep on the bed. I looked at him lying on his side, breathing deeply, and I could feel the affection I had for him when he had been much younger.

Right now, I wished Ammi would feel one-billionth of that affection for me. It was hopeless. Did she love me at all? Abbu and Chacha hadn't seen me standing at the door, looking despondent. Even if they did, what could I say without looking and feeling foolish? This time, I had to face Ammi without Abbu's protection.

I looked around nervously and saw her sitting in the other room, where Asifa Chachi was lying down on her bed. Fouzia Phuppu and Farha had apparently left. I walked inside, wondering if it would be wise to talk to Ammi in Chachi's presence. Ammi looked up when I came in. Her mouth tightened. She looked away and continued talking. Chachi and I exchanged looks. She seemed sympathetic, and I assumed that Ammi had told her everything.

"Ammi, I'm sorry," I said. What else could I say? Ammi didn't turn around to even acknowledge my presence. God, this was going to be horrible. I wished I could fast forward the day until it was night and it was time for bed and then time for another day in college. Right now, the possibility of college being taken away from me was the only thing that kept me standing there. "Ammi, I am really sorry. Please," I said, walking around to face her.

She looked at me and said harshly, "We'll talk about this at home, Mehnaz. Right now I'm having an important discussion with Asifa."

I sat down on the bed. Ammi looked surprised. "I told you we'll talk about it at home," she said, her voice tight.

"Please, Ammi. I'm sorry for all that has happened. I never intended to annoy you or hurt you or make you angry. I don't know why but whatever I do, it turns out to be wrong. I never seem to do anything right and I don't know why it's like that."

Ammi shut her eyes. I didn't know how to proceed or what to say but I just continued.

"Ammi, I went to Mrs Dahlia's house because I consider her my friend. The poor lady's son died and she lives all alone, with no one to help her." Ammi looked at the window, her gaze distant. I didn't know if she had heard what I was saying.

"Ammi, please, for whatever it is I have done, I'm sorry. Today also, I went upstairs because I was feeling bored. I had no idea you would bring those women up and my *dupatta*..."

Ammi's cheeks had turned red. She got up in a hurry and I got up too. I held her hand to prevent her from going.

"Leave my hand, Mehnaz," she said, her voice breaking. I almost let go of her hand in surprise.

"No, Ammi. Listen to me, please," I begged her. Chachi was looking at both of us and I was getting embarrassed playing out such a personal scene in front of her. But it had to be now. Once we reached home, Ammi would toughen that hard and unyielding shell that surrounded her whenever I was near, and I would never be able to explain.

"From the time I was small, I have always felt that no matter what I did, you would never be happy about it. Why is that so, Ammi? Just because I am not the way you were when you were my age?"

Ammi looked at me for a long moment, her eyes shining. She shook her hand until I was forced to drop it. She walked out and I stood there squeezing my eyes tightly to prevent myself from crying in front of Chachi.

Chachi, thankfully, didn't say anything. She smiled at me and patted my hand. "It's okay. Everything will be all right," she whispered.

Should I bring Abbu into this? But to be honest, he didn't really solve any of our problems. He just fixed them temporarily, removed the cause of our distress for the time being, and let us continue pretending that everything was all right with the world.

When we left, I decided that I wouldn't apologise anymore. I would handle whatever happened. Ammi ignored me and continued discussing Rehana's marriage plans with Abbu. The women had hinted that they would probably angle for an engagement ceremony in another month and maybe the wedding itself in three or four months.

I listened to them discuss gold rates and the possible household items that Sadiq Chacha would want to buy for Rehana. I leaned my head against the seat and shut my eyes. Life seemed so simple just a few years ago. Our wants were less complicated and more straightforward. At least, we had known what we wanted.

I recalled Rehana's beautiful face as she had gone down to face her prospective in-laws. There was none of the usual calm I associated with her. Instead, there seemed to be a desperate and frantic searching look in her eyes. I could only guess that she was worried about her parents and Chachi especially. Or maybe the house. That was a possibility, yes. Knowing Rehana now, after a gap of all these years, when we had bloomed into women from girls, I realised that for her, this house was very important. There was a sense of ownership that she was not ready to relinquish even to her mother. And the idea of living in a strange, new family in their new house, learning to call it her own, but never owning it completely...

Rain lashed outside and Mateen drew circles in the steam that condensed on the car windows. The rain was an ever present source of fascination for me and I could look at it for hours as it pulped the mud outside and gauged potholes out of mere puddles on the road. It wasn't until Mateen poked me in my waist and I turned to him angrily when I realised that Abbu was asking me how many more years of college I still had to complete. I looked at him dazed. Ask him how many containers of goods he had brought from Madras and the numbers would roll off his tongue. But to expect him to remember which year I was in? "Final year, Abbu," I mumbled.

"Then it won't be long until our daughter also gets married," Abbu said.

I tried to assess the emotion that he was feeling as he said that. Was it regret or satisfaction? But I did know that Abbu would miss me when I was gone. However, whether Ammi would appreciate me more when I was married was irrelevant now as I heard her damning words.

"What is in her fate will happen," Ammi said quietly.

It sounded ominous, almost as if Ammi was wishing me to have the worst fate possible. But what if that nebulous creature '*naseeb*' that everyone thanked and blamed in equal measure was actually good and I got all that I wanted in my life? Would she resent it?

My thoughts went to her childhood and adolescence and I wondered if she had got everything that she had wanted. I wished that at least one of her parents were still alive to tell me how she had been as a child. From her own recounting of events I knew she was a near perfect daughter, but despite all that, had something important changed in her life?

Was it possible that Ammi had been denied most of the things that she wanted in life despite being the perfect daughter? One who obeyed her parents completely, one whose life was solely concentred around the kitchen, who never argued with her elders, who did just what was asked of her? And despite all this, had she not been given something that was important to her? Maybe that was why she was so short-tempered with me. I too was her daughter. Yet I was nothing like how she had been. I still got away with all the things that I wanted out of life. At least, most of them.

27

Keyed up

Rehana was getting married in February and my pre-final exams started two days before her wedding. Ammi didn't consider any of my exams to be important and so every day she insisted on taking me along to Rehana's house. So many things were happening there and each day there seemed to be some crisis, which Sadiq Chacha or Asifa Chachi seemed totally incapable of resolving.

Ammi stayed calm and she often steered the arguments and discussions to their proper conclusion. They packed Rehana's clothes in shiny cellophane sheets. Every little thing was bought for her, right from safety pins to toothbrushes to even buckets and washing powder. Chachi spotted me looking at all the things dubiously.

"Your parents will get you all this and more too," she smiled.

"But why? Why do you have to give her all this? Won't her in-laws have buckets?" I asked incredulously.

"They will, but when we marry a daughter and send her away, we give her everything that she will need in her new life. She needn't go and ask anyone for anything."

When I still didn't look convinced, Chachi continued, "For a new bride, everything is so strange and scary na? She will be comforted to know that her parents have taken care of her basic requirements till she gets used to her new family."

"So how long will six toothpastes last? And all these soaps? What will she do when it gets over? Come back here for more?"

"Mehnaz!" Ammi had overheard our conversation and she looked angry. "Think before you speak!"

"Wha..." I decided to keep quiet, but Chachi felt compelled to complete her explanation.

"See, by the time she uses all these things, her in-laws will no longer be strangers to her. She will be happy with her husband and her in-laws and she will not want to come to us for anything."

And that was what every mother hoped for as they got together a dowry for their daughter. In my community, dowry wasn't a bad word. It was something that parents gave willingly to their daughters to make lives more comfortable for them. But there had been cases where in-laws had turned nasty and demanded things, which made 'dowry' into the ugly word it was.

Fouzia Phuppu fuelled Ammi's anger against me by constantly taunting her that I should have been a boy, because being a girl I never did what other girls did. Ammi often took out all this on me at home but I ignored it. If I got into an argument, things would get heated and unnecessarily complicated.

I often looked up from my books and would see Rehana staring out of the window. If I had so much free time forced on me, I would probably read all the novels I could lay my hands on. Rehana, however, spent each day sighing, looking sad and distant. The thought that she probably liked someone did cross my mind, but then, I dismissed it.

"Where are your friends?" I asked her once. "Why haven't you called them?"

She shrugged, looking weary. "I lost the diary where I had everyone's phone numbers."

"But..." I stopped. Surely she would remember the phone number of at least one or two girls. But then I had never heard Rehana mention anyone from her school or her pre-university college. Maybe she didn't have friends.

My first exam was on Rehana's *chor-haldi* day. Weddings in our households started on Friday. If the wedding were on Sunday, the first function would begin on Friday, I mean. No one I asked, not even the old ladies, knew why it was called *chor-haldi*. During the *chor-haldi,* the bride was dressed in a simple yellow outfit, completely devoid of any jewellery, and her family members gathered together. *Mehendi* was also usually applied to the bride on this day.

Ammi, Abbu, and Mateen had breakfast and left for Chacha's house. I had my exam in the afternoon, and after I finished it I would join everyone for the wedding festivities. The *chor-haldi* wasn't a very big affair, limited to just close relatives. It was all right if I wasn't there from the morning. Ammi had taken another *salwar* of mine, so I could change into it after the exam.

I sat alone in the house feeling entirely free and exhilarated. Sahana had agreed to pick me up from home at 11.00 a.m., and we would go to college together, an hour and a half before the exam started. The exam we had today was Sociology and I had finished studying most of it. I watched TV for some time and then I sat sprawled out on the sofa. Ammi wasn't there to berate me, to tell me that no decent girl ever sat like that. The feeling of freedom lasted for ten minutes. After that it was boring, and the pain in my back wasn't worth it.

I sat up straighter and watched TV for some more time before switching it off. There was no fun in watching alone, especially without Ammi to berate me about watching too much.

The hours dragged. Eventually Sahana came and we left together for college. Ammi had told me at least five times that I should lock the house properly before leaving. Just as I was locking the main door, the gate opened. I looked up and saw Mateen.

"What are you doing here?" I asked him alarmed. Mateen said nothing.

"What happened?" I asked. Sahana looked at me and held my hand. Had something terrible happened? Why wasn't Mateen saying anything?

I ran up to him and shook his arm. "What happened? Say something! Is everyone all right? Ammi? Abbu?"

He shook my hand off, irritated, and said, "Ammi just wanted me to check if you had locked the house properly."

I felt a hot flush run up my face. My mother didn't trust me to even lock the house properly. She had to send my younger brother, ten years younger, to check on me. The thought made me furious, but I didn't want to create a scene in front of Sahana. She already looked amused. Forcing myself to keep quiet, I handed the key to Mateen and said coldly, "You can check if you want."

I went out to the road and blindly got into an auto. I didn't stop to see what Mateen was doing, whether he had left or if he had entered the house. How had he come? I couldn't believe that Ammi had sent him alone from Rehana's house just to see if I had locked up the house properly. The thought was so infuriating that if I had to write my exam in a proper frame of mind, I had to stop thinking about it.

28

Missing Love

I didn't feel like going to Rehana's house for her *chor-haldi* that evening. But I had given the house keys to Mateen, so I couldn't return home either. I went to Rehana's house hoping that no one had come yet but outside the door there was a huge number of glittering sandals and scruffy shoes. Everyone had apparently come.

Someone opened the door and I walked in feeling self-conscious without my *burka*. I should have at least taken it to the college today and worn it when I came here. Feeling a little daunted I looked around for Ammi because she had my new clothes. I found her in the kitchen, laughing with three other women. They were related to us, and as it often happened, they knew who I was but I didn't know them.

"Mehnaz, how was your exam?" one of them asked me.

"It was okay."

Ammi didn't comment on this. "Your clothes are in Rehana's room. Get ready soon," she said briskly.

I looked at her, some of the morning's anger returning to glower inside me. "Why did you send Mateen home? Didn't you think I could lock up the house properly?" I asked her.

The other women looked at us curiously.

"What are you talking about?" Ammi asked. I described what had happened that morning and with a feeling of dread saw shock spread on her face.

"Mateen went home? Alone? Where is he now? I thought he was with your father or someone. Why didn't you tell me before?"

she said in an accusing voice. I looked at her, not understanding what she was saying. She hadn't sent Mateen?

"Mehnaz, say something," she said, shaking my arm. I looked at her confused and shook my head. She left the kitchen to look for Abbu. I followed her, wondering what had prompted Mateen to do such a thing. I found Abbu and Ammi standing in the middle of the hall, talking and both of them looked worried. I approached them cautiously. Ammi looked up and glared at me while Abbu's expression was serious. "Come here, Mehnaz," he ordered. I walked up to him. Taking me by the arm, he pulled me into the nearest room. Ammi followed nervously. "When did Mateen come home? What did he say?"

I repeated what I knew. Looking at my mother I said, "He told me that Ammi had sent him to check whether I had locked the house properly."

Abbu looked genuinely surprised. "Why would she do that?"

I wondered too. Abbu really had no idea about how it was between me and Ammi. He seemed to believe – no, he wanted to believe – that everything was perfectly fine. As for Mateen, I wanted to believe that he was a normal boy, who lived a carefree life. And I believed it, not bothering to know whether it was true or not.

"Abbu, why are we wasting time here? Let's just call up home and see if he is there. He might pick up the phone," I said. I did not tell him that I had assumed Ammi had actually sent Mateen because she had such little faith in me.

Abbu nodded. "Good idea," he said. He quickly dialled the number and we watched his face for any indication that Mateen had picked up. His face remained blank. Hanging up, he said, "There's no response. I think we should go home and see if he is there."

Ammi looked fearful. "What if he went off somewhere? What if he isn't there at home?" I looked at her, feeling sorry and a little ashamed for thinking whether she would worry about me, if it had been me instead of Mateen. Maybe she would. Right now, we had to ensure that Mateen was safe. Sadiq Chacha was speaking with Abbu and offered to go with him, but Abbu refused. Asifa Chachi looked troubled.

"No, I'm coming," Ammi insisted. I wanted to go too. I had to know if he was all right. As we drove home silently, I looked out at the darkened streets of Bangalore. Cars and scooters flashed past as it was nearly 6:30 and there was heavy traffic of people returning home from work. Something suddenly occurred to me. "Abbu, how will we get inside the house? Mateen has the keys."

Ammi said without turning around, "I have another set. If I had known that you would actually give the keys to a little boy... *ya Allah!*" Abbu looked at me and then at Ammi. The car had stopped at a traffic light. Abbu sighed. "Nothing will happen. Don't worry."

The car jerked forward when the traffic light changed. We were near home now. Passing the familiar landmarks, I started feeling nervous. I prayed frantically for Mateen to be in the house but other thoughts also came into my mind, and I felt a churning in my stomach. What if he wasn't there? What if he had gone out? What if he had got lost? That wasn't likely, I tried to think rationally. He was old enough to come home from Rehana's house alone. So why would he get lost? But what if something else had happened to him? The words 'kidnap' and 'accident' formed in my head nebulously before I banished them frantically in fear.

Abbu pulled up outside our house and I quickly got out. Abbu and Ammi had already scrambled outside and rushed to open the gate. I followed them anxiously, praying all the while. "Please let him be inside. Please let him be inside." Ammi twisted the key in the lock and turned it in a hurry. The door opened, and we walked inside, calling out to Mateen.

My stomach dropped. My parents were looking for him in each room calling out his name, but standing in the hall I knew that Mateen wasn't there. It was empty and there was a slightly musty smell in the air. The house hadn't been closed for even an entire day. Somehow, this smell was never there when we were at home. I always felt it when the house was closed.

I stumbled forward, ready to collapse. What if Mateen had run away like Basheer? What if we never found him? Abbu and Ammi came out, Abbu's face pale and Ammi's dark with fury.

"Because of you, my son isn't at home!" she shrieked, shaking my shoulders until they hurt. "Didn't you have any sense at all? All you think about is your exams and your studies. Where is my baby?"

Abbu took hold of her arm and pulled her away. In all my years, I had never seen Ammi so angry. Whatever had happened before, all her anger and all her rage at me, was nothing... nothing compared to this moment. I stared at her, scared. It was an odd moment to realise that I didn't love my mother. I just didn't love her. I looked at Abbu's tired face. In spite of what happened, he didn't look angry. He was just very upset. But Ammi looked ready to kill me. And if it had been me instead of Mateen, I was now sure she wouldn't have been this upset.

Knowing, this wasn't going to help me in anyway now. We first had to find Mateen. With that resolve in mind, I walked to his room shakily. Maybe we could find out something from his friends. I rummaged through his desk drawers and found a diary. Flipping the pages, I saw a lot of entries, paragraphs scribbled here and there. There was no time to read anything so, I looked quickly through his other books and found a few phone numbers. Abbu paced the room and Ammi sat on the sofa, tears running down her face. To be constantly reminded that this was my fault compounded my guilt.

She wiped the tears from her face and took the book from me. "Give it to me!" I handed the book to her mutely and watched as she flipped the pages.

"The numbers are at the back," I volunteered. Ammi glared and turned to the last few pages.

Abbu turned to face us. "What if he's on the terrace? I'll take a look."

I watched him go. Ammi dialled the first number. I stood near the hall window which looked out into the street. What if he was at the park? I badly wanted to tell that to Ammi and suggest we look there. Despite my sudden realisation about how I felt for her, I wanted my brother back and I also wanted to console her.

Abbu came down with the same look on his face. He sat down on the sofa wearily. I stood behind him and pressed his shoulder. His head was thrown back and his eyes were closed. Ammi had called up the first number but hadn't found Mateen there. She continued with the other numbers, her face crumpling a little bit each time she spoke to someone.

"What if he's in the park?" I asked. Abbu opened his eyes.

"At this time, the park is already closed," Ammi replied scornfully. "You would know if you ever got your nose out of your books."

Abbu kept quiet at the unfair accusation. I wished he would defend me instead of leaving us to sort it out by ourselves. Ammi had finished calling up all of Mateen's friends and he wasn't with any of them. She looked at Abbu with despair. "Should we call up the police?"

Abbu sat up but said nothing. I sank down on the sofa and watched Abbu and Ammi in horror. No one spoke. The phone rang, breaking the silence. We all looked at it fearfully. Ammi was sitting right next to it, but she didn't seem to have the will to answer it. I got up and lifted the receiver from the cradle and said, "Hello."

It was Sadiq Chacha. Mateen had just stepped inside his house.

❖❖❖

29

Painful but True

I spent Rehana's *chor-haldi* alone, at home. Ammi and Abbu rushed off the moment they heard that Mateen was at Rehana's house. They slammed the door and sat in the car. I was still feeling a little dazed that they hadn't even checked if I was there or not, when Abbu hurried inside. "Come quickly, Mehnaz. Let's go to Sadiq's house," he said. I shook my head.

"Please go, Abbu. I have to study for my exam tomorrow." My voice wavered. I felt childish even as I refused to go. Ammi never came inside.

Self-pity was sickening. It was like a huge abyss into which I wanted to drown painlessly. I could have gone to Chacha's house, attended Rehana's *chor-haldi,* but here I was, in this darkened house, alone, with just my books for company. I didn't know if anyone would even miss me.

In the morning I was feeling ravenous. Ammi, Abbu and Mateen were probably still asleep and I wanted to leave for college as early as possible, but I couldn't avoid them all day. Today was Rehana's big *haldi.* Like yesterday, I would have to go to Rehana's house directly from college and get dressed there. But unlike yesterday, the function would be held in a wedding hall.

I saw a covered plate on the dining table. I lifted the cover and saw that Ammi had heated the *biryani* that Asifa Chachi had probably sent for me last night. I was really hungry.

Ammi stepped out of the kitchen. There were huge smudges under her eyes. She looked exhausted. "Have some breakfast," she said.

"I just want some bread," I said, reaching for the butter dish.

"Why?"

"Because *biryani* will make me sleepy and I won't be able to write my exam properly."

I was surprised when she didn't argue with me further. She sat down and rested her head on the table.

"Are you all right?" I asked her anxiously.

She said something that sounded like "Uhm". I buttered a slice of bread and took a bite. My stomach felt like a huge hollow. Ammi looked up when I sat down opposite to her at the table. She seemed like a different person now. Maybe I felt like this because at the moment she wasn't looking or behaving like she was superwoman.

"Mehnaz," she said softly, looking at me. Maybe she was feeling bad about last night.

"Yesterday, Mateen had me so worried. What do you think is the matter with him? Why did he do that?"

"Why don't you ask him yourself?" I got up in a hurry, but she stopped me again.

"I know you were upset last night, but try to think of things from my perspective also, sometimes."

I turned around, surprised to see Ammi looking at me solemnly.

"I have always looked at things from your perspective. That's why, I know that you love Mateen and not me."

The words had escaped and I couldn't take them back. Ammi looked at me, her eyes large and hurt. But it was the truth.

She didn't say anything after that. I left early for college, even though my exam was in the afternoon. I told Ammi that I wanted to do some reference work in college. But before leaving, I turned around and said, "And you can go to Rehana's house without any apprehensions, Ammi. After all, you didn't leave the responsibility of locking the house to me." Ammi didn't reply.

In college, I looked at the campus with longing. Classes were over for the year and everyone was busy studying furiously. The atmosphere was charged with anxiety, yet there was also a sense of excitement. College was finally getting over. It meant independence for so many of them overhere. I didn't want to think about what it meant for me.

Sahana was sitting under our tree, skimming through the pages of a book. We had found this tree in a secluded corner of the college, near the huge ground, and it had become our tree ever since. I sat down beside her.

"Where's Jyoti?" I asked her.

"Here she comes."

The three of us didn't do much studying that day. We spoke about many things under our tree, and I wished that time wouldn't hurry off so soon. Sahana, who always found something funny in everything, was very quiet today. Her mother wasn't keeping well and she was worried. Jyoti and I sympathised with her. I told them about what had happened last night. They both listened to me intently.

"Something exciting is always happening in Mehnaz's life, isn't it?" Sahana said to Jyoti. I resented that. My life wasn't exciting at all. When I said this much, she protested.

"But, Mehnaz, your father and your Chacha, how they had fought and how they got back together, later. Isn't that like a filmi story? Too bad, your Chacha doesn't have sons. You could have fallen in love with one of them."

Sahana was back to her usual jokes but I didn't like it one bit. It wasn't funny to be in the centre of something so intense.

"Don't forget Imtiaz," Jyoti added slyly. "After all, how many of us have faithful boyfriends who would wait for us on their terrace?"

My face flushed and I wanted to get up and walk away. But this would create an unnecessary scene, and then there would be a lot of awkward moments. We had such little time in college and I didn't want to waste it. I didn't reply. These two were my closest friends. They knew things about me that no one else knew. Yet I couldn't bring myself to tell them what I had realised yesterday. That, I didn't love my mother. I couldn't tell that to anyone.

I changed the subject and soon, Sahana and Jyoti were discussing their plans after college. Sahana wanted to pursue her masters in Psychology. She wasn't sure what she wanted to do, however. Jyoti was more clear. She just wanted to get a good job, something that paid well and made her independent. When they turned to me, I looked at them blankly. They knew that I had no career planned out and yet, every time this topic came up they always looked at me expectantly. As if, I would have realised what I wanted to do in life, between the last time they asked and now. As if, I would be allowed to.

I shook my head. Sahana clicked her tongue impatiently. "Enough, Mehnaz! Stop feeling so sorry for yourself. You're much better than that cousin of yours who's getting married tomorrow. You have a college education."

"So?" I asked bitterly. "Do you think that makes any difference? My parents won't let me go out and work. They're too conservative." Both, were silent for some time and then both started speaking together. They laughed but I sat grimly. Sahana said, "Look, I'm sure there must be something that you're good at. You don't have to have a career like all of us. Just try to find out what you're good at and at least don't let it die. Keep working on it. Nurture it."

I looked at the ground in the distance, at the empty basketball court. “There’s nothing I’m good at. I can’t sing, dance, cook, sew, paint, play basketball or any other sport.”

“Well, you’re good with words,” Sahana said.

“What good is that?” I asked her bitterly. “I’ve never won a single creative writing competition, nor do I get good marks in English.”

“But I’ve read what you had written the other day, about Imtiaz, and I think you write very honestly.”

I looked up, startled.

“Where did you read that?”

She looked embarrassed. I scrambled up, furious. She had actually read my diary! Sahana and Jyoti got up too, looking worried.

“I’m sorry, Mehnaz. It was a mistake. Your book was open the other day, on the desk during Sunaina Ma’am’s class, and I saw Imtiaz’s name. I just thought I’d read one sentence.”

“How much did you actually read?” I asked through clenched teeth. She looked down and didn’t answer. I walked away, needing the wind to cool my anger. Jyoti didn’t follow me, and I was hurt expecting at least her to come after me and say something.

My diary was still in my bag. I wanted to tear it apart. Today, yesterday... they were turning out to be days full of pain. Would tomorrow be the same? Tomorrow was Rehana’s wedding.

30

Mehendi

Rehana's *haldi* had been a huge success. So many people had come, Ammi gushed. I had gone to Rehana's house in the evening, straight from college, where I had taken my *burka*. From there, we all got ready and left for the hall where the function would take place.

Rehana looked ethereal in her pale-yellow *ghaghra*. Again today, no jewellery adorned her arms, her ears or her neck. Her simple attire was meant to be drastically different from the *nikah*, when she would be dressed in a rich *ghaghra*, complete with jewellery. I watched as she was led to the dais and seated on an ornate chair that was placed in the centre of a cage-like structure decorated with flowers. Her head was bowed down and her eyes closed.

I tried to be as inconspicuous as possible and I wasn't in the mood for exchanging small talk with anyone. Ammi stood near Rehana and adjusted her saree *pallu* so that it framed her face properly. One by one, women came up on to the dais and rubbed talcum powder on her cheeks, nose and forehead, and then bent down to hug her.

I watched the proceedings with interest. For the past few years, Ammi and Abbu had left me at home with Mateen whenever they attended the weddings of acquaintances. Unmarried girls like me were not taken to such weddings because the parents didn't want anyone to think that they were parading their daughters in front of interested women, who would immediately send off proposals for their male relatives.

Since Rehana's wedding was the first one in the family, and also since she was my cousin, I couldn't be left at home.

I looked around at the numerous women in brightly sequined sarees, *pallus* draped modestly over their heads, as they sat on plastic chairs, gossiping loudly about other weddings and other brides and people. Quite a few ladies hadn't removed their *burkas,* and they sat demurely, watching everyone. Asifa Chachi or Ammi or someone else would tell them to remove their *burka,* but they would smile and demur.

It was only at a wedding that one's community became apparent. I had never given much thought about being a Lababin Muslim from Tamil Nadu. Most of the people sitting here were Lababin, although there were a few people from other Muslim communities too, invited because they were business associates of Chacha's. Some had arrived without a *burka,* heads uncovered. One lady had even brought along a girl about my age, and I stared at her as she entered. Her hair was loose, her *dupatta* slung carelessly around her shoulders. She wore glossy lipstick, and she sat with her mother, one leg crossed over the other, and looked straight ahead.

Asifa Chachi had been standing on the dais, a little away from Rehana. I could see that the excitement was making her extremely nervous. She looked tired and fatigued too. I got up hesitantly with the intention of getting Asifa Chachi down from the dais, so that she could sit down.

Ammi had told me last week that during the wedding she wanted to see me in the background. She didn't want to tell people that I was her daughter, and yes, that I was older than Rehana and that I still wasn't married. So, she stared at me as I led Chachi down the steps.

Farha sat alone in the middle of the hall, unmindful of the people staring at her as they walked past. Fouzia Phuppu stood on the stage near Rehana, hovering over her, smiling fatuously at people who stepped on the stage. I imagined a scenario, where I was sitting on the dais like Rehana, and one push from me would send Fouzia Phuppu sprawling into the crowd below. I smiled for the first time that day.

It was past midnight and the hall had emptied quite a bit. Most of the guests had left, and I envied them. The few people who remained were close relatives. I wondered why Afzal Mamu hadn't come. After all, Rehana was his only niece. Did Abbu still hold a grudge against him? I remembered the feud that had given me so much to think about, so much to feel. Without it, life had slowly returned to its earlier state of normalcy. But somewhere, everything had changed.

We reached home at two in the morning. After the *chor-haldi* incident, Mateen had grown even more subdued. I don't know what Abbu had said to him. I wanted to talk to him, but oddly I was scared to ask him anything.

The next morning, Ammi and Abbu were waiting for me and Mateen to come out. I looked at the empty table. No breakfast? Ammi answered my unasked question. "We're having breakfast at Rehana's house."

The car window was rolled down, letting in the cool breeze, as we drove to Rehana's house. All these days, I had never asked Rehana if she ever wondered what her husband looked like. Of course, we had the engagement photos, and in those he seemed like a nice person. But to pledge your life to someone you didn't know at all, someone you hadn't spoken to, hadn't even seen... required a lot of faith. I didn't think I had it in me.

We reached Rehana's house and got down from the car. Yesterday, I had glanced at the house just before leaving for the *haldi*. The house had been decorated with twinkling fairly lights. They still blinked weakly in the morning light.

Inside there were some relatives who had stayed overnight in Rehana's house. Upstairs in Rehana's room, the door was locked. I knocked gently and walked in when she opened.

She was wearing a resplendent pink *ghaghra* that swirled around her ankles like liquid silk. It was embellished with tiny sequins and maybe a million of crystals, which twinkled in the morning light. There was a lot of *zari* work that climbed all up over the *ghaghra* and reached the waistband. She hadn't worn the *dupatta* as yet. We had seen the *ghaghra* as it arrived from the bridegroom's family, wrapped in the cellophane paper, covered with thick, glittering ribbons. Someone from his side had handed over the *ghaghra* to my mother who had undertaken the responsibility of making sure it reached Rehana's house properly. Along with the *ghaghra,* they had sent a pair of elegant slippers that was a more muted shade of pink, also glittering with crystals.

"Wow!" I said. She looked spectacular. She was adorned with gold ornaments, which dangled from her ears, lying quietly on the centre parting of her hair, shimmered on her neck, clinked on her arms, and winked on her fingers.

"Your husband is really going to get flattened!"

She looked at me in surprise.

For a moment I had forgotten that it was Rehana and not Sahana and Jyoti with whom I could talk freely. I had vowed that I wouldn't think of them today. Rehana smiled a little nervously. "You really think so?" she asked softly.

Catching hold of her arms, I turned her to face the mirror. "Look," I whispered. She looked straight ahead. Her face was almost angelic in the morning light, fresh and radiant. She had used kohl to darken her eyes. A light dusting of powder lay on her back, and I brushed it away gently. She turned around to face me, and it was then I realised that despite all her urgency and need to run a house, she was still a young girl. There was so much to see in life, and she was giving it all away. One night would transform her from a girl to a woman. It seemed to me that it was only now she had realised the enormity of the situation.

She didn't say anything and I felt curiously protective towards her. She sat down gingerly, holding the *ghaghra* above her ankles so that it wouldn't trail on the floor.

"Shall I get something to eat?" I asked. She looked at me, her eyes brimming with tears.

"I'm so scared," she whispered. I bit my lip. I pushed her hair back from her forehead and patted her back gently.

I went downstairs where everyone had woken up, and there was a lot of noise. In the kitchen, a middle-aged woman stood at the stove, stirring a huge *lagan*. I assumed she was the cook who had been hired by Chachi to do the cooking at home for the guests. I picked up a plate from the stand and went up to her. She turned towards me and raised her eyebrows.

Throwing down the huge ladle with which she was stirring the flat bottomed vessel, she turned to me and started a tirade.

"Just now I told that fat girl that breakfast will be ready in five minutes. I'm also human. And now she has sent you to get food for her?"

I looked around and saw Farha outside the kitchen, sulking. Oh! I returned to Rehana's room, thinking of amusing her with a description of the incident. Farha getting a dressing down from the hired cook!

I changed in Rehana's room, slipping the dove-grey silk *salwar* over my head. Ammi had done all my shopping and showed me the clothes one sunny afternoon while I was having lunch. I didn't protest. If she wanted me to wear it, I would wear it, as long as it wasn't outlandish or garish.

Rehana watched as I forced the gold studs into my ear lobes. She winced when I winced, and we both smiled. I examined myself in the mirror. I looked all right and I was satisfied. I didn't want any proposal coming my way because some woman in the crowd had taken a fancy to me as her prospective daughter-in-law.

Some time later, the women started leaving. The guests would start arriving by eleven, and we had to be there to receive them. As the bride's family, we had to welcome the bridegroom's people as well as the guests we had invited. Ammi left with a few women in the first group of people. Mateen was sitting with the men, quietly. There were other boys of his age, but he didn't seem interested in talking to them.

Rehana would go right at the end and I would accompany her. The house had been crammed with the furniture that her parents had bought for her. Downstairs, one of the rooms had the huge bed, the sofa set, the dining table, the dressing table, and other things that her parents had got made especially for her. Yesterday, all the furniture had been moved to her in-laws' house. Today, little by little, the house was emptying of all the people who had filled it up for the last few days.

Rehana was tired of sitting in her room and wanted to go downstairs. By now, almost all the people had left, including Fouzia Phuppu and Asifa Chachi. We were waiting for the car to arrive. I helped Rehana walk downstairs, holding her so she wouldn't trip on her flowing *ghaghra*. We had to be ready for the car. So I seated her on the sofa and ran back upstairs to collect my *burka*. Rehana's was already downstairs. Someone had been sewing silver sequins along the hem.

We waited in the quiet house, a slow breeze rippling across us from the open window. It had been carelessly left open. I got up to close it. Rehana's eyes were downcast. I watched a tear trickle down. Feeling choked and unhappy, despite all the gaiety that had been there from morning, I hugged her hard. Her many necklaces poked my chest, and I quickly moved away. I didn't want to ruin her hair or her clothes.

I was afraid of speaking because I felt that if I spoke, I would probably start crying. I was here to help her, not to induce a crying fit. But she looked at me and wiped her eyes gently with a tissue.

Some of her kohl got smeared on her eyelids. I took the tissue from her and gently wiped it away.

"I'm sorry, Mehnaz," she said in a soft voice. I looked at her surprised.

"For what?"

She looked down once more. "I'm sorry for the way I had treated you all those years ago," she said. "I'm sorry for being so jealous of you, sorry for trying to be like you, sorry for thinking that you were conceited."

Whatever was she saying? What was there to apologise? All my life, I too had been jealous of her, of her place in my parents, affections, of the calm and serene way she managed her house, of her quiet and gentle beauty. I opened my mouth to say all this but I couldn't. I didn't want her to be burdened with my guilt, that too just before she got married. I wanted her to go to the wedding hall happily.

So I told her about Imtiaz. The entire story, of how our friendship had developed from the time he threw those *chappals* to the time he was almost going to tell me he loved me. She listened to me, amazed. I gauged her reaction to the story by her expressive eyes, which grew round when I told her how he had held my hand.

"Then?" she asked breathlessly.

I told her about each meeting, including the last. I told her that I thought I was in love with him, but the whole thing was so ambiguous.

"What are you going to do?" she asked me finally. Her face was animated and there was a sparkle in her eyes. I shrugged. "Oh, I do so hope it works out for you, Mehnaz. This is so exciting! Why didn't you tell me about this?" she asked. I didn't know what to say. The door bell rang. Rehana looked up. It was time.

I dropped my *burka* over my head carelessly and quickly helped her into hers. Her hands shook as she tied the string that held the two sides together. I took it from her and bent to tie it for her. The strong smell of the *mehendi* on her palms reached my nose and I felt like gagging. I hated the smell. I looked at her as she tried to regain her composure. She looked almost regal, and I was proud of her. I was also glad that she wasn't looking teary-eyed or getting sentimental about leaving the house she had cared for so much.

An uncle stood at the door. I was glad it wasn't my father or Rehana's who had come because that would have made her more emotional. She looked fresh and in great spirits, while strangely I felt subdued. As we sat in the car, I saw her looking out of the window. Soon I too would be leaving my house like this. But I had no idea about how I would be feeling.

31

Ahead

It's been two months since Rehana got married and I had no idea how she was. Her in-laws preferred to stay most of the time in Vellore, and they often took her there with them. While studying for my finals, I would look out of the window and suddenly think of her. What was she doing now? What was her husband like? At the *valima,* he looked straight ahead, not even turning to look when Rehana was brought by a couple of women from his family and was made to sit next to him. There was no smile on his face.

Rehana was in a rich green saree, with lots of gold sequins, lots of jewellery, and lots of *moghra* flowers. I couldn't see her face as her head was bowed down, even on the day after the wedding. From the back row, I observed the wedding that everyone had waited for so long in my family, was finally over.

I looked at Ammi talking with some women. She looked happy, almost radiant and wore a blue silk saree, looking very elegant for a change instead of looking harried, as she almost always did. The *pallu* of her saree was draped modestly over her head, and she kept adjusting it as she spoke to the women. I looked around for Asifa Chachi. She was sitting in the front row, her back towards me. I couldn't see her face, but I knew that she was tired from all the excitement and needed to rest for at least a week.

I wanted to talk to Rehana, but there was now a wall between us. It had been there ever since we had left our childhood behind. It had grown stronger as our differences had increased, its foundations deepening with the feud, brick by intangible brick.

It was now there between us, the final brick in place, with her marriage. We hadn't identified with each other for a long time. But now, it was even more real. With the jewellery, the flowers, the rich sarees... she was not the Rehana I had thrown *chappals* with.

It was the last day of my final exams today. I entered the exam hall feeling a little numb. This was the last time I would sit on these scarred benches. The last time I would hold pen to paper and write furiously, vigorously, till my fingers ached. I surveyed the neatly ordered benches and found my roll number inscribed on a bench with wet chalk. I took my seat. Jyoti was seated in a different room. Sahana's seat was at the back of my room. I turned around to see her. When she saw me turn around, she quickly looked down. I continued staring at her bent head. We hadn't spoken for many days. I had thought that she would seek me out and apologise. I wanted to be a little pricey, but I was going to forgive her eventually. After all, friendships that have grown over five years cannot be flicked away with the page of a diary. But she didn't approach me at all. I was hurt but chose to remain silent. Jyoti spoke to me but it wasn't like before.

I willed her to look up. She continued staring at her answer sheet. The teacher would distribute the question papers in a couple of minutes. While I wrote my exam, I was often so engrossed that I didn't realise the time or the number of people left in the room. After each exam, I would look up and would discover with surprise that Sahana had already left.

The teacher came in and I reluctantly turned away. On a quick impulse, I turned back and saw that she was looking at me. I quickly smiled at her. She looked surprised and then she smiled tremulously. I wrote the exam with a happy heart. I knew I had forgiven her. After the exam, she waited for me outside, with Jyoti. We sat down in the canteen, realising that we would miss all these little things so much now.

After an awkward silence, Sahana finally spoke. "I'm sorry, Mehnaz. I wanted to apologise to you but you looked so angry and unapproachable that I was almost afraid."

I didn't know what to say. I couldn't say, "It's okay." Because it wasn't really okay, that she had read my diary. But then it wasn't something that I wanted to hold against her and make her feel guilty.

"Let's not talk about that," I said forcefully. She looked at me surprised. Once again, we went back to talking about where life would take us now that we no longer had the same goal of reaching the classroom on time, or getting enough attendance in all the classes, or even trying to score good marks.

We chatted for some time. Jyoti bought a bar of Cadbury's Dairy Milk and we broke it into pieces and popped it in our mouths as we talked. The chocolate stuck to our tongues and the roofs of our mouths, making it difficult to say anything properly. We laughed at each other, at how funny we sounded. With sticky hands and sweet mouths, we hugged each other and walked out of the college gates. Here was life.

Part 3

32

Old Houses

Sitting at home all day, I stared out at the road from my room. The world had a purpose. People striding to offices, children skipping towards school, maids slouching to work... everyone had something important in their lives. Everyone, except it seemed me. It was five months since the final exams were over. The results were out, and I had passed with a first class. I sometimes took out my mark sheet and spent at least 15 minutes going over it, looking at the Bangalore University logo and the subjects that I had taken and my marks.

I helped Ammi in the kitchen but despite that, there was so much time on my hands. What bliss it was to be busy, I wished, when I heard that Jyoti had found a job immediately after college and was earning 6,000 to 7,000 rupees a month. I was happy for her but more envious. Sahana was doing the rounds of admissions for her postgraduate course. And Rehana, my sweet little cousin, was now four months pregnant.

It felt strange that we would never do anything together now. She now had another family whose priorities came first. Would I also have to distance myself from my parents and stop thinking about them, like Rehana when I get married? But was it ever possible to stop caring about one's parents? Sons are expected to take care of the parents, while daughters... are expected to leave and join another family. It was unfair, the assumption that daughters would not care for anyone except their in-laws after marriage.

With my exams out of the way, I had heard Abbu and Ammi talking about my marriage more frequently. It was a matter of time before people came to see me, and for some reason I wanted to go to Vellore before that. At steady intervals, I dropped huge hints to Abbu about our house there, wondering loudly about the state of the house since we had last visited. He would mutter something and would get back to his work. Basheer and Vellore were the thoughts that occurred simultaneously. How different things would have been if he had been in Vellore! Without him and Zohra Phuppu, the house seemed to be sapped of everything living.

And that Ammabi? How was she getting along? She must be nearly hundred. Well, no, that was an exaggeration, but to my eyes she had always looked old and scraggy. And now, without Zohra Phuppu, she must have become even more emaciated. I felt sorry for her sometimes and wondered about her life too. Where was her own house? Didn't she feel odd living in someone else's house? Didn't she have anyone else, except Basheer's father?

My obsession with Vellore grew along with my realisation that I knew very little about Ammi's family. Some of her relatives still lived in Vellore but she hardly ever took us there, almost as if she wanted us to grow up ignorant about her life before she became our mother. I wanted to visit them, learn from them what they knew of Ammi, and try to see if I could see her from a fresh angle.

There were times when the intensity of my longing for Vellore and that house was so much, that it unnerved me. What I probably needed was to join some cooking course or something, where I would meet other young girls and housewives looking to whip up new and exciting dishes for their families. But that wasn't what I have wanted to do. I wrote in my diary extensively, although being rather careful not to mention Imtiaz again and lamented about the inertia that had swept over my life so irrevocably. Imtiaz was also one of the reasons I wanted to revisit the place of my childhood fantasies, although I didn't know what I could possibly do once I was there, because I had no way of contacting him at all.

One Monday, Abbu announced that we were going to Vellore on Thursday. We were leaving by train, as it had become the norm now. Ammi looked surprised.

"Why?" she asked him.

"I want to look up on some old friends. I thought we could spend the weekend there. We'll come back on Sunday," he said and got up slowly because of the arthritis in his knees.

"I'm not coming."

Abbu turned around. It was Mateen. "I have school!" he protested. "I can't take two days off just like that!"

My heart sank. He was right. Attendance couldn't be ignored. "Why can't we go on Friday after he returns from school?" she asked guardedly. Abbu shook his head. "I'm not driving down. You know that, and there's no train for us at that time. There's no point in going on a Saturday and returning the next day."

"Abbu and I can go on Thursday and Mateen and you can come on Saturday," I suggested slowly. My heart bobbed about in my chest as I looked at Ammi's face for any kind of indication. We had almost reached a truce now that I never stepped out of the house. I was quite comfortable with her now, but there was still the uncertainty. Abbu looked undecided. Mateen looked mutinous. Finally, Ammi spoke.

"I think she's right," she said. "It has been a long time since we have been to Vellore. Because of her exams we never managed to go all of last year. Yes, I think that's a good idea."

My heart was now knocking around in my chest wildly. Vellore without Ammi meant freedom of a totally different kind especially if I was going to try and meet Imtiaz. This trip to

Vellore had become all the more important now and before I got married or engaged, I wanted to be in Vellore if only to remember the old days.

The tickets came and I had already packed my clothes. Without Ammi, it indeed felt like an adventure. It was odd that she wasn't organising my things or telling me how to arrange my clothes in the travel bag, instead of stuffing them, but that could be because she had so many other things to do, although the tiniest bit of me hoped that maybe she was now ready to treat me as an adult.

Abbu and I took an auto to the station, and I watched Ammi wave at us from the window. It was early morning, the air fresh and crisp, and I felt a soaring sense of freedom. The train arrived at the station and Abbu and I got inside, found our seats and sat down. The train started sluggishly after some time.

I looked out of the window for some time, cupping my chin in my hands and dreamed. The trees, bushes, mountains melted past in a blur and I felt the warm wind on my face. I closed my eyes, and breathed in deeply. Wondering what would become of me it had become such an ingrained habit that when my mind wasn't occupied with anything else, I started thinking about my future.

School and college had passed by and the only objectives we had were to pass exams. But at least, by the last year of college most girls knew what they had wanted to do. My friends from PUC who had taken up professional courses like Medicine, Engineering etc. were far removed from my mind. They had become mere acquaintances, and there wasn't the close bond that Sahana and Jyoti seemed to have with me. But now, both of them too were busy with life. Life apparently had taken them with open arms, telling them exactly how exciting it was going to be. They didn't have much time for me, and I was the one who persistently called them up.

I had called up Sahana yesterday and when I told her about my Vellore trip, she had been surprised but she didn't probe further. Jyoti didn't have time at all to call or even receive calls. I opened my eyes as the blur outside slowly became Jolarpettai Station. Vellore wasn't far away now.

The train picked up speed after some time. Abbu asked me if I wanted to eat something. I shook my head. He had started a conversation with a Gujarati man sitting opposite us. They spoke about business and government policies, and I yawned.

Everyone seemed to know what they wanted. I wished I had paid a little more attention to the career guidance classes we had in college. I hadn't attended a single lecture because I felt it was a waste of time. What career, after all? I chewed my lips and shook my head. Writing? I twisted my lips in distaste as I remembered Sahana admitting to having read my diary. She had said something good about my writing, although at that time, the words didn't cling to my mind.

It had been months since I had met Mrs Dahlia and I thought of her now and then. I hadn't wanted to displease Ammi more, by going there again. But Mrs Dahlia had looked so old and tired the last time, and I really ought to have gone and seen how she was, because Ammi would disapprove of everything I did anyway. Suppose she was better now? Maybe she would guide me about my future. With that faint possibility spurring my hopes, I closed my eyes and slept.

Abbu shook me awoke after some time. "Vellore is here," he said. I shook my head to dispel the sleep and got up unsteadily. The train had screeched to a halt at Katpadi. It would move on to Madras in barely five minutes. We got down from the train, and I looked at the station fondly, a blast of warm air hitting my face as the train moved on. I closed my eyes briefly and muttered a short, very short prayer to Allah, thanking him for bringing me back here.

Outside the station we got into an auto and Abbu bargained with the auto driver. As we neared Vellore, I thought it would be better if I told Abbu about my plans to visit Ammi's relatives. He looked taken aback when I brought it up.

"Does your mother know?" he asked.

I shook my head.

"I don't think she will like it."

I stared at the passing vehicles spewing black smoke. "But, please, Abbu!" I implored turning to him once more. "I really do want to meet Ammi's relatives. Why doesn't she ever bring them home? Why doesn't she even talk about them? What is so shameful about them?"

Abbu grew silent. He shrugged. "Do as you wish," he said. Feeling confused, I looked at him. Had I offended him with my outburst?

"Will you take me there?" I asked timidly. "I mean, I can't just land up at their house and tell them that I'm Shabana's daughter."

Abbu looked at me curiously as the auto turned inside one of the *gallis*. We were near to the home now. "Did you plan this beforehand?" he asked. I didn't say anything. The auto weaved in and out of potholes and gutter-lined streets and finally stopped at the tiny *galli* that led to our house. Abbu and I got down and I started walking with my bag, while Abbu paid the auto driver.

I walked towards the house, feeling a strange combined sense of anticipation and longing. No matter how much I longed for it, the old days would never come back. I would never see Zohra Phuppu standing at the door, looking out for us, her saree *pallu* twisted around her slim fingers. I would never see Basheer distracted and slightly dazed as he sat on the bench outside his house, waiting for me to freshen up so I could rush out to play with him.

Coming here, without Ammi seemed like a mistake. With her crisp instructions and her constant orders, I often forgot what this house really meant to me. But now, I walked in silence towards the grey house, with the cracked pillars and dusty bench. I stood outside, waiting for Abbu to catch up with me. We didn't ring the bell. Ammabi wouldn't hear it anyway.

Abbu inserted the key into the key hole and it turned rustily. We pushed open the door and stepped in. Ammabi was sitting in front of the *divan,* watching TV. I took in, her appearance. She was quite tidy, and yet I felt a surge of sympathy and compassion for this old woman. She may have taunted Zohra Phuppu, but she had at least given her an identity, despite her son, Phuppu's husband having taken it away from her.

She was still engrossed in the programme. It looked like Tamil news. She watched the newsreaders as they spit out the news with great gusto and she was completely taken in. Abbu and I moved forward and we placed our bags beside the *divan.* Ammabi looked up, and smiled a toothless smile.

33

Clues

Vellore didn't seem to have changed much. At least not the Vellore I knew. The *azan* still sounded out loud, clear, and strong, five times a day. I listened to it, letting the sound soak into me, reaching all corners of my being until I felt whole again. Ammabi was so happy to see us there that she offered to make *biryani* to celebrate our arrival. Abbu refused. He knew it was no easy task and he didn't want her going through any trouble for us.

"Make *dal* and rice," he told me. "I'll go get the ration and maybe some chicken. You can make something nice this evening."

I nodded, feeling a little disconsolate. Abbu wanted me to cook! But then I could finally cook something without Ammi looking over my shoulder, berating me constantly. The kitchen was hot, I decided after being there for ten minutes. How could anyone stand here and cook a decent meal without melting first? I fanned myself furiously with my *dupatta* and quickly cooked *dal*. I had no idea how to cook rice without a rice cooker. Ammi had never shown me any other way. I went to Ammabi hesitantly and asked her.

She was watching a cookery show where a rotund Tamilian lady was stirring something in a brass pot over a stove. I went back to the kitchen and brought the cleaned rice in a plate to show her. She waved me away, when I thrust the plate before her but I persisted and she got up with great difficulty, mumbling something, and took the plate from my hands and walked towards the kitchen. Abbu took care of everything for her, right from phone bills to rations and everything that she needed, but what would she do if she ever fell sick?

After lunch, Abbu went out to meet some friends. I spent the hot afternoon on the terrace, waiting for Imtiaz to appear. But how would he know I was in town? I suddenly remembered an old conversation where he had mentioned something about a friend who informed him when he spotted our car. Maybe I could call him up and inquire about Imtiaz? The idea excited me tremendously, and I flew downstairs. It was only when I came up to the telephone that I stopped.

Who was this friend? What was his name? I sat down on the ground. Ammabi was taking a nap on the *divan*. How was I going to find out the number of this person? I shut my eyes and tried to recall the name of the person but it kept eluding me. I wished, I had brought along my diary because I was sure to have written something in it about this. The name of the shop popped into my mind all of a sudden and I got up and jerked the receiver from its cradle.

I called up Enquiry and asked them for the number of Sundaram Jewellers. After jotting it down quickly, I called up the number. While the phone rang, I ran through all possibilities in my mind. Maybe he didn't work there any more. Maybe he had lost touch with Imtiaz. Maybe Imtiaz had got married. The ringing stopped with a click when someone picked up the phone but I didn't know what to say. I still hadn't been able to recall the name of his friend and feeling rather foolish, I hung up to the sound of hellos echoing in my ear.

I sat there for some time, wondering what to do. Maybe I could call up, and ask for Imtiaz. But he didn't work there. Still, it was worth a try. The *asr azan* started and Ammabi stirred on the *divan*. Covering my head with my *dupatta,* I pressed redial. This time, I said 'Hello' softly. The voice on the other side, male and slightly impatient said 'Hello' gruffly.

I cleared my voice and spoke. "I'm actually Imtiaz's friend, Mehnaz. He once told me that his friend worked here. Am I speaking to him now?"

There was silence. I wondered whether he had hung up. I wished I knew Tamil. I wished I hadn't sounded like I came from a convent, sounding so cultured and academic. When the silence continued, I cleared my throat a little loudly and spoke again. "Are you Imtiaz's friend?"

The voice on the other side said "No" and hung up. I stared at the receiver and replaced it in the cradle. I would try once again this evening. Ammabi got up and sat on the *divan,* swinging her frail legs down. She looked shaken. What was it, about old age that you woke up from a nap looking tired?

I made tea for both of us and watched her sip it noisily. "Did Basheer ever call you?" I asked her loudly. She had slowly turned deaf and I usually avoided conversations with her because they stretched my patience. She looked at me, and put her tumbler of tea on the ground. She shook her head and mumbled something about being the unluckiest woman on earth. "My son left me, my grandson left me, my daughter-in-law died... how will I live?" she asked. I looked at her in surprise. What did she mean? She was living, managing somehow. But then, this wasn't really life. This was just waiting for death, for oblivion. I shuddered involuntarily. My life would never amount to this, I resolved. Never.

"Why don't you come and live with us?" I asked her, shouting once more. She shook her head and said, "If Basheer comes, then what?" I looked at her in understanding. She didn't know how much longer she had to live, but she wanted to be here, in case her only grandson decided to come back. I wanted to tell her that he wouldn't ever come back. But then, who was I to take away her hope, the reason for her existence?

Later in the evening, I tried the number once more. This time, I spoke slowly, clearly. "I'm looking for Imtiaz's friend." Once more, there was silence. I stared at the blank blue wall in front of me in frustration. "One minute," the voice said, and I kept quiet. No point in getting my hopes up. This really didn't mean anything. Another voice said, "Hello, this is Suresh." I sighed in relief and spoke to him quickly. "Suresh, I'm Mehnaz, Imtiaz's friend. He told me about you once. I'm in Vellore right now. Do you know how I can contact Imtiaz?"

There was a silence. I wondered if this man would berate me for calling him up or simply hang up. "Mehnaz, Imtiaz doesn't live in Vellore now. He lives in Madras. He has a business set up there," Suresh said. I fought down the disappointment. "But I could give you his number," he continued. My throat seemed to have closed up. Hurry up! Say yes! Take it down... but I just couldn't. The possibility of having Imtiaz's number made my head spin. "Yes. Please give me his number."

I took down the number and noticed with irritation that my hands shook slightly. This was nothing. Nothing really. It was just a phone number. "Why don't you give me your number so I can ask him to call you?" he offered. I thought for only a second before giving the number to him. Maybe it would be better if Imtiaz called, I thought. After all, Abbu paid the phone bills here, and Ammabi never made any STD calls. Ammi called her every week to ask how she was. Abbu would surely get suspicious if he saw Imtiaz's number in the phone bill.

"Will you be in Vellore for a few days?" he asked.

"I'm not sure," I said. I didn't want to tell him.

"Okay," he said. "I'll ask Imtiaz to give you a call." He promptly hung up. I wanted to ask him when Imtiaz would call. Now? Tomorrow? When?

I replaced the receiver and stared at the digits I had scribbled on the paper. I sat there, staring at the number for nearly ten minutes, memorising them. Then the phone rang. I looked at it, scared and excited. I lifted the receiver from the cradle and croaked out a "hello". Damn! Why did my voice have to sound like I had laryngitis or something?

The voice on the other end spoke warily, "Mehnaz?"

Just listening to Imtiaz's voice made me feel warm. "Hi!" I said.

"It's really you!" he said surprised.

"What did you think?" I ventured, feeling slightly at ease.

"I didn't know if Suresh was telling the truth or simply pulling my leg."

"Why would he do that?" I asked wondering if my smile could be manifested through my voice.

"That's just the way he is. Forget him. Tell me how you've been."

I told him that I had finished college and Rehana was now married. "What about you?" I asked him warily. "Are you married yet?"

He laughed. The sound of his laughter, rich and resonant, reverberated in my ears. "Not yet, but my mother has been pestering me to get married soon. What about you? Any plans soon?" he asked casually.

Almost too casually, I decided. "No, not yet. My parents are looking for a groom," I replied. When he didn't reply, I wondered what had happened. "Imtiaz?" I asked him.

"Hmm. I'm here," he said.

"I heard you have set up a business there. How's it doing?" I asked. He spoke for a while about his hardware business. It sounded a bit boring.

"How long will you be in Vellore?" he asked. I didn't know what to tell him. Taking a deep breath, I said, "I'm here with only my father. My mother and brother are coming here on Saturday, and we'll be going back on Sunday."

The silence stretched. Then he spoke quickly. "I'm coming to Vellore tomorrow. Wait for me."

I didn't know what to say to that. I felt like holding the receiver and jumping up and down a hundred times. "Wait for me!" Those three words made me so happy that my temples ached from grinning so much. "Why?" I asked, feeling slightly more confident.

"This time you're going to listen to what I have to say," he said gruffly. "You're not running away again."

I didn't reply to that. His tone made me slightly nervous. "Okay. I'll listen to what you have to say," I said. "Whatever it is."

"Okay, so I'll see you tomorrow on your terrace, after *Asr?*" he asked.

I clung to the receiver, feeling absolutely foolish, drunkenly happy as I said, "Yes!"

34

Zulekha

Ammabi looked at me myopically.

"Who were you speaking to?" she asked.

"A friend," I told her. It was the truth.

Abbu came home later that evening. He had brought chicken *tikka* from a stall and we ate it from the newspaper wrapper and banana leaf in which it was wrapped. Ammabi sucked and chewed the succulent chicken pieces with her gums and then finally swallowed. She looked happy.

Abbu also looked relaxed. He was different in Vellore. Almost larger than life. Bangalore seemed to dwarf him with its progress and fast way of life. But Vellore was still Vellore for him.

I was euphoric about Imtiaz. No longer did things feel vague. I knew there was something between us, and maybe tomorrow I would know what it was. I reminded Abbu to take me to Ammi's relative's house and he looked away, sighing for the first time that day.

"Why do you want to go there, Mehnaz? What will you tell them? Do you think they will recognise you?"

"That's why, Abbu! We have to go there, increase our acquaintance with them. After all, even if Ammi has forgotten them, they wouldn't have forgotten her."

Abbu shook his head. "I don't think they would have forgotten your mother."

I continued staring at him.

"If your mother finds out..."

"She won't. We won't tell her."

He stared at his knees for some more time, and then finally agreed. "Okay, come," he said.

I ran to the room where Zohra Phuppu used to stay. I had kept my clothes and *burka* there. I quickly opened my hair and braided it once more, smoothening the parting at the centre. After quickly washing my face, I slipped my *burka* over my head and went outside. Abbu hadn't changed from his trousers into his *lungi* as he did whenever he got back home. He slipped his feet into his slippers and waited for me at the door. I rushed outside, feeling breathless.

We walked up the *galli* and when we came to the main road, he stopped a cycle-rickshaw. He spoke to the man on the cycle and gave him an address. I couldn't quite hear the name of the *galli* as I got into the rickshaw and Abbu clambered in beside me. It was getting dark as the rickshaw puller led us through winding, narrow, gutter-lined *gallis*.

We reached a slightly broader road with a huge *masjid* at the beginning. Goats loitered around, sniffing piles of rubbish. Schoolchildren clamoured around an ice candy man, and we skirted around them, the rickshaw wobbling precariously. The cycle-rickshaw pulled us forward, every inch we moved, the strain clearly visible on the man's arms and chest. Abbu asked him to stop before a nondescript house. It was painted a dull shade of cream. We got down and Abbu paid the rickshaw puller ten rupees. I stared at the brown door. I hadn't asked Abbu who these people really were. How were they related to Ammi?

Too late, I thought, as Abbu rang the bell. We stood in silence. I wondered once more why Ammi had never brought us here. Ammi never took us anywhere in Vellore. Only once, I had been inside CMC, and we only passed by Gandhi Road whenever we came. I had never really seen anything inside this town. I didn't know the street names and I didn't know the directions to any place. At twenty-one that was pretty shameful I thought, about how little I knew about my birthplace.

The door opened slightly, and Abbu leaned forward and said, *"Salaam"*. The woman behind the door shrank back. Abbu lowered his gaze and talked to his feet.

"I'm Shabana's husband. I've brought my daughter, Mehnaz. She wanted to meet you."

The door didn't open any further as I had expected. The woman behind seemed confused.

"Your sister Shabana," Abbu said once more. I looked at him, shocked. Ammi's sister? Surely he meant cousin. How could Ammi have a sister and never tell us about her? My eyes bored into his head, wishing he would look up from his feet. I tapped his arm and he looked up. There was something in his eyes. Embarrassment. And it was laced with anger. If I wasn't careful, Abbu would just take me back to our house.

The door opened fully. The woman standing there had draped her *pallu* around her head with extreme modesty so it covered half her face and she held it there with her fingers. She said *salaam* to Abbu and invited him inside. Abbu looked hesitant, and then shook his head.

"I'll come back for you in an hour. I hope your curiosity would be gone by then," he said to me. He turned around and left. I looked after him and then turned to look at the lady behind the door. She too was looking at him as he walked away.

"Come," she said, motioning me to step inside. I walked inside and faced her. Her *pallu* was still draped around her head, but I could see her face now. She was fair and plump, a lot like my mother. But there were many differences in their physical features. I didn't know what to say to her when she asked me to sit down. I looked at her, then at the house, at the uneven, crumbling walls, and cracked pillars that mated the red, dusty floor with the cobwebbed ceilings. This house was ancient.

Behind the pillars was the sitting area where a few mats were rolled out neatly. I sat down, without removing my *burka* and she didn't ask me to. Maybe she thought I wouldn't remove it even if she asked me. I folded my legs under my knees and asked her, "Are you really my mother's sister?"

She sat down beside me and didn't say anything. I noticed a girl standing at the door of one of the rooms. Her head was covered with her *dupatta*. She looked at me curiously while I tried guessing her age. She was probably a couple of years older than me.

"Yes," the lady said. I looked at her in shock. She was really my mother's sister! My aunt! And this girl, she was my cousin! The joy of having discovered new relatives rushed through me and stopped just as soon. Why hadn't Ammi told us about her? Why had she hidden it so much? Was she ashamed of them or something?

The woman, my aunt, looked at me and smiled.

"What's your name?" I asked her.

"Zulekha," she said softly.

"Can I call you Khala?" I asked her hesitantly.

"I would like that," she said smiling again. She turned to her daughter and asked her to get some tea for me. I started to refuse and then kept quiet.

"How is Shabana?" she asked.

"Ammi is fine," I replied. She nodded and then looked down at the dull colours woven in the mat. I followed her gaze and fingered the ragged edges. What could I ask her? Why was she so quiet? I decided to be straightforward.

"Ammi never told me that she has a sister. Are you her younger or older sister?" I asked her.

The woman looked at me, her eyes shining with tears. "She didn't tell you about her own sister?"

It hadn't been the most diplomatic thing to say, but there was no time for niceties and Abbu would be back soon.

I shook my head. "Can you tell me why?" I asked her. If she was anything like Ammi, she would just get angry and decide that if her own sister had thought she wasn't worth discussing with her children, she wouldn't say anything either. I held my breath and waited. She wasn't Ammi after all.

35

Hopes, Dreams and Reality

"I'm two years older than your mother. This was the house we lived in when we were small. We were only two sisters. My parents had hoped for a son, and Ammi did have two sons. Both of them died when they were only a few months old. After that, Ammi didn't have any more children.

"Abba didn't send us to school. He was so ashamed of us. Wherever he went, he saw other men talking about their sons and their pride in whatever they did. Other men boasted of how their sons would help them in their business once they grew up. In all these conversations, Abba could never say a word. He always sat silently and listened.

"But he always came back home in a foul mood and snapped at Ammi and thrashed Shabana and I if we happened to make too much noise while playing. We never could understand the reason for his fury. But that was how life was for us. Ammi persuaded Abba to send Shabana to a local Urdu school at least and he agreed reluctantly. Not so with me. I stayed at home and helped Ammi. I did wish to go to school, but Abba was not willing to spend more money than what was necessary on a girl's education–one that would not be of any use to him.

"When I was sixteen, some people from Hyderabad visited us. There was a young man in their group, and he was the only young man I had ever seen. You see, I hardly ever stepped out of the house, and although I had seen the men who came to our house, they were mostly Abba's age and there was nothing attractive about them.

"I didn't speak a word to him, but I would always look at him from the kitchen window or would try to hear his conversations with Abba. He was a student and he soon was to join his father's business. I dreamt about him, about his life in Hyderabad, and simultaneously about my life here. Without knowing it, I had entwined my dreary existence to his more exciting life, hope and a meagre faith in life making me wish for what I could never have. Your mother was in school then and whenever she returned, he would be sitting outside in the hall, almost as if he were hoping to run into her. As if he was waiting for her.

"She was only fourteen then. And he was twenty. But they seemed to have a lot to talk about. I would look at them laughing sometimes and wonder why I couldn't talk to him so openly. She was so easy-going! She giggled at his jokes, and he would come up with so many! Ammi didn't want her to talk so much to him. Shabana was going to finish school in a couple of years and she would be waiting to get married. Like me.

"He went back after a few days, and we slowly got over the excitement of having so many people at home. Life resumed the way it was, and soon Shabana had finished school. I was getting quite a few proposals but Abba didn't seem to like any of them. He was looking for a pair of brothers to whom he could marry both his daughters. Someone had told him that it would be a good idea and he had firmly decided that he wanted it that way.

"I was nearly twenty, and other family members were anxious that I hadn't been married yet. That was when we got news of the Hyderabadi people. They had sent a proposal for Shabana. I couldn't understand what I felt. Whether it was a disappointment, or anger... it was confusing. Abba was confused too. He didn't refuse straightaway. After all, they were relatives and wouldn't take it lightly if we refused outright.

"Abba had liked him, but he didn't know if it would be a good idea to get a daughter married and sent so far away. Shabana was rather anxious. I could see from her face that she was extremely happy to have received that proposal. But she was also unsure of what would happen from there. What if Abba refused?

"I couldn't bear to see her looking so happy and so anxious. I watched her pray, her *duas* after *namaz* were interminably long, and I knew what she was praying for. In my own prayers, I silently lamented about the injustice of life.

"I dropped hints to Ammi a few times after that. I told her how Hyderabad wasn't a nice place, and Ammi would look at me and frown. "What would you know?" she asked. I couldn't answer, but I thought of other ways to ruin the alliance. Finally, I did the one thing that I regret to this day. I told Ammi that he wasn't a nice man. I told her that he had once caught my hand and kissed it.

"I remember becoming red and uncomfortably hot, just saying it and imagining that it had happened. Ammi made her decision then. She slapped me and hit me, calling me all kinds of names for having allowed him to do that. But she was also angry that I had ruined a perfectly good proposal and soured things between relatives. She and Abba discussed it, and I didn't know how much they told Shabana, but they called it off, naturally.

"Shabana was broken-hearted. She cried for days and Ammi was alarmed. Abba just glared at me whenever I walked into a room. Shabana stopped talking to me completely, and I became uncomfortably aware of what I had done. Ammi had probably told her about what I had said, and Shabana was aghast.

"The days continued and my guilt kept growing inside me. It grew so big that I decided I couldn't continue living with it. But I didn't have the courage to face Shabana and come clean with her. I got a proposal from a family in Vellore, and Abbu stopped looking for brothers to whom he could get both of us married.

"The day I got married, I purged myself of my guilt and wrote everything in a letter. I placed the letter on Shabana's pillow and went to get dressed. She came into the room. I was wearing my jewellery and I saw her open it curiously. From the mirror, I saw her reading my clumsy Urdu scrawl, and saw her frown. She looked up at the mirror at my reflection a couple of times. Quickly, I averted my gaze.

"She wasn't one to let things go easily. She came up to me and demanded an explanation. She was always the stronger one among us both, and I felt a bit scared of her. Just then Ammi came in and took me away for my *nikah*. My eyes were closed throughout my *nikah,* but I knew that my younger sister hadn't attended my wedding. She had chosen to stay at home.

"Ammi told me later that Shabana showed her my letter. Maybe she hoped that things could still work out in Hyderabad. Ammi once again discussed things with Abba and they didn't know what to do. Those days, we didn't have a phone in our house, and neither did they. So, Ammi wrote a letter to them, apologising for the misunderstanding and hoping that things would be well between them. Towards the end, on the last side of the blue inland letter, she added that she was willing to give her daughter in marriage to their son.

"Abba posted the letter hesitantly. He didn't want to approach them again. He felt that it would make them lose face, and they would receive no respect. But Ammi thought that maybe there were chances that it would work out. Ammi had liked him too. We waited for three months but there was no letter from them.

"I visited Ammi's house, this house, regularly. My husband was an indifferent man. He lived his life and he expected others to live theirs too. However they could. I was soon pregnant with my eldest daughter, Razia. I came home for the delivery, and your mother still didn't talk to me. The Hyderabadi people hadn't even bothered to respond.

"After the delivery, I stayed for the required forty days. Just when I was going to return, your mother got the proposal from your father's family. Abba agreed quietly. Your mother didn't say a thing. She just sat quietly at the *nikah*. After Shabana got married, Abba slipped from the stairs and fell down one day. The woman who cleaned the house had been swabbing, and in one corner of the stairs, the water hadn't dried completely. Abba slipped, broke his neck and died. Shabana left for Bangalore after that. I saw her only once after that. At Ammi's funeral. After that, I haven't heard from her, and I don't even know how she is."

I stared at the tray before me. The girl had kept a cup of tea on it and a plate of biscuits. A brown wrinkled skin floated on the surface of the tea. I couldn't believe a word of all that I had heard. Khala had to be joking. She must have made it up, living here all alone these days. But then, why would she do that?

I lowered my head and stared at the pattern on my *burka*. This had to be true. So much of Ammi's past – obliterated by her marriage. Ammi had deliberately distanced herself from her sister and her house. Why? What Khala had said implied that Ammi hated her for interfering in her life. But so much hatred that she had ignored Khala's very existence?

I was still having trouble taking it all in. My mother! I shook my head and lifted my face. Khala was looking at me, smiling a little vaguely. Her story still hadn't answered many questions. Why was Khala living here instead of living in her own house? Why had Ammi broken off all ties with her only living relative? Why had Ammi never told us about her sister? Why did Khala look so old, if she was only two years older than Ammi?

I leaned forward to ask her when the doorbell rang in shrill bursts. The girl hurried to open the door, and a young boy stepped in. He looked around my age. He walked in complaining about something, but stopped when he saw me. Without asking who I was, he removed his slippers, washed his hands and feet in the *aangan,* and went inside one of the rooms. I turned to face Khala. She was looking at him with adoration. Who was he?

The sky had darkened completely, and the *Isha azan* rang out clearly in the warm, still air. The door bell rang once more. I looked at the door in dismay. It had to be Abbu. He said he would return in an hour. But I wanted to know more. So many things were still not answered. I heard Abbu's voice calling out to me, "Mehnaz! Come, let's go."

I scrambled up, the tea untouched. Khala got up with me shakily. She looked at me sadly. "Are you going away?"

I nodded. I wished I could stay and ask her more questions, but it wasn't possible with Abbu at the door. I didn't know if I would ever get another chance. I walked to the door slowly, wishing Abbu hadn't returned so early. I turned to Khala who was trailing behind me.

"What are the names of your children?" I asked her.

"Razia and..." she said and looked at her son, who was inside, sleeping on a cot, "Raheem." Their names were now etched in my memory. New cousins... but what was the point if I was never going to meet them again? I wished there was some way I could tell Khala that I would be back. I smiled at her, hoping that my smile conveyed what was in my mind.

I gathered my *burka* around me, feeling a chill on my arms. I was feeling cold in warm and torpid Vellore.

36

Imtiaz

We reached home to find the house swamped in darkness. Ammabi had forgotten to switch on the light bulb outside. Abbu hadn't spoken to me at all; he looked forbidding. When and how had he changed? I had always been able to confide most of the things to him. There was an urgency to his step as we walked towards the house.

I knew he was worried about what Ammi would say if she found out. Obviously, he was not so comfortable with hiding it from her, as I had suggested. Perhaps he was thinking that he had made a big mistake. I wanted to tell him not to worry as this was between Ammi and me, as most things were. But I remained silent.

Once inside, Abbu washed up, wore his *lungi* and sat down to eat. I made *rotis* and served him silently. I felt uncomfortable now, as he avoided meeting my eyes. I hated it when things reached this... this discomfort and we swept it under forced cheerfulness and mindless blabber. Why couldn't we tackle it head on? I wanted to, but I was also exhausted. It seemed like we had been in Vellore for weeks now.

Ammi telephoned. Abbu spoke to her curtly and was about to hang up when she asked for me. He looked reluctant as he handed the receiver to me. I took it and spoke to her. She didn't say much, just asked about Ammabi and when the water would come. How would I know? Being here for a day would make my mother a native, and she would immediately rattle off all things that only someone living in Vellore for the past six months would know. But me? I hadn't even bothered to ask Ammabi about water. Yes, precious water in Vellore. I mumbled something, and she sighed in irritation. "When will you learn which things in life are important, Mehnaz?" she asked. I had no answer to that. When I learnt that, I would know what to do with my life.

She hung up after some time and I prepared for bed. It was warm and Abbu wanted to sleep in the hall. Ammabi slept in Phuppu's room and I slept in the room opposite that. Only in the quiet darkness of the night was I able to sort out some of the things that were vying for attention in my head.

What could I do about Khala? I wished I had had the presence of mind to ask for her phone number or address, some way I could maintain contact with her and children. But I had just been too stunned and didn't think of practical matters. How was I going to contact her again? How would I know so many other things that I wanted to know?

When I woke up, the sun shone through the windows brightly. I stretched, and scrambled out of bed. So many things were going to happen today!

For all my excitement in the morning, the day seemed to drag on painfully. Another fear suddenly captured my mind. If Abbu stayed at home all day, how would I meet Imtiaz?

After lunch, it was only three more hours until five. But I still went to the terrace on the pretext of drying my hair. Abbu had thankfully gone out after lunch and had told us he would be back only after *Maghrib.* The sun was uncomfortably warm and my yellow cotton *kurta* seemed to be absorbing all the heat. I looked at Imtiaz's terrace and wished that he would come up. But he had said 5 p.m. With a sigh I walked downstairs.

At four o'clock, I combed my hair and, feeling a bit foolish, I dabbed my face with some powder, hoping my nose wouldn't turn oily. Feeling more out of sorts, I rubbed a gloss stick on my lips lightly. At exactly five, I was upstairs. There were children on the terraces and they were flying kites in the strong wind. I remembered the first time I had met Imtiaz on such a day.

How happy the three of us had been! But none of us had been able to recognise that happiness and cling to it. It just wasn't possible. I didn't want to think about Rehana and Basheer at the moment, so I trained my eyes on Imtiaz's terrace waiting for his tall form to emerge. I looked at my watch after a few minutes. It was 5:15. The sky darkened a little and birds flew across it. What if he didn't turn up? I looked at the other terraces and every two minutes, my eyes would return to his terrace, willing him to come up. At quarter to six, I felt resigned. Maybe he had been joking. Maybe he wasn't going to come.

I placed my hands on the parapet, wondering how he could jump across terraces with such ease. I would never be able to do it. The terrace wall felt warm under my hands, gritty with pebbles. Maybe I should just go. I turned around, and like so many times before, my heart stopped for a moment before resuming its mad, erratic beat. He was standing behind me, leaning on the parapet on the other side.

I didn't know how to react. Anger? Surprise? Joy? I didn't know which would be appropriate. And although I had realised long ago that he was no longer the old Imtiaz with whom I could talk freely, I was reminded of this when I saw him now. He was wearing a loose shirt, of some nondescript colour as always, and a pair of jeans. But he didn't look like a boy now. He had filled out appreciably and I realised I had been staring at him, just as he was staring at me. The realisation made me uncomfortable and I wanted to break the silence.

But we stood there for what seemed like ten minutes, and neither of us spoke a word. I felt a warm glow inside me, but there was also some discomfort. Why wasn't he saying anything? Finally, he opened his mouth to say something, and I spoke at the very moment. "Where were you?"

He shut his mouth and smiled. He straightened up and walked towards me, standing just a little away from me. "This time, I was on that terrace," he said, pointing to the terrace behind our house. "I've been waiting there from four o' clock, waiting for you to come out."

"If you had told me you would be here so early, I would have come upstairs too," I said, feeling a little peeved that he had wasted so much time.

He shrugged. "I wanted to see how interested you were."

"I don't like such games Imtiaz!" I said, feeling breathless and angry.

He grabbed my hand and pulled me down suddenly. I looked at him, not sure of what was happening. I understood that he wanted me to sit down, but I was taken aback by his peremptory manner with me. It excited and scared me at the same time.

I folded my legs under my knees and looked down. I wished we could converse like before. We were both quiet for some time.

"Why are you so quiet?" he asked.

"I don't know what to say," I said truthfully.

He turned to look at me. "Okay. Let me start then," he said. My stomach churned. "First things first. Before I forget, here, take this," he said, and shoved a small note pad and pen in my hand.

"What?" I asked surprised.

"Write down your Bangalore phone number and address in it."

I looked at him, horrified. "But why?"

"Just do it, and then I'll tell you why."

I clicked the pen, and holding the notepad against my palm, I wrote down my phone number and address with a shaky hand.

He took it from me, looked at it thoughtfully, and nodded.

"You said you have finished all your education, everything right?" he asked.

I nodded. What was this all about? "Imtiaz! What's happening? Will you please tell me?" I asked. He kept quiet. I wished we were children, so I could prod him with my finger and push him till he spoke. Controlling myself, I waited for him to speak again.

"If I don't have your address or phone number, how will my mother contact your mother?" he asked calmly.

Wishing I could speak just as calmly, I asked, "Why? Why does your mother need to contact my mother?"

He snorted. An angry sound that made me look at him. There was something else I couldn't identify in his eyes, as he spoke, "How else will she send my marriage proposal to you?"

I couldn't breathe suddenly. I wanted to get up and run back downstairs. What was he talking about? Surely, he didn't mean... but I should be happy. I should be thrilled that it was what he wanted too. But was it what I wanted? And why didn't this make me happy? Maybe it was the way he had said it.

"Oh!" I said, sounding haughty. "What makes you think my mother will entertain a proposal from your mother?" At this, he caught my arm and forced me to look at him. But he didn't say anything. His eyes searched mine. He flung my arm away in anger.

I looked up, at the first star that had popped up in the sky. This wasn't what I had imagined when I had met Imtiaz again. I didn't know what I had wanted, but this anger and unpleasantness wasn't it. He made an effort to get up, and this time I caught his arm and pulled him down. He sat down with a grunt and looked at me.

“What went wrong?” I asked softly. “This wasn’t what I had thought would happen. We’re meeting after such a long time, and all we can do is disagree.”

He looked straight ahead, at the wall opposite us. “Do you want to marry me?” he asked. He looked serious.

“Do you?” I asked him, instead of answering him.

“Of course! Why else do you think I would take your number and address?”

“But why do you want to marry me?” I asked, my breath catching in my throat.

He shrugged. “If you had listened to me then, you would have known why. I can’t believe you still want to know why I would want to marry you,” he said.

I looked up at the sky. It was dark and there were more stars. I should be going downstairs very soon. Abbu would be home.

“What makes you think I will make a good wife to you?” I asked. He may have been thinking that I was just egging him on, but truthfully, I was worried most about this. First of all, I couldn’t imagine myself becoming someone’s wife. And becoming the wife of a total stranger? And here was Imtiaz. Someone I knew and he wanted to marry me. I must be insane to have this conversation instead of agreeing straight away.

“I must have been mad,” he said. I looked at him, puzzled. I poked my finger into his ribs. He looked up, startled. “I was mad to think of marrying you,” he clarified. But he didn’t look angry and that made me smile a bit. “Any other girl would have...” he didn’t complete the sentence.

“Any other girl would have?”

“No other girl would have dared to do that,” he said. I didn’t know whether that was a compliment. It didn’t sound like one.

I felt some of the irritation coming back. He still hadn't answered my question about why he wanted to marry me. In a swift change of mood, he caught my hand and held it hard. I pulled my hand away but he held fast. Feeling annoyed, I tried to yank it away once more and ended up falling on top of him.

I scrambled to get up, pinpricks of awareness shooting all over me. It was the first time I was in such proximity to a boy and the feeling was pleasant and yet it made me feel angry and flushed. "Why did you do that?" I asked. My hand was still caught in his. He didn't answer. He was looking up at the stars that had popped up everywhere. I was getting extremely anxious now. I hadn't managed to get up completely, and my arm was still lying across his chest.

"Imtiaz," I pleaded. "Let go of my hand!"

I felt tears rushing to my eyes but he didn't budge. Abbu could come up any moment now, and this was how everything would end with Abbu seeing me sprawled on top of Imtiaz on the terrace of our Vellore house.

He loosened the grip on my hand and I lifted my head slowly. I looked at him. He smiled as he sat up. "I'm sorry," he said, grinning.

I pulled my hand back and shook it vigorously. It was red and throbbed painfully. "I'm really sorry. I didn't mean to hold your hand so hard," he said. I didn't say anything. I arranged my *dupatta* carefully on my shoulders.

"Mehnaz, I'm sorry. Don't go," he said suddenly. I looked at him, teary-eyed. He took my hand once more, and this time, he pressed it gently. My hand didn't hurt now. It felt warm and I let him continue rubbing my hand but when I looked up, I realised that he was looking at me intensely.

He stopped and I realised I had liked the sensation. He pulled me towards him, gathering me in his embrace and I felt warm breath on my neck as he pressed small kisses there. I stiffened. Why was I letting him do this? I stepped back, and he lifted my chin. I knew then that I was really attracted to him. But to marry him on the basis of that? Or marry someone on the basis of nothing, like Rehana? I didn't know which was worse.

I just knew that I wasn't ready for it yet. I hadn't found anything I really wanted to do yet. Everyone I met in the family thought it was a strange hankering I had. 'To do something.' What? You get married, you have children, and you manage your house. What else can you do? I was asked sceptically. I didn't know. I knew Ammi and Abbu wanted to get me married. And here was Imtiaz, after the same thing too.

He was looking at me, puzzled. "What's going on in that mind of yours?" he asked. I knew I had to explain it to him. But where was the time? Would he understand if I asked him to wait? How long? And even if he agreed to wait, would my parents understand? Would they wait?

I took a deep breath. "It's complicated, Imtiaz. I don't have time to explain it to you right now. I have to go. Abbu would have come back home and he will be wondering where I have been."

"Mehnaz, I'm not letting you go until you answer my question," he said firmly. I shook my head. I walked away and turned around to see him once more. I didn't know when I would meet him again. He looked upset as he ran his hands through his hair. He came running towards me and caught my arm.

"Wait. Can I meet you tomorrow morning? Before your mother comes? Early tomorrow morning, before *Fajr*."

I nodded. I knew I couldn't just walk away without giving him an explanation but I also wanted to meet him again.

"Okay. I'll meet you here at 5 a.m." I told him. It was dangerous. Abbu would be at home, and there was no saying what could happen. He let go of my arm and I walked away.

When I myself didn't know what I wanted, it was useless to expect him to understand. It was a lost cause, but I still wanted to meet him. I stopped and turned to look at him once more. He watched me leave.

37

Unmade Decisions

I stayed awake for a long time trying to go over things in my head. So much had happened in last two days! I had discovered Ammi's sister and Imtiaz wanted to marry me. I still didn't know why Ammi had hidden her sister away from us, and I didn't know if marrying Imtiaz was the right thing to do.

Imtiaz was still a stranger to me, I realised. Just because I had met him a few times, I didn't know what went on in his mind. I lifted my hand in the dark and stared at it. I remembered how it felt to be in his arms, to feel him so close to me, and I felt warm. After a while, I started wondering what it would be like to be married to Imtiaz. I enjoyed the fantasy until I fell asleep, with what I was sure, a silly grin on my face.

I had no alarm clock, so I kept getting up to see if it was time yet. I couldn't ask Abbu to wake me, which was what I used to do when I had exams or tests. I got up quietly at 4 a.m. and walked outside the room. Abbu was sleeping in the hall. I walked to the bathroom slowly, trying to quell the rustling of my *salwar*. Half an hour later, it was still dark, and I felt slightly scared to go upstairs alone.

I walked up the stairs slowly, with a heavily thudding heart, my mouth dry. At other times, I could always claim that I had gone upstairs for the fresh air. Now, if I got caught, I didn't know what Abbu or Ammi would do. They couldn't take away my education from me. Maybe Abbu would also start giving me the silent treatment, I thought. The thought of Abbu not talking to me made me stop at the turn of the stairs. Light was slowly draining the dark patches in the sky and I continued upstairs, feeling shaky and irresolute.

Once outside, I felt even more scared. I had never seen Vellore like this, early in the morning. The houses were silent, and the terraces empty of people. A cold wind blew across the terraces, making me shiver. I covered my head with my *dupatta* tightly and twisted one edge of it nervously. Where was he?

I would have enjoyed the calm serenity of the moment had it not been for my fear of being caught by Abbu. The still air, the cold terrace, and the mountains in the distance looked awesome, and for a minute, I tried to forget about Imtiaz and the real reason I was up here. I jumped when I felt a finger tapping my shoulder. I whirled around to face Imtiaz.

He looked tired. "Haven't slept all night," he said. My face flushed when I remembered the thoughts I had before falling into a deep sleep. We sat down at our usual place on the terrace and I hoped I could finish this soon and go back downstairs. But Imtiaz had other plans. He leaned across and kissed my cheek. I felt shaky and overpowered as he moved my *dupatta* away from my head and freed my hair. I wanted to stop him, but I also wanted to see what he would do next. He pulled me closer to him, and continued kissing my neck, my jaw line, as if he couldn't stop himself. He was on his way to kiss me properly on my lips and I was excited and scared when the *Fajr azan* broke through the silence of the morning, startling me and I pushed him away. "We have to talk. This is important," I said.

He took a deep breath and sat back, looking at me. I looked at the mountains and the mist melting in the morning sun. The vibrations of the *azan* seemed to reach out physically and unclasp something from my chest. I turned around to speak to Imtiaz, but the expression in his eyes made me stop. I think he had a different idea of me as a person, and I had a different one of him. What we needed to know was if both our ideas had something in common at least.

"Imtiaz, I don't want to get married right now," I said.

He leaned back and looked at me. "Why? You're old enough to get married, right?" he asked.

I took a deep breath. "Okay. Let's not talk about marriage. Don't think of me as the girl you want to marry. Just think I'm a friend. Someone who needs some advice."

I sat cross-legged and moved away from him sideways. The space between us helped me breathe a little more comfortably.

"I want to do something, Imtiaz. I want to be something more than what I am. I don't want to be just a housewife or a mother. I'm not saying that there's anything wrong in being that, but I want more. And is that wrong?"

There was no reply so I looked at him. He was studying me, his hands resting on his knees, his eyebrows raised.

I continued, "I don't really know what it is that I want to do with my life. I'm still looking. If I get married, I will never be able to know what it is. I don't know if you will understand what I want."

I didn't want to say anything more. On a nearby terrace, a woman came up. I looked at her, feeling terror run through me.

"I can't marry you..." I said quickly and got up hurriedly.

He took a deep breath and said, "Okay. You want to wait for some time, right? I'm willing to wait."

I shook my head as I ran towards the door. "I don't know how long you can wait, Imtiaz. I don't know how long it's going to be."

"What about your parents?" he asked, getting up and running after me. I opened the door and stepped inside. But he held my hand. "Do you think you can tell them to wait? Will they? You told me they are looking out for you. What if, right now, they have spoken to someone for you?"

The words scared me. I looked at the woman on the terrace. She was spreading soaked rice on an old cotton saree to dry. Thankfully, she wasn't standing, but she would get up soon. "I'll refuse," I said, looking at her and then at him.

He looked at me sceptically. "That won't work. I know how these things are. They will simply force you into it."

What he said was true. They could do it, and with all my education, I wouldn't be able to stop them. My eyes strayed again and again to the lady on the terrace. There were chances she would know who I was. As it often happened in Vellore, I was often accosted by people at gatherings who asked me if I remembered who they were. I would be clueless and look at them embarrassed while they would talk to me like an old acquaintance.

"Marry me, Mehnaz," he urged. "I'll help you with what you want. I'll help you realise your dreams." I looked at his earnest eyes.

"I'll think about it," I heard myself saying as I withdrew my hand from his clasp.

His lips tightened in a grim smile as I turned away from him. I could only hope that the woman on the terrace hadn't seen me. Even though it would have been hard for her to recognise me, she could easily surmise who I was from the house on whose terrace I was standing. Other *azans* from different *masjids* had started. Ammabi would have woken up by now. Abbu too.

"We know each other, Mehnaz," Imtiaz said softly. Startled, I turned back to face him. "I already love you. Maybe you will too one day. Give me this chance, please. I promise I'll try and help you."

I stared at him and nodded slowly. Later, I would think of this moment and relive it, but now all that mattered was Abbu getting up. I couldn't say anything. His eyes lit up when I nodded and he smiled. "Shall I ask my mother to..."

I thought for a moment. He was right. If not him, then it would be someone else. My parents were waiting for the right proposal. With Imtiaz's proposal, at least I had some control. I nodded. The enormity of it struck me only when I started walking down the steps. Imtiaz. Proposal. Marriage.

38

Revelations

Ammi and Mateen arrived by the Lalbagh Express and Ammi look more harried than usual. Maybe it was because she had never travelled without Abbu and the experience frightened her. Mateen sat on the *divan* after washing up, thumbing through an old comic he had brought along.

Every time I looked at Ammi, I remembered her sister's words. It made me flush with guilt that now I knew something about Ammi's past, something that she had deliberately wanted to keep hidden. I watched her as she sat on the sofa, looking tired as she sipped a cup of tea I had made for her. She didn't speak much. Abbu looked at the floor instead of looking at her when he spoke. He was probably feeling guilty too, about having taken me to her sister's house.

I watched them silently. I realised that Ammi would find out about that visit from Abbu as soon as they were alone. The thought made me afraid but Imtiaz's words reminded me about the things to come. I wondered how Ammi would react when she received the proposal. What if she refused?

Ammi made lunch and we all sat down to eat together. It was almost like the old days; only Zohra Phuppu and Basheer were absent. I started wondering about how life would turn out for me eventually. If I was going to be busy in another life with other people, I didn't want to isolate myself from my own family like how Rehana had done, albeit inadvertently.

The day moved on peacefully and nothing interesting happened. After dinner, Mateen lay sprawled on the *divan,* and Ammabi looked at him peevishly. It was her place, where she sat and watched TV. In minutes, he had fallen asleep. Murmuring something, Ammabi walked painfully to the room and lay down to sleep. Ammi, Abbu and I sat in the hall, with the TV droning quietly in the corner. Ammi was making a *paan* for Abbu. I wanted to get up and go but I lingered, wondering whether Abbu would tell. Abbu cleared his throat and snapped the TV shut with a flick of the remote. Now. He was going to tell her now.

"I got a very good proposal for Mehnaz," he said, his face turning a deep red that looked slightly demonic in the light of the evening. This day had already come! I was terrified about what was going to happen.

Turning towards Abbu, she folded the *paan* in three neat folds and handed it to him. "Who are they?" she asked. Abbu took it from her and folded it further before placing it in his mouth. He chewed for a moment and then spoke. "My friend Murad's son," he said. I looked at Abbu, my mouth dry but he wouldn't look at me. I could see all the plans that Imtiaz had made for me dissolve. I could see all my plans of making something out of my life evaporate into oblivion.

Ammi didn't say anything. She was making a *paan* for herself. I watched as she dropped broken betel nuts on the glistening *paan.* I had to hear her reply soon or I wouldn't be able to hold myself back. She folded the *paan* and placed it in her mouth. She spoke, her cheek wadded with *paan.* "I know this man... he lives in the next *galli* right?" Abbu nodded.

Ammi shook her head. Hope flared in my chest. I looked at Abbu. Surely Ammi wasn't thinking of getting me married in Vellore? I would suffocate here. I took a moment to consider when I had begun to think that way. Vellore was fine for me in small doses, and I even loved it, but to live here for the rest of my life?

Ammi shook her head. "His son, if I remember correctly, used to tie up the servant boys on the terrace and leave them up there. The poor things would stay in the cold wind, all night sometimes, if no one discovered them there. They wouldn't even shout for fear of that boy. It was known all over Vellore that he had an evil streak. I can't imagine why you thought of that boy for Mehnaz."

Ammi shuddered. I looked at her surprised. Her words made me shudder too. What a sadist! "Not him," she said emphatically.

Abbu protested. "Of course, I know about that boy. I'm talking about his younger brother. He's a very nice young man and he works with his father in their hardware shop."

Hope flared in my breast was crushed again, but once more, it was looking up hopefully at Ammi from beneath its broken wings. Ammi was quiet. Then looking up from the plate where the bunch of betel leaves lay, she spoke to Abbu, "I don't have a right feeling about these people. Let's not hurry into something like this. She's our only daughter."

Ammi spoke about me as if I wasn't there. For the first time, I didn't really mind, as long as she stopped things from getting out of hand. Suddenly, I wanted to return to Bangalore, and stay there. Both the objectives of my coming to Vellore had been accomplished. I got up. Abbu looked at me. He probably thought that I was feeling shy and wanted to go inside. But then, when was life ever so simple?

I opened my mouth to protest but stopped when I saw Ammi looking at me interestedly.

"What is it?" she asked me.

I thought of what to say. "I d-don't know," I stammered. "I know you want to get me married, but, Abbu, please, not in Vellore."

Abbu looked at me, his face becoming redder. "Why? What is wrong with Vellore?" he asked and I could sense something in him resisting and urging to break free.

I shook my head. I thought of a lot of things. "If you were going to dump me in Vellore, then you should have never shifted to Bangalore. You should have never given me any education. You should never have made me the person I am today." I didn't say it aloud. I wanted to! Oh, I so badly wanted to tell them how I felt. But I didn't. Because my own thoughts shocked me. I was a hypocrite then. Everything about Vellore appealed to me in a quaint manner. But to live here, and become one of them – I was horrified at the thought. I shook my head once more and only said, "I don't think I will be comfortable here."

I looked at Ammi. It was a rare moment when she could glimpse what I was feeling. She turned to face Abbu. "Let's forget about this proposal for now. I'm sure we can get many better proposals for her."

Abbu was silent but he was breathing heavily. How could he be the same man who doted on me so much, and yet today he was peeved by my resistance? I was the same daughter. I was his baby, the one he held so lovingly in his arms in old photos.

I was still standing, my form throwing a shadow over Ammi. "Go and sleep if you don't have anything else to do," she said.

I hesitated. What if Abbu told her about the visit to Khala's house after I went to sleep? How would I know whether he told her or not? I had to be prepared. But then Abbu could tell her any other time, and I wouldn't know.

I sat on the floor next to Ammi. "No, I'll go to sleep a little later," I said. She didn't say anything.

Abbu and Ammi started talking about some relatives. I leaned against the wall, feeling drowsy and even a bit tired after everything that had happened in the past two days. I wanted to go home to Bangalore and sleep contentedly in my own bed and I was glad we were leaving the following morning.

Abbu and Ammi's combined voices were a steady hum. They spoke softly about water shortage and Ammabi's health. Abbu was worried about who would live here if Ammabi died. In a foggy corner of my mind, I was a bit shocked that Abbu would talk about someone's death so openly while she slept in the adjacent room. Ammi said that we would have to rent out the house. My eyes were shut now. If someone prodded me, I would have fallen down in a heap.

Then Abbu said something that banished all sleep from my mind. "We could ask your sister to come and stay here with her family."

I was sitting next to Ammi and I knew they thought I was asleep. I wanted to open my eyes and see Ammi's expression, but I didn't. Maybe she would say something that would solve some of the mystery surrounding Khala. I felt Ammi stiffen and turn around to look at me. My eyes were shut lightly, calmly, because I knew if I shut them too tight she would know the pretence.

She swivelled around to face Abbu and spoke in a furious whisper. "How can you even think of something like that? You know how I feel about her."

Abbu was silent. "Look, Shabana, you saw how my fight with Sadiq ruined the bond that was between us as brothers. Why do you want to continue something like that with your sister?"

I was excited but had to still pretend to be asleep. I was astounded that Ammi hadn't discovered I wasn't sleeping, as she always did when I was younger.

"Your problem with Sadiq Bhai was different. With Apa, you know I can't stand her," she said fiercely.

"Shabana, I have been telling you so many times. Very soon, we'll be going on *Hajj*. How can you keep such hatred for someone in your heart and face Allah? You have to forgive her."

Excitement and fear dodged around inside me. Abbu was going to tell her about our visit there. I knew it.

Ammi was silent. "After her husband died, how could she have an affair... with... I can't even say it... I can't believe she was once my sister. She even had his son. How can you expect me to forgive that? How can you even think of asking her to come and stay in this house? I would rather see strangers living here than that... that woman come and live here with her bastards."

Ammi's voice quavered in my ears. Khala had an affair?

Ammi shook me. "Mehnaz, go and sleep in the room."

I pretend-slept for a few more seconds to avoid Ammi's suspicion. When she shook me once more, I opened my eyes sleepily. I got up and staggered to the bed in the free room. Mateen was sleeping on the *divan* and Abbu would be sleeping in the hall on a mat.

Ammi joined me after some time.

I stared at the ceiling in the darkness. Ammi hated her sister because of this. I shifted uncomfortably. Having an affair, well, that was indeed shocking and most probably even sinful. But Ammi's stance towards it disturbed me, especially her harshness and her judgemental attitude.

Ammi turned to face the other way. I saw her sleeping profile and shut my eyes. What if Khala had never been happy with her husband? What if she had found happiness with this other man? Who was he? Where was he now?

39

Finally, the Proposal

In Bangalore, I waited every single day for Imtiaz's mother to call. What had he told her about me? How had she reacted? I spoke to Imtiaz so much about my own family and hardly ever asked him about his.

Life fell into the normal routine. I watched each day begin, move, and end in the same monotonous way. We visited Rehana's house when we heard that she had come there to stay for a few days. Ammi made *dum ka roat,* Rehana's favourite *mithai,* and we took it with us.

Asifa Chachi looked subdued and pale as if Rehana's absence had aged her. We sat in the hall, in our *burkas*. Chachi kept insisting we remove them. Ammi waited for some time, and after Chachi had asked a couple of times, she got up and untied the flaps that held her *burka* together. I got up and did the same. Ammi folded her *burka* neatly and kept it on the side table, while I let mine lie in a heap beside me.

Rehana emerged from the downstairs room where she had been taking a nap. I took in her appearance; she was wearing a loose *salwar,* but it couldn't hide the bulge of her pregnancy. Her face looked a little puffy and she walked slowly. She smiled when she saw us and sat down beside me. I felt like going back home. It was hard for me to take in this new Rehana.

"How do you feel?" I asked her.

"A little breathless now and then," she said and beamed at me. "I can feel the baby move, Mehnaz."

My mother looked at her, as if to tell her not to share all this with me. After all, I wasn't a married girl. Ammi probably thought I was really ignorant about matters of sex and babies and all that. I should have showed her my tenth standard Biology textbook.

I pressed Rehana's hand tightly and smiled at her. "That sounds wonderful. How does it feel?"

"I can't really describe it, Mehnaz. It feels like something small, yet vague, turning over inside me."

I lifted my eyebrows. Sounded a bit creepy. "But how do you feel about it?"

"It's amazing."

We spoke for some more time. She wanted to continue talking about her visits to the gynaecologist and I felt disconnected from her, listening to everything she was going through. I looked at Ammi hoping to give her some indication that we ought to leave. Ammi was talking to Chachi but her gaze kept moving to Rehana's face, her swollen hands, her belly, acute reminders that Chachi would soon be a grandmother while she, had not even progressed towards becoming a mother-in-law. Chachi asked us to stay for dinner but we left after making the usual excuses.

I often thought of the day when I had visited Khala's house. Abbu hadn't even come inside. Did he also harbour misgivings towards her? But then he had considered bringing her to live in his Vellore house and that would have been a drastic step considering the scandal Khala's affair must have caused in Vellore. Why hadn't she simply married the man?

Abbu's sympathy towards her surprised me. After all, this was the very man who would turn red with anger just thinking of his own brother. But compassion for Ammi's sister? I wished I knew more about the matter. But then what would I accomplish by learning more? There didn't seem to be any way in which I could help Khala. And Ammi's antagonism towards her sister would be directed towards me if she found out I had visited her.

There were times I was tempted to call Imtiaz. But the phone bills would reveal the Madras number and could cause problems. Sometimes, I was just scared that he would call and ask to talk with me and although I knew he wouldn't be so foolish, the fear was there. On some days when all I could do was brood, I would sit quietly at my window and look outside at the rain, wondering why I had ever given him my number and address. Was it because I too loved him? I wished someone could define love for me or that I could look it up and compare it with what I felt and see if it tallied.

The call from Imtiaz's mother came on a rainy evening when Ammi and I were making *paneer pakodas*. They hissed and sputtered as Ammi dropped the batter coated pieces in hot oil while I fried them, hoping my daydreams would not intervene, blackening the pakodas irreparably. When the phone rang, Ammi went outside, wiping her hands on a towel to pick it up. When she didn't return to the kitchen after ten minutes, I switched off the gas and went outside.

She was sitting upright, the phone in her hand and I couldn't read her expression. Was she smiling or grimacing?

"What's his name?" she asked. "Imtiaz Ahmed," she repeated, and I felt my scalp tighten.

I didn't know anything about Imtiaz's family, but now I would know what Ammi thought about them. I didn't step out, but watched Ammi from the kitchen door. She hung up after five minutes. She sat still for some time and then she looked at the phone thoughtfully. "Mehnaz!" she called me.

Jumping almost in fear I walked up to her. What had Imtiaz's mother told her? Had she implied that I had a hand in this? Oh god! Feeling nervous and shaky I stood in front of her. She looked up at me. "Do you know the people who live three houses away from our house in Vellore?"

I shook my head. Ammi was quiet. Was she suspicious? What had Imtiaz's mother told her? "True. How would you know them..." she seemed to be speaking to herself.

"I got a call from this lady. I have met her at weddings and all that. She had come for your Phuppu's *chehlum* also. We have known them for a long time. Not very well, but they are after all our neighbours."

I stood quietly, knowing that Ammi didn't really expect an answer from me.

"Did you switch off the gas?" she asked, and I nodded impatiently. She thought of cooking gas at a time like this?

"That lady has a proposal for you, for her son. I know you don't want to live in Vellore, so I refused."

I looked at her shocked. This was it?

"But she wouldn't listen. She said that her son lives in Madras and he's doing really well in business. He's quite young, actually. I had someone older in mind for you. Anyway, I told her, no, we're not interested. She said that she has already seen you at the *chehlum* and she liked you, and if she brings any people to see you, it will directly lead to the engagement. I told her no, and still she talks as if we're going to agree any minute. I don't know why she was being so stubborn!"

I stared at the floor. Imtiaz's mother was probably like him.

Ammi continued, "She told me that her son has a house in Madras and you would probably have to live with him there. That's the limit! Here I am, not willing to even show you to them, and she's talking about engagements and living arrangements."

I bit my lower lip angrily. "Show me?" But now didn't seem to be the right time to launch into an attack over that.

"Finally, she hung up, but only when I told her that okay, we will consider it. I asked her son's name and I thought I will speak to your father about it. Actually, I don't really want to. I would rather get you married in Bangalore, so you can be close to me."

Ammi could really surprise me sometimes. When she spoke like this, I was tempted to believe that she really cared about me and I felt uncomfortable when I remembered my startling realisation at Rehana's wedding that I didn't love her. "Still, I'd better speak to your father about it."

Gloomily, I walked back to my room. My heart was hurting, but my mind refused to accept that there was very little hope unless I spoke to either Abbu or Ammi, and told them of my interest in the matter. The very thought made my throat dry. Whatever love that seemed to have sprung up for me in Ammi's heart would be instantly quelled.

I sat at my desk, rifling through my old books in the hope of finding one that would give me some relief. I found the copy of *Pride and Prejudice* that Mrs Dahlia had given me. Pursing my lips, I opened it. Oh, all about marriages and husbands in this too, I thought, annoyed. My attachment to the book was forgotten momentarily as I wondered how Mrs Dahlia was doing.

I should go and meet her. Maybe I will take Ammi along, I thought. If Ammi saw her, and how old she had become, she might not resent my visiting her so much. With that idea taking root in my mind, I pushed my desk drawer back and kept the book on the desk. I put my head down on the desk and shut my eyes thinking about how frustrating it was that my life and happiness lay in the hands of others. And once that was decided, I had to make do with whatever I had and just be happy.

I slept for some time and when I got up there was an awful crick in my neck. The house was silent and dark. I could hear the sound of the rain beating furiously on the roof. Why was it so dark? A power cut probably, I thought as I walked into the hall.

Abbu and Ammi were seated in the dark, talking softly. Mateen was also sitting with them. Sometimes, I felt like taking hold of his shoulders and shaking him till he became the sweet and naughty brother he had been a few years back.

Abbu looked at me. In the dark, I couldn't figure out his expression.

"Mehnaz," he said simply.

"Yes, Abbu?"

"Come and sit here. We have been talking about you."

I sat down. The sound of the rain buzzed in my ears.

"Why didn't you light a candle, Ammi?" I said.

"I hadn't realised it had become so dark," she replied. "Your father and I were talking about you. About the proposal you got this evening."

I didn't say anything. Ammi spoke again. "Your father knows this boy, Imtiaz."

I swallowed. Really? Imtiaz had never told me about it. I wonder what he knew of Imtiaz. "He had met him during one of his trips to Madras."

Abbu took over at this point. "I've been to his shop. It's a good business that he has set up. He is also a very sincere and honest boy." I nodded. Imtiaz was sincere, but honest? How would I know either way? But it felt good to listen to him be praised by Abbu.

"Why we're telling you all this is because I like him. He's smart, good looking, and he's handling a branch of his father's business so well that I think his father doesn't need to worry if his Vellore shop does well or not. We would like to get you married to him."

Thank god, it was dark. What a relief they couldn't see my face at the excitement that surged through me when I heard those words! It was actually happening!

Abbu leaned forward. "Since you are not like other girls in our family, meaning that you are educated and all that, I want you to have a hand in this decision. Let me tell you that I will be really disappointed if you refuse, but I will respect your wish. What do you say, Mehnaz?"

Feeling idiotically like a Hindi film heroine, and with absolute insincerity, I murmured, "It's your wish, Abbu. Whatever you think is right for me." The words came out from my mouth in a rush, and I wanted to get over this silly precursor. I wanted to scream, "Yes! I'll marry him."

Abbu hadn't heard me. "What?" he asked. I repeated what I said and looked at him, trying to ascertain his expression in the darkness. Ammi sat still. Was she happy? Abbu heard my words and he said, "That's great! I knew my daughter would never go against me."

The power blinked on at his words. My face was red and I felt a twinge of guilt, but one look at Ammi and Abbu and I knew they were happy. Only Mateen looked at me curiously.

40

Sisters

Nothing usually kept Fouzia Phuppu away from our house. Even after Abbu had yelled at her because she exasperated him so much, she was never affronted enough to swear that she would never step inside this house. She always came every Saturday with Farha in tow. But her visits had been drastically reduced in the past few months.

Abbu didn't really notice her absence and Ammi was relieved. She had stopped calling up, but one day, out of sheer guilt, Ammi called to ask her how things were with her. She also knew she had to inform her about my proposal. Ammi and Abbu had talked it over, and Ammi called up Imtiaz's mother to inform her that we were interested.

Fouzia Phuppu answered the phone. I sat in the hall with Ammi, reading a magazine as she spoke to Phuppu. At one point, Ammi had to keep the receiver away from her, and even then we could hear Phuppu's shrieking voice. I winced and looked at Ammi sympathetically.

Phuppu had not been visiting us because her husband had stopped giving her money for the auto fare. Normally that shouldn't have stopped her, because she could always call up Abbu and tell her that she needed money to come and see him. Also, I was surprised that something as small as that had stopped her. After all, she had often landed up at our house and demanded that Ammi pay the auto driver. I sat up straighter to listen. Something didn't seem right here.

Ammi said it was too bad her husband was such a mean person. She promised to talk to Abbu about sending some money for her. Then she told her tentatively about my proposal. At this, Phuppu started crying loudly. I could hear her wails over the receiver and Ammi once more kept the phone at arm's length.

When her crying had subsided, Ammi listened to her for nearly twenty minutes, and became very quiet. Finally, she said, "Okay, I will talk about this with your brother." Phuppu protested I think. "But Fouzia Apa, if we don't tell him and if he finds out from someone else, he will be livid."

I shoved the magazine and leaned forward. What was this all about? Finally, Ammi hung up and sighed. She rubbed her forehead and sat back, shutting her eyes. She sat that way for some time.

"What happened?"

She opened her eyes and looked at me. Taking a deep breath, she looked me in the eye.

"Farha has eloped with a tailor," she said.

If she had knocked me down with a hammer, I think I wouldn't be as shocked as I was at that moment. When had Farha taken time out from her preoccupation with eating, to pursue a tailor?

"When did this happen?" I asked, wondering what the implications of this could be.

"A few months ago. That's why your Phuppu wasn't coming here."

"But didn't they try to find her?" I asked surprised.

Ammi nodded. "They did, but by then, they had already got married."

I was stunned. "When your Phuppu heard about your marriage, she couldn't suppress it any longer. Sometimes I hate her so much," Ammi said vehemently. I stared at Ammi. What had got into her? She never admitted this openly.

"You know what she said? She said that she had always thought that you would do something like this, something silly and scandalous like running away. My daughter. She never thought her own daughter would rub their noses in the dust this way. She actually said that to me."

I felt indignant. How can Phuppu think about such things? I may have met Imtiaz secretly and arranged for all this. But I wouldn't have run away with him. Still, it felt good to hear Ammi vent some anger against Phuppu.

"What did you tell her?" I asked Ammi.

She shrugged. "No point in telling her anything. She's being punished enough," she said. I fell silent at that. "I have to tell your father about this. If he finds out from elsewhere, he will be really angry. I still can't believe Farha would do something like this."

I thought of the podgy girl who I had always seen chomping on something. When had this upheaval happened in her life? How? What did she feel, stepping away from her mother, cutting off ties with her?

That night, I thought about Farha a lot. I wondered what might have prompted her to do run away with this tailor. Was she really in love with this man, or had she been carried away with the glamour of falling in love? I marvelled that she could feel so strongly for someone that she could leave her home willingly. Was it also foolishness? The more I thought of it, the more I realised that I admired her. It was a foolish and cowardly thing to do, but I admired the way she had taken control of her life. Even if it meant leaving behind everything that she knew and loved. But what would I think if ever she returned in defeat? I didn't know. It was rather confusing. I was happy for her, but I also knew that doing something so rash could hurt one's parents. Not to forget the huge scandal. From what I knew, it was better if girls didn't become popular, especially for the wrong reasons.

Abbu was furious when he heard about Farha. He immediately called up Fouzia Phuppu and spoke to her for half an hour. I realised, with a certain amount of surprise that he continued his heated conversation in front of me. Either he was too angry to bother, or he now considered me an adult. And it was the high time too!

I could hear Fouzia Phuppu's quivering voice at the other end, alterning with her wails. Abbu was really angry that she had hidden the matter from him for so many months. "Why didn't you get her back?" he yelled into the receiver. The cord dangled as he shook the receiver, wishing it were Phuppu's neck I was sure. "So what if she got married? We can go to the *jama'at* and do something about this."

I looked up surprised. How could they undo a marriage? It wasn't a game. Abbu's anger had really crossed all limits. He wasn't thinking straight.

Finally, he replaced the receiver. I saw Mateen standing near the sofa. He had probably heard everything. He sat down silently. Abbu lowered his head into his hands and Ammi crept up behind him to massage his neck. We watched in uncomfortable silence.

"I think now it's equal," he said. Ammi continued massaging his neck, not really listening to him.

"Your sister and my sister's daughter! They have really done it!" Ammi's hands stilled. I watched her face crumple in horror. Abbu was talking about Khala, and in front of us!

Abbu's head was still lowered and his voice came muffled as he spoke once more. "I think it's time we told the children about your sister. Although Mehnaz knows. She even visited your sister this time when she was in Vellore."

Oh no. Ammi collapsed on the sofa. "What?" she asked. My mouth was dry. Mateen looked surprised. At least there was some reaction from him. "What are you saying? Why did you take her to that house?"

Abbu didn't answer. Like a movie shot, the scene cut from Farha's wrongdoing to me. My close-up. I didn't know what to say. Whatever I said, Ammi was bound to get angry. But she wouldn't let me remain silent. "Answer me, Mehnaz!" she said loudly.

Mateen spoke up then. "Are you saying you have a sister about whom you never told us? Were you even intending to tell us about it? Who is she? Where does she live? Does she have children? Why did you hide her from us?"

Ammi stared at him in horror. "How could you do this?" she asked Abbu. Yes, I wondered. How could Abbu do this? In one moment, the shame and guilt had moved from Farha to Ammi. He could have told this to her in private.

Abbu looked up. Since I hadn't answered, he spoke. He told of how I had wanted to visit Ammi's relatives and how he had taken me there. All the while, I kept my head lowered. I carefully noted the swirls on the carpet, counting them carefully. My life depended on it. If I looked up at Ammi's accusing eyes...

We went to sleep without dinner that night. Ammi got up and quietly went to her bedroom. I looked at her worried. Abbu followed her. Mateen got up to follow them but I stopped him. "Let them talk it out. Ammi is angry with Abbu, and they have to resolve it between themselves."

"Why didn't you tell me anything?" he asked. "I'm still confused. Why had Ammi hidden something so important from us?"

I looked at him uncomfortably. I had heard Ammi talking about Khala's affair but she didn't know that I knew. Anyway, how could I possibly relate that story to Mateen? How could I tell him everything that Khala had told us?

"I don't know," I said simply.

"What does she look like? Where does she live? Does she have children? Do I have cousins?" he asked excitedly.

I nodded. "She has two children. A son and a daughter."

His eyes lit up when I said that. But what was the point, I thought. Ammi would never let us visit them.

"She looks like Ammi, but she's a little more older. She looked quite old, actually," I said.

Mateen and I were having a decent conversation for the first time in months. I had Khala to thank for that. Without telling Mateen anything about the Hyderabad boy who Ammi had liked, I told him briefly about the house.

"I wish we could go there the next time we visit Vellore!" he exclaimed. That was a wish that wasn't going to come true any time soon, I knew. "How come Ammi isn't making dinner? I'm hungry," he said.

I looked at the door of Ammi's room. She wasn't going to make *roti* or anything for a long time, I realised. I made a couple of *rotis* for Mateen and sat down at the table, watching him as he ate. At times like this, I could glimpse the baby he had been, the adorable toddler and the slightly serious five-year-old. He talked continuously with his mouth full. Discovering new relatives had given him a huge appetite and had also made him more talkative.

At night, my thoughts wandered to Farha. If she hadn't run away, if she had been married in a proper manner, Phuppu would have gloated and crowed that her daughter, though younger than her brother's daughter, had been married first.

I shifted uncomfortably when I realised I would be married soon. Where was that elusive thing that I wanted from my life? Was I going to bury it under matrimony and household chores like Rehana and now Farha? I hoped they were both happy. If it was exactly what they wanted, then why wouldn't they be? But was it exactly what I wanted?

41

Truth

Ammi spoke only when it was required. She didn't look at us and an uncomfortable silence swept our home. Abbu left for the shop every morning, looking bitter and glowered if I tried to ask him what the matter was. Mateen filled up the silences for everyone. Mateen's chatter echoed across the house, his sudden garrulousness surprising me immensely.

But how bothersome this whole thing was! Ammi wasn't speaking and neither was Abbu. What had transpired between them that night? I wished Ammi would realise that I was an adult and would talk to me about it. If she wasn't going to, then I would have to ask her. And how I dreaded that!

Three days later, we were quietly making lunch. Ammi was making the curry and I was chopping tomatoes. My mind wandered and I thought of a number of things that I would rather be doing. Ammi was standing at the stove, stirring the pressure cooker in a steady rhythm. "Mehnaz, tomatoes," she said. I handed the chopping board to her and spoke. "Ammi, what's the matter? Why are you behaving like this?"

Ammi was sliding the tomatoes into the pressure cooker and her hands stilled. The tomatoes still slid in, and one or two small pieces fell outside. She lowered her hands, switched off the gas and walked away. This was really ridiculous. I followed her outside. No one else was at home. The maid had come and left, Mateen was at school, and Abbu at the shop. I stopped her before she could enter her room. "Ammi, I'm not a child any more. You can tell me what's bothering you. Please!"

Her eyes had become really small in the past few days. Was it because the bags around her eyes made them look that way? Why was she crying over something her sister did? If she thought it was shameful, still, why was she getting so upset that we now knew about her sister?

She sat on the floor near her room, leaning against the wall. I had never seen her in such a dejected state. I crouched down beside her and took her hand. She abruptly withdrew her hand from me. Then with her palm resting on her forehead, she started speaking.

"She was just a few years older than me."

I kept quiet. I wanted Ammi to talk. For the first time, Ammi looked like she was going to tell me something significant. Her palm now covered most of her forehead as she murmured, "And yet I always thought we were from different generations. She was always so serious. She didn't go to school. She stayed at home with Ammi and managed the house. I never thought about anything, never thought about what I was going to do, like you do." She didn't look at me as she said this. "What option was there for me but to get married? I thought of each day as it brought me closer to womanhood, away from being a carefree girl. Yet I tried to be happy most of the time. Until he came into my life."

I looked at Ammi as she said this. Would she tell me her version of the story? Would she dare to continue? How much did Abbu know? Ammi looked straight ahead at the wall and spoke once more.

"He was from Hyderabad. He had come with his family. He was one of Ammi's relatives and they stayed in our house. They stayed for ten days, and in those ten days, I was a changed girl. I was no longer a girl even though I was only fourteen. I had become something else. He was such a handsome fellow, very jolly, and would always make me laugh. I loved to hear him talk, loved to hear him speak Urdu so unlike ours. When he left, I was really sad, but I let it go.

"A couple of years later they sent a proposal for me. I couldn't believe it when I heard it. You don't know what it was like to just dream about it then. I would close my eyes at night and dream about a different life. An exciting new life. But it never happened. She intervened. She made up some story to Ammi about him and discouraged Abbu from going ahead. In a few days, once again my life had changed for ever."

"She got married and on the day she was married, she told me the truth that she had lied. I showed the sick letter she had written to Ammi and Ammi too was horrified. But she was such a sly woman. She revealed all this on the day she was getting married, when Ammi wouldn't be able to berate her as she was going away. I hated her for doing that to me. For having changed the course of my life."

Ammi looked at me then. I felt red heat climbing up my neck. This was so strange. Ammi had behaved all this while like she was in a confessional, but now she had acknowledged my presence. "You must remember, Mehnaz, that I don't regret marrying your father for even one moment. There isn't another man in this world I would rather be married to."

"Then why do you hate her so much?" I asked her abruptly. Wasn't this something that had happened years ago? If Ammi had found happiness with Abbu, why was she being so recalcitrant?

Ammi looked at the wall once more. "Her husband died after a year of her marriage, leaving her with her daughter. Her in-laws were unkind people. They harassed her because she was a widow and because she didn't have a son. Abbu had died by then, and I had got married. Ammi brought her back to live with her."

I chewed my underlip. I knew about Khala's affair. But it was better if I didn't let it out to Ammi. Ammi might just change her mind and not tell me anything about it again. So quietly with a puzzled look, I said, "But she has a son also, right?"

Ammi looked at me. "Today, I think you are no longer my daughter."

I was startled. What did she mean? I tightened my grip on her hand and said, "Ammi!"

"The things I am about to tell you now, I don't think I should be telling my daughter. I realise that you are an adult now, Mehnaz. I can tell you this."

I wanted to hug her. This was a different Ammi. Still, she scared me too. Her calmness in the face of such painful memories was unsettling. "That son of hers is a bastard." She looked at me, waiting for a reaction. I gasped, as was expected of me. "What?" I asked incredulously. All this wasn't acting. Hearing the words out aloud did shock me.

She took a deep breath and said, "She had an affair with a man and her son is a result of that."

I wished I could say, "So what? Why are you so bothered about it? Why do you hate her so much for that?" But my new-found courage wavered. I kept quiet, knowing that Ammi would continue.

"She had an affair, Mehnaz. An affair. With that Amaan... that man from Hyderabad." She looked at me to see my reaction. I think she was satisfied with what she saw. I was truly, exceedingly shocked. WHAT? The word reverberated in my head. HOW?

"He was married when he came to visit Ammi after Abbu's death. He hadn't brought his wife and child along. He stayed with them for a week. And when he left, she was pregnant. He never returned to Vellore, but I'm sure he knows about his son. He didn't take any responsibility. At least he could have married her. And to think that I... I had wanted to marry such a man." Ammi shuddered and looked at me, with fierce anger in her eyes. "Can you believe the scandal it caused in Vellore? Can you even begin to think?"

I shook my head. I really couldn't.

"Mehnaz, my Ammi died because of that shock and scandal. I saw her at Ammi's funeral. She was eight months pregnant. You were a year old then. Do you realise now what I had felt when I saw her? She ruined her life and our family name. And caused my mother's death. Obviously, I don't want a reminder such as that in my life. I no longer consider her as my sister."

I kept quiet. Ammi's revelations had shocked me into silence. Thinking quietly, with Ammi breathing heavily beside me, the person I really felt sorry for was Khala. Ammi got up and went to her room. I sat there for some more time, letting everything sink in. Did Ammi really hate Khala because of the scandal and how it had affected her mother? Would Ammi have hated her so much if it had been another man? Did Abbu know about this man from Hyderabad?

For a moment I thanked Allah that I was from a different generation and that I lived here in Bangalore. An inner sense, an uneasiness, however, gripped me. If I had been in Khala's place, my education or my living in Bangalore would certainly have helped me. I wouldn't have been reduced to misery like Khala. But even then, such hate and such anger would have made me question the choices I had made. I knew then that no matter where I went, what I did, how I did it... without Ammi's approval my success would still be meaningless.

42

Beauty and Sorrow

In October, Rehana came to stay with her parents. She was in her seventh month. After a lavish feast, her in-laws sent her to her mother's house. After her marriage, she had mostly lived in Vellore. Only once in a month, when she came to Bangalore, did she stay with her parents for a few days.

Rehana had come to Bangalore with her in-laws a few days earlier and Ammi had attended the function. Ammi returned looking bitter. Ah yes... the competition between me and Rehana. I was way behind now. She was going to have a baby and I wasn't even engaged yet. However, I think Ammi was pleased that things had worked out well for me with Imtiaz's family.

Imtiaz's mother called up one day and announced that she wanted to bring a few of her family members to 'see' me. When the day came, Ammi was like a woman possessed. She wiped every surface in the house, every table and mirror, until there were no spots, no thin film of dust, nothing at all. Asifa Chachi came over and the two women spent the whole afternoon in the kitchen, frying *keema samosas* and making other savouries. Abbu got *rasogullas* and *rasmalais* from K.C. Das and then, not satisfied with this, he bought pastries too. I thought it a bit ridiculous that Ammi should go through all this trouble. But then making the right impression on the prospective groom's family mattered the most.

Ammi and I had gone to Fazal's a few days before and picked up a rich cream-coloured *ghaghra*. I was stunned when I saw the price tag but Ammi wouldn't let me change it for something simpler and less expensive. The *ghaghra* was of soft satin and silk and had a diaphanous chiffon *dupatta* with glittering sequins. I was secretly very pleased that Ammi and I had settled on something so tasteful and elegant.

At 4 p.m., Ammi told me to get dressed. She came into the room and gave me her jewellery box. I stroked the soft material of the *ghaghra,* not really thinking about what was happening.

"Mehnaz," she said. She looked worried. "I'm really happy today. Just make sure that you don't do anything stupid, okay?"

Why would I do anything stupid? When they finally came, I was dressed and wearing all the jewellery Ammi had kept out for me. Rehana wasn't feeling well so she hadn't come. Asifa Chachi smiled at me and I smiled back at her. I felt a different person, with the gold adorning the parting in my hair, the *dupatta* covering my head and falling around my shoulders in soft folds. This didn't feel like me. How was this new me supposed to behave?

I would know soon enough. Asifa Chachi escorted me outside, telling me to bend my head. I did, but not low enough apparently, for she pressed her palm on my upper back gently, forcing me to bend more. I couldn't bring myself to bend any more and I stood straight. She looked at me surprised. "What happened?" she asked.

I shook my head. "I can't bend like that in front of anyone. Please don't expect me to close my eyes also," I said curtly. She looked hurt but didn't say anything. I was still seething for some unknown reason. Imtiaz didn't have to bow and scrape before my father, I was sure.

Still, thinking of him gave some direction to my thoughts. I was not being coerced into this. I was doing this willingly. I lowered my head just enough so I could see the tips of my slippers peeping from under the *ghaghra*. Looking at the marbled designs on the floor, I walked from the corridor outside my room to the hall. Feeling nervous and edgy, I stepped inside the hall and let Chachi escort me to the centre where a single chair had been placed.

Chachi helped me sit down. I still looked down, eyes lowered. Where was Ammi? I felt strange and forlorn sitting in the chair while I didn't even know how many people stared at me.

Maybe the best thing to do would be to pretend I was somewhere else. I closed my eyes and let myself be transported to Vellore. The terrace. Rehana and Basheer popped into my head. I almost smiled but just then my head was being lifted. Determined not to think about what was happening, I saw Imtiaz standing on the terrace cockily. I felt an urge to throw my slippers at him again for making me go through this. But then it had to be done. It was just one step in the middle. And what about the end, I thought. What was all this leading up to? Marriage with Imtiaz, of course. And was it really what I wanted?

I let out a breath and suddenly realised that the person standing in front of me had become still. Oh god! But then I had to breathe. I couldn't behave like I was some mannequin. Did they really expect me not to breathe loudly? What if I wanted to sneeze?

When it was finally over, I walked out of the hall in a dignified manner and broke into a run the moment I reached the corridor leading to my room. I was breathing heavily when I collapsed on the bed. Ammi and Chachi were still talking to the guests and would probably come after some time. I still had a few minutes to think things over.

Getting up wearily, I pulled the *dupatta* from my head and let it fall on the bed in a heap. Imtiaz hadn't spoken to me even once after that day in Vellore. I knew it was a little risky, but I wished he had taken that risk. I wanted to talk about so many things with him. I wanted to ask him how our life would be. What would I have to expect from him?

When they left, Ammi and Chachi came to my room. They looked horrified when they saw me removing the jewellery.

"Mehnaz!" Ammi admonished. "Your father hasn't seen you as yet. He wanted to see how you looked, all dressed up as a bride."

Wearily I wore all the jewellery once more and sat outside in the *ghaghra* with Abbu, Sadiq Chacha, Asifa Chachi, and Ammi. Mateen hadn't bothered to come outside for the entire evening. Abbu kept looking at me, almost unbelievingly. I was longing to change into something comfortable. Chacha and Abbu spoke about how Fouzia Phuppu had missed this event. Ammi and Chachi looked thankful she wasn't here with her loud mouth and raucous laughter. For once, I didn't care. I listened as Abbu and Chacha discussed Imtiaz's family, while Ammi and Chachi did the same. They all sat eating the *samosas* and other delicacies that Abbu had bought.

Chachi arranged some *samosas* and a pastry on a plate and handed it to me quietly. Feeling contrite, I apologised to her for being rude earlier. She smiled and nodded. I took the plate and got up. I wanted to see what Mateen was doing. I hadn't even seen him come back from school, and Ammi had been too busy to notice.

I went to his room and found it locked. I knocked and waited. There was no response. I knocked a little loudly once more and called out. When there was no response, I felt uneasy and banged on the door with my free hand.

"Mateen! Are you there inside?"

Silence. I walked back to the hall holding the ghaghra in front of me so that I wouldn't trip on it. "Ammi, I don't think Mateen is in his room. Did he tell you where he went?"

Ammi looked up surprised. "No. I'm sure he's in his room, maybe asleep or something." But she got up and so did the others.

We went to Mateen's room and all of us called out his name. When he didn't respond, Ammi's face paled. She looked at Abbu, worried.

"What do we do?" she asked him.

"Why don't we go from the outside and look into his room?" I suggested. Abbu nodded and ran outside. Ammi banged on the door once more. Her eyes grew round with alarm when we heard Abbu's voice calling from outside that the room was empty.

We went back to the hall. Apparently, Mateen had got out through the window. The window grilles were quite broad. Even then, how had he managed to squeeze through them to the outside? I went to my room to change, feeling subdued. Where was he? What was happening to him? Why was he no longer the happy little boy I loved? What was troubling him? For once, I stopped worrying about what was going to happen to my life. I had been so engrossed in my own life that I hadn't even watched my brother grow distant and withdraw from all of us.

Chacha and Chachi stayed with us, waiting for Mateen to turn up. Chachi looked a bit distracted. She had left Rehana alone, with only the little girl to take care of her. She telephoned Rehana, telling her that they would be home in a while.

Ammi and Chachi started reading Yaseen and I joined them. Wherever Mateen was, I hoped he was safe. At 8 p.m. when there was no sign of him, I had a worrying thought. I went to Abbu.

"Break down Mateen's door, please."

Abbu looked at me surprised. "Why? What's the point? He's not there."

I shook my head. "Please, Abbu. I have a feeling. Please break down the door."

Abbu agreed reluctantly. Abbu and Chacha looked through some of the tools in the garden. When Ammi saw what they were doing, she was horrified. The tears were already flowing down her face.

Grunting heavily and perspiring, Abbu and Chacha broke the lock on the door. The door gave away limply. I rushed inside and pushed open the bathroom door. The bathroom was wet. Mateen cowered under the shower, fully clothed, dripping wet.

43

Mateen

The doctor was unable to tell us what was wrong with Mateen. Abbu and Chacha had dragged him out from under the shower, and Ammi had removed his wet clothes, drying him with a towel silently, while tears flowed down her face. Chacha had by then rushed outside and called the doctor from the nearest clinic who came very reluctantly.

Ammi had dressed Mateen in warm clothes, covered him with two blankets and yet he shivered uncontrollably. His condition made all of us feel helpless. I was furious with myself. I had let the same thing happen to Mateen. The same thing that happened to Basheer. Even before he ran away, he had become a stranger to me. He had firmly enclosed himself in a shell, and made it so thick and strong that no one could force even a crack in it. Here was my little brother, who had been such a chirpy little fellow... he too had changed so much. Why hadn't I seen it? Why had I been so self-absorbed?

Aren't we all self-absorbed? Abbu in his business, Ammi in the house and the million other things she takes care of, and I was so taken up with what was going to become of my life. What I was going to do, and how I was going to do it... and here, something had happened to Mateen's life that had changed him irrevocably.

I sat at the end of the bed and watched Ammi stroking his forehead with a shaky hand. The doctor had come, checked his pulse, saw that he had a fever. He was a nervous and fidgety man, who kept tapping his fingers on the side table. Mateen's eyes had a glassy look. He stared at us vacantly, as though he did not recognise us.

The doctor prescribed antibiotics for the fever and got up to leave.

"What should we do, doctor?" Abbu asked.

"Keep him warm. Give him some soup. I hope he doesn't get pneumonia. Also, someone should stay here with him tonight."

Ammi spoke then. "But why did he do something like this?" she asked.

"I think it's better you ask him that question," said the doctor, shrugging his shoulders. He left.

I looked at Mateen, who was now staring at the ceiling unblinkingly. Ammi shut her eyes tightly. Asifa Chachi clasped Ammi's hand and tried to comfort her, but Ammi wasn't willing to listen to anyone.

Abbu sat on the bed. "Mateen," he said softly. Mateen looked at him and then looked back at the ceiling. I wished I could do something. I wished I could make him respond in some way. I tried to think of something funny that he and I had shared recently. But we hadn't spoken for ages. Mateen had spoken only when we had discovered the truth about Khala. After that, he had once more become withdrawn and I hadn't given much thought to it.

"Don't worry," Asifa Chachi comforted Ammi. "He will be all right soon. It's not like he has some life-threatening disease or anything." At that Ammi started crying loudly. I tried to suppress my irritation with Chachi. That wasn't what Ammi wanted to hear. However, I also knew that Ammi would cry at whatever we said now.

Abbu looked at Ammi and then at Chacha and Chachi, who were silent. "Rehana is alone at home. I think you should go now," he said. Chacha protested, but Chachi got up. "Yes, we should go home now. She must be really worried," she said. I was the only one to come outside Mateen's room to say goodbye.

I watched Chachi wear her *burka*. Already she was thinking of Rehana. I knew it was natural. Watching someone else's child suffer had reminded her acutely of her own daughter and her condition. Still, I wished they wouldn't go. It was like a mourning house here. I wished life were a slate where we could just rub clean everything and start afresh. I looked at the food still lying on the plates in the hall and sighed. Ammi wasn't going to do anything. It was up to me now.

Feeling like a martyr, I cleaned the hall, stashed the remaining food in containers, and put the pastries in the fridge. My stomach rumbled. I hadn't eaten anything since lunch. I wondered if Abbu and Ammi would eat dinner. Feeling oddly selfish and guilty, I ate a chocolate pastry hurriedly. I wouldn't be having any dinner either, and I was hungry.

After making sure everything was cleaned up, I went to Mateen's room. Ammi had switched off the harsh tube light. She and Abbu spoke in low tones in the dimly lit room. Mateen appeared to be asleep. When I went closer, I realised he wasn't asleep. He was still staring at the ceiling vacantly. This disturbed me immensely.

Something overwhelmed me at that moment. My heart felt full and my throat itched. I ran to my room and cried. I sat on the bed, holding my head in my hands and cried for a long time. I splashed water on my face and rubbed my eyes. Finally, I went to his room. Abbu and Ammi looked at me when I came in. I sat near his desk and cleared my throat.

"Mateen has been having some problems from quite some time, Abbu," I said, looking at Abbu. I felt Ammi's eyes on me, but I wasn't sure if I could look at her.

"Do you know something that you haven't told us, Mehnaz?" Abbu asked.

I shook my head. "I don't know. I'm just guessing. But he has been having some problems, I'm sure," I said. I looked at Mateen, who seemed to be asleep now.

Ammi spoke. "If you knew something, why didn't you tell us?"

The soft accusation gripped me, but I refused to get cowed down. "Ammi, I am as guilty as you are in this." I looked at the ground as I spoke. "If I have noticed something different in Mateen, then at least I have been noticing him. You and Abbu have ignored him for some reason."

Ammi got up and left the room. Abbu looked at me and then at Mateen. "He'll be all right. I'm sure there isn't anything wrong with him." He too got up and went.

Feeling angry and powerless, I sat by Mateen's side for a long time. I brushed the hair from his forehead and watched his face, remembering the tiny little thing he had been when he was born and how I had been thrilled to just hold his soft body in my arms. I remembered the little toddler who followed me everywhere, annoying me, yet in a disarming way. Where was he? What had happened to him?

But what irked me most was my parents, absolute, refusal to believe that anything could be wrong with their son. Who knew... maybe it ran in the family. Why else did Zohra Phuppu deliberately not take her medicines? Why had Basheer run away? It was because they couldn't face the stinging reality of everyday life that had been flung on their faces every now and then.

My brother wasn't going to lose this battle. Whatever it was. I was going to be with him every step of the way. My brother wasn't a loser.

I knew Ammi would be back to sleep here tonight. I didn't move from there until she came much later. She had a plate with a bowl of steaming soup on it. She didn't talk to me, but sat down beside Mateen. She was about to wake him up, when I laid my hand on her arm.

"Ammi, when was the last time Mateen spoke to you about anything? When did he tell you about his school or about his friends? Does he even have friends? Why does he remain so silent? I'm not blaming you for all this, but we all share the blame for not being aware of whatever that was happening to him."

Ammi stared at me. She didn't say anything. I turned to Abbu who walked in that moment. "Ammi has had her arguments with me, and she has had her fights. But in the end, things almost always got resolved and we would continue. But with Mateen, there's nothing anyone knows about what's going on in his head. How can you ignore that? Yesterday he was sitting under the shower for so long. What if today he did something like... like..." I couldn't bring myself to say the words.

Ammi looked horrified. Abbu glared at me. "How can you even say such a thing, Mehnaz?" he thundered. I flinched. But I had to carry on. "Abbu, these things are common. We read about it in the newspapers all the time. You're just finding it hard to believe that it can happen to your son. Do you want to wait until it happens?"

****

Ammi sat by Mateen's side all night. When I came in at midnight, she was dozing off, and looked very uncomfortable. I placed my hand on her shoulder and she got up immediately, "Wha... Mateen! I..." she mumbled. She saw me and narrowed her eyes, trying to think why I was there. "Ammi, you sleep for some time in your room. I'll sit with him." She shook her head. Shrugging, I pulled up the chair near his desk and sat down.

Ammi was awake now. "Do you want some tea?" I asked her. She shook her head, and then nodded. I got up reluctantly and went to the kitchen. The kitchen seemed odd at this time of the night. A few cockroaches scurried past me when I switched on the light. A lizard darted back from view and hid behind a switch board. Grimacing, I pulled out the sauce pan from the cupboard. I went back to Mateen's room with the tea and saw Ammi standing near the window. She turned when I entered.

She took the tea cup silently and then sat down once more, caressing Mateen's forehead gently. He slept soundly.

"Does he have fever?" I asked.

Ammi nodded. "We'll have to check his temperature when he wakes up," she said, her voice sounding hoarse.

I sat near his desk once more, and sipped the scalding tea. I tried sleeping but couldn't. Oddly, I was thinking about Imtiaz and what his mother had thought about me. I had completely forgotten about him for the past few hours. The day had started with so much excitement at home. I found it hard to believe it was the same day. It seemed like many days ago that his family had come home.

Maybe his mother would call up tomorrow. I suppose he would be anxious too to hear from his mother about whatever details she had to report to him. Strangely, I wasn't anxious. Right now, only Mateen mattered.

Ammi had spoken to me, but preoccupied as I had been, I hadn't heard. "Umm... what?" I said. She expelled a deep breath and spoke once more. "I said I wonder what could have gone so wrong for Mateen. What has caused this? Why? I thought he was such a happy little boy."

I nodded. There wasn't any answer to that rhetorical question. But was it a rhetorical question? There had to be answers. We had to talk to Mateen and find out what was happening to him. "He has been really quiet for quite some time, Ammi. I think there is something that is really bothering him. Remember how he had us all worried at Rehana's *chor-haldi*? Even now, I don't know why he did that."

It was the first time I had brought up the *chor-haldi* incident myself. I had avoided talking about it as far as possible. But right now, there was probably some relevance to it, with what was happening with Mateen. Ammi was silent. She sat back in the chair and yawned. "Are you going to sit here for some time?"

I nodded. "You go and sleep for some time. Come back after an hour. I'll sleep then."

She looked hesitant. I knew she still didn't trust me with her baby. She thought that I wouldn't take care of him or that I would fall asleep. But she didn't know that Mateen was like my baby too. "Go, Ammi," I said. Finally, she went.

I stood at the window for some time. Feeling cold, I wrapped my *dupatta* around my arms tightly and came back to the desk. That was when I remembered. The last time I had rummaged through his desk, looking for his phone book to call his friends, I had found Mateen's diary.

I walked up to him quickly to see if he was still sleeping. He seemed sound asleep. I walked back to his desk and slid out the drawer carefully. There were a number of things he had kept here. Some games, a few comics, an old battery and there, under an old tin box, was the diary. I pulled it out slowly, and yet the tin box banged softly against the drawer bottom as I did it.

I looked once more at Mateen. Asleep. Feeling nervous and rather anxious, I sat down by the desk. I switched on the table lamp and opened the diary.

Part 4

44

Voices

"It's a beautiful day today and yet Ammi won't let me go out to play. I've tried asking her, but she just doesn't listen. I wish my friends, Nikhit and Suhail, lived near my house. Even then, I don't think she would let me go outside...

"Sometimes I sit in my room and I imagine the world is going around in circles and I feel all dizzy. I close my eyes and everything is just going round and round. Mehnaz yelled at me today... I wanted to borrow her colour pencils to finish the drawing I was making. She didn't even listen to what I was trying to tell her... My colour pencil collection doesn't have dark green... that Ankit broke it in two... how I hate him... I finished the drawing without it finally. It looked horrible so I tore it up...

"Ankit stole my lunch today.... I know it was him... Ammi had made *gobhi paratha* and I was waiting to eat it, but I stayed hungry that day... how I wanted to bash him up... but I didn't... I'm scared of him... he's so much bigger than me....

"Today Asifa Chachi went back home... I watched them leave and felt sad... it had been nice having them at home.... Ammi is always so busy with something or the other, and Mehnaz never has time for me... I wish I was more important... Asifa Chachi spoke to me sometimes and I liked sitting beside her, watching her sleep....

Nikhit and I thought we could bunk school today and we were on our way to the park when Mr Kumar saw us. He made us kneel down in class and caned us. I didn't show the cut on my back to Ammi....

"I don't know why Mehnaz likes going to that Dahlia's house. Her house smells so funny and I don't like her dog. He always growls at me... Sometimes I don't think I belong to this family. Mehnaz doesn't love me, Abbu always scolds me, and Ammi is always busy... sometimes I wish I could run away... I know that Basheer Bhai ran away... I was too young then, but I know what they were all talking about...

"I remember seeing Zohra Phuppu's dead body. I have never seen a dead body... it was the first time... it looked so strange... I wanted to go near her and touch her... when no one was looking... they were all crying... I walked up slowly and touched her hand... it was cold and hard....

"That night I couldn't sleep... no one slept that night... I went with Abbu to the burial ground... Ammi hadn't noticed or she wouldn't have let me go... I watched as Abbu and Chacha lowered the covered body inside the ground and then covered it up.... There were so many ants in the muddy ground... I watched them crawl over the mound of earth where Phuppu was buried... Would they do this after I died also? The thought scared me so much that I didn't speak to anyone until we returned to Bangalore....

"Today Mehnaz went to Dahlia's house even after Ammi told her not to... Ammi asked me where Mehnaz was and I told her... when Mehnaz came back, Ammi was very angry with her.... I enjoyed watching Ammi get angry with Mehnaz... Ammi is always angry with her for something or the other....

"Ammi is hard to understand... sometimes she smiles at me and I remember how she used to hold me tight when I was small... but at other times, I think she forgets that it's the same me....

“I don’t know why Mehnaz wants me to call her ‘Api’. It’s not like she behaves like she’s my elder sister... at least when Aasia was there, she would try to be with me... but now, it’s like I don’t exist for her....

“Rehana is getting married in a few days. Abbu and Ammi keep taking us there and I get so bored.... I just want to get back home and curl up on my bed and sleep....

“Today, I came away from Rehana’s *chor-haldi* without telling anyone. I had some money in my pocket and I took an auto... it felt so free to be all alone without anyone... when I came back to the house, Mehnaz was leaving for college with her friend... I don’t know why, but I lied to her and made her give me the keys... it felt good to see the expression of hurt on her face. Afterwards, I felt bad but what could I do... when I got bored of sitting in the house, I locked up and went to the park...

“I sat there till the evening and then a drunk man came and asked me to get up... I got up feeling scared... I was scared now... Abbu and Ammi would be mad with me... they wouldn’t listen... I was scared to even take an auto back to Rehana’s place... I wanted to go back home and sit there... but I don’t know why I was so scared... I started walking and then when I came to a main road I took an auto back to Rehana’s house... that night Abbu hit me with his belt... I have seen him angry many times, but it was never at me... does he hate me so much...?

“Ankit cornered me in the ground today. He pushed me down and sat on me and hurt my legs. Suhail and Nikhit were playing hide-n-seek with me... they didn’t know Ankit had caught me... a group of eleventh standard boys came and they started laughing at us... they caught Ankit by his collar and pulled him up from me... they said some things to each other and laughed and laughed....

“I got up from the ground the moment Ankit moved and I ran away from there as fast as I could. Only when I was very far,

I turned back and saw that Ankit was still with those boys... they were dragging him behind the bathroom... I don't know why...

"Today some people are coming to see Mehnaz... when she goes off from this house... how will it be? It's getting late for school... I have to go now..."

I looked up from the diary, my eyes blurred with tears, my heart aching unbearably. Mateen was awake and he was looking at me.

45

School of Horrors

I got up from the chair and rushed to his side. The diary was still in my hand and his eyes followed the diary. I felt heat rush up. I had been caught reading my younger brother's personal diary. "Api?" he spoke softly. I sat beside him and looked at him gently. All along, only one question burned in my head. Had someone taken him behind the bathroom too? Was this his reaction to it? My heart lurched when I realised what this could mean.

"Yes, Mateen?" I said. He looked at me, and then at the diary. "Did you read everything?" I nodded. My throat was choked up. I was sure I wouldn't be able to speak. "Today..." he started. He looked away from me and directed his gaze at the ceiling. I looked at his face and then at his bed covers as he spoke. "I went to school and Ankit wasn't there. He was absent today. I wondered what had happened yesterday with him."

"Suhail, Nikhit and I were playing football during lunch break when those boys came and joined the game. They were not playing, but they kept tripping up one of us each time. In five minutes, all three of us were muddy and Nikhit even had many scrapes on his hands. I got angry but I was scared to say anything."

There was silence. I didn't encourage him to proceed. I didn't know if I had the courage to listen to him, but it was important to let him continue talking. "Nikhit finally spoke up and said that he would complain to our class teacher. The boys got angry when they heard that and they caught hold of Nikhit by the collar. Like yesterday they dragged him too behind the bathroom. Suhail looked scared and he said we should better go back to class. I wasn't happy about leaving Nikhit like that."

"Suhail said he was going back to class and he ran away from there. I walked up slowly behind the bathroom."

I held my breath. Oh god, what had he seen there that had reduced him to this state? I knew the answer but I was afraid of acknowledging it. "Api..." he said. He looked at me and I tried to muster enough courage to look him in the eye.

"They had his pants down, Api... they..." he broke off with a sob. I got up, feeling sick and horrified. I had guessed what had happened, but to hear it actually from Mateen made me feel shocked. "They saw me, and one of the boys said that tomorrow it's going to be my turn. I'm never going back to that school."

Saying so, he turned to bury his face in his pillow and sobbed. My heart heavy, I looked at him, not knowing what words would soothe him.

"Mateen, we have to tell Abbu and Ammi," I said softly. He looked up and shook his head. "No! No! They won't believe me, Api."

"But there is no other choice, Mateen. We have to tell them that this is what is happening in the school. Did you speak with Nikhit? How is he?"

Mateen didn't speak. "I don't know," he said finally. I got up, anger pounding my brain, making me feel impotent with rage. How come the school authorities were so oblivious to this?

"Api, please let's not tell Abbu and Ammi," Mateen pleaded. "I sat under the shower today for so long because I wanted to make sure I would get fever. I don't want to go to that school ever again."

I reasoned with him. "Mateen, when your fever goes down, Abbu and Ammi will expect you to return to school. You can't keep hiding at home for ever."

"Who is he hiding from?" Ammi's voice interjected sharply. I saw her standing at the door. How long had she been there? Mateen looked at her horrified, and then once again started sobbing. I got up, my heart pounding madly. Would Ammi believe us?

"Ammi, you have to come here and sit down. It's something important. I'll go and call Abbu," I spoke confidently, but I dreaded their reaction. Ammi sat on Mateen's bed, looking angry and a little cynical. She had already decided that she wouldn't believe me. Abbu looked sleepy but worried.

I told them everything that Mateen had told me, and watched Abbu's sleepiness disappear and Ammi's anger being replaced by disbelief. Abbu turned to Mateen. "Are you telling the truth?" he asked. Mateen cowered. I addressed Abbu. "Abbu, he won't lie about such a big issue. We have to complain to the school authorities."

No one spoke. Ammi turned to Mateen and gathered him in her arms where he cried loudly. I felt relieved on seeing that. My heart, however, was still troubled. What about Nikhit and Ankit? Had they told their parents? Would they be able to tell the school authorities what had happened to them? Without them, the school wouldn't believe Mateen. The easiest option would be to put him in a different school. But those boys had to be punished. Or how many other little boys would be victimised?

"I'm going to his school tomorrow," Abbu said. "I'm coming with you," I told him. Mateen and Ammi were silent. "Mateen, you have to come with us," Abbu told him. Mateen looked stricken, but I held his hand. "If you don't come, how are the school authorities going to believe what we say?"

He shook his head firmly. I spoke again, "Abbu, we have to speak to Ankit's and Nikhit's parents and tell them what has happened. I have a feeling both the boys wouldn't have spoken about it to their parents. We have to go to their house first and then take them with us to school."

Mateen held on to Ammi tightly. She stroked his forehead but he still looked troubled and scared. I sat beside him. "Mateen, trust me. We're going to make sure those boys get expelled."

The next day, I got up in the morning, dread filling my heart. What was going to happen today? All four of us drove down first to Nikhit's house. His mother said he wasn't feeling well, so he wouldn't be going to school. As we sat in the drawing room of their house, I looked at her as she spoke to us calmly, wondering what her reaction would be when she learnt the truth.

Unexpectedly, her reaction was one of denial. She refused to believe what I had told her. "You're l-lying!" she said, her eyes registering shock and the beginning of anger.

I tried speaking to her reasonably. "Why would I want to lie about something like this? My brother sat under the shower yesterday for two hours, hoping he would get fever so he wouldn't have to go to school."

She shook her head. "Why don't you ask Nikhit?" I asked her. Mateen looked uncomfortable and he squirmed in his seat. "My son would have told me if something like this had happened with him."

When she made no move to go to Nikhit's bedroom, I looked at Ammi and Abbu, feeling annoyed. Why weren't they saying anything? Why couldn't they tell this woman that she was wrong?

But they both sat straight, on the edge of their seats, looking as if they would bolt and run any moment. I got up. They looked at me. Abbu and Ammi were both treating me as an adult. In fact, they seemed to be looking to me for direction. This wasn't the time to feel triumphant about it though.

Nikhit's mother looked hostile. "I don't believe you," she said to me once more. I took a deep breath. "Why don't you just ask your son? That will be enough."

Her eyes flashed with anger. "You don't have to tell me what I should or shouldn't do," she said. Abbu and Ammi got up and all of us left the house.

Subdued, we all went to Ankit's house. There we found that Ankit had gone with his parents to his grandparents' house in Cuddalore and wouldn't be back for a few days. I felt frustrated. Abbu looked unsure. Somehow the onus of handling this whole thing had fallen upon me, and I wasn't sure how to do it. Ammi and Mateen were very quiet in the car. They sat at the back, while I sat in the front with Abbu. "What do we do now?" Abbu asked.

"Maybe we should go home and wait till Ankit returns. It won't be of any use to go to school and accuse those boys without these two children," I said. Abbu was silent. "What if Ankit's mother also refuses?" he spoke loudly. I instinctively turned around to see Mateen. His face was blank.

"We will just have to wait and see," I said. Ammi spoke then. "Why can't we just enrol him in another school?" Abbu pondered that for some time and nodded. "Mehnaz, I think that's the best thing to do. Otherwise, his studies are going to get affected badly." Abbu looked relieved while I felt frustrated that they had arrived at this conclusion so soon.

"But Abbu, those boys... they have to be punished," I protested. Ammi spoke up then. "Mehnaz, all this isn't as easy as you think. The school authorities won't believe us and what if those boys find out where Mateen lives and try to harm him as revenge?"

I had no answer to that. I craned my neck to look at Mateen in the back seat. He was looking out of the window, trying to desperately pretend that this hadn't happened to him. I sat back with a sigh. I shut my eyes and thought of what he had written in his diary. So many feelings and so many emotions he had bottled inside him and vented briefly in his diary. Did he really think that Abbu didn't love him and that Ammi didn't have time for him, and I too wasn't bothered about him?

Seeing things from his perspective had shaken my views about him. Suddenly, I realised where the little boy I was missing had gone. We all had driven him away.

46

Coffee House Meeting

We reached home and everyone seemed to want to shake off the whole episode, maybe even pretend nothing had happened. Abbu sat down to watch TV and Ammi went to make lunch. Mateen sat down to watch TV, but when Abbu wasn't looking, he got up slowly and went to his room. I followed him there and found him sitting on the bed, studying his fingernails intently.

I sat beside him. We didn't talk. I didn't know what words I could say. I felt impotent and angry, and deep inside me, there was a turbulence that ceased to go away. We sat in that position for quite some time. I heard Abbu leave the house to go to his shop. I heard cooking sounds coming from the kitchen.

The phone rang. Mateen jumped but sat still again. I got up to answer it. I was feeling so angry, I wished I could kick something, throw something at someone to make me feel better. Even my throat hurt from keeping quiet. I wanted to just scream.

I picked up the receiver and said "Hello." There was a brief silence at the other end before, I heard Imtiaz's voice whispering loudly, "Mehnaz! Thank god, you picked up the phone."

I quickly looked around. Ammi was in the kitchen and Mateen in his room. "Why did you call here?" I asked him, whispering furiously. Thoughts of Imtiaz didn't bring any pleasure at the moment. Anger and helplessness raged inside me and I was afraid I would tell Imtiaz something I would regret later.

"My mother is very happy. She said she will try and arrange our wedding really soon." He spoke normally now, and I could hear the excitement in his voice. Hearing his mother's plan, however, didn't do anything for me. I blamed it on my present state of mind. "Are you there?" he asked cautiously.

"Umm."

"What's the matter?"

I wished I could tell him, but it wasn't something I could explain over the phone. "It's nothing. I'll probably tell you if I meet you, although that's an unlikely possibility," I said, trying to sound light.

"But you can!" he urged. "You can meet me. I came with my mother to Bangalore. We are leaving tomorrow. Can we meet somewhere today?"

My throat felt dry. What was I supposed to answer? I did want to meet him and speak to him, but as a friend to whom I could unload my troubles. Right now, I didn't feel like telling any of this to Sahana and Jyoti. They were too involved in their own lives. "Where can we meet?" he asked once more.

My mind refused to oblige. Not that I knew of many places where I could meet a boy and not be seen. "I don't think I can meet you," I said firmly. Right now, I didn't feel like leaving the house and going anywhere. "But we have to!" he urged. His enthusiasm just bounced off me and I felt like hanging up the receiver.

"I hate lying to my parents. I don't think they will be too eager to send me if I told them the truth."

He snorted. "Oh, please! Don't give me that rubbish about not lying to your parents. I've known you for many years now. Just tell them you have to meet your friends. Come and meet me somewhere for coffee."

We decided to meet at the Coffee House on MG Road. I knew it was foolish to meet him in such an open place. But I would be wearing my *burka*. Of course, this would be possible only if I got permission to step out of the house.

Ammi wasn't convinced that I wanted to go to the library. "Why do you want a book now?" she asked. "Spend some time with your brother. I don't want you going out anywhere."

"But I'm going to see if I can get some nice books for him. By the time he gets admission in a new school, he is going to be really bored at home, Ammi."

Ammi looked at me over the fumes of the *baghaar* she was preparing for the *dal*. "Take him and go," she said. "What about his fever?" I asked. Finally, completely annoyed, she poured the *dal* over the *baghaar,* filling the kitchen with smoke. "Do what you want," she said. "Do what you want" implied a 'yes' and 'yes, she wasn't happy with the situation'.

I quickly washed my face and slipped my *burka* over my head. I would have to remember to stop by at the library while coming back.

In the auto, the excitement of seeing Imtiaz in a totally different environment had finally registered. When I got down at the busy road in the middle of the day, drinking coffee suddenly seemed a good idea. Once I was inside the old and rambling building, I tried to calm myself. I took a few deep breaths and looked around. I had been here earlier with Abbu once and for some reason I liked the place because it was not exactly dazzling. There was a relaxed and gentle air which appealed to me enormously because it seemed like a place where I could fit in.

He was sitting at a corner table and he waved when he spotted me. I walked up to the table, my heart doing a number of flip-flops. He looked the same. Of course, I hadn't expected him to look any different just because we were meeting outside Vellore. I sat down and said "Hi!" breathlessly.

He smiled and didn't say anything for a while. I looked around. There were quite a few people seated at the tables, sipping coffee, reading newspapers, or just gossiping idly. I looked at him.

He was still smiling at me. “What?” I asked him finally. “Why are you smiling so much?”

He shrugged and finally spoke. “I’m looking at the future Mrs Imtiaz Ahmed,” he said with a grin. I kept my face expressionless for a moment. Mrs Imtiaz Ahmed was a name that didn’t become me. Still, I tried to smile. He told me how his mother and his aunts had thought that I was lovely and they had really admired my house and liked my mother and everything seemed to be headed in one direction now.

When I didn’t respond, he looked at me concerned. “What is it, Mehnaz?” he asked. I sighed. I told him everything that happened with Mateen and watched his animated face lose its sparkle. “What are you going to do now?” he asked. I shrugged. “I don’t know. I don’t think we’re going to do anything.”

The waiter placed a tray with two coffee cups on the table and swished away, flicking a towel at his shoulder. Imtiaz leaned over and took my hands in his. I let him hold my hand for some time and then removed it slowly. “Don’t worry. Everything will be fine,” he said. I looked at him, irritated for saying that. How could he be so banal about it? This was my brother! My baby brother who was undergoing so much trauma!

When I didn’t say anything, he started talking about our marriage plans. He went on about how his mother was trying to get a December date and how she wanted to speak about it with my parents. She was hoping to have an engagement next month and then the wedding the following month. I stared at him, and thought that both mother and son could really be presumptuous.

“What?” he asked, noticing the expression on my face.

“Have you ever thought that my parents might not want to get me married so soon in December? They may have other plans for me?”

He was taken aback. “What other plans?” he asked. “Whatever they are, I’m sure they include me.”

I sat back and took a deep breath. "Imtiaz, I can't marry you in December. It's only two months away. How will my parents arrange for everything in time?"

He looked thoughtful. "It's not like my mother and I are expecting anything. We want a simple marriage. Grander marriages have taken place in less than a month's time. Why not ours in two months?"

Before I could stop myself, I blurted out, "I can't marry you, Imtiaz."

He looked shocked but then he smiled. "You mean you want to extend the marriage date?"

I nodded. "By at least a year," I said.

Imtiaz's eyes grew round and then he looked at me angrily. "Don't be silly," he said. "Why do you want to wait for a year?"

I looked down at the cooling coffee on the table. Neither of us had touched the coffee. "Imtiaz, I already told you about my desire to do something in life and..."

He cut me off. "And I told you that you can think about it after you marry me."

I took a deep breath to steady my voice. "It's not just that now, Imtiaz. There are things at home that need to be resolved before I can leave that house and come to yours."

He shook his head. "I don't understand. What can be more important than this?"

I looked away, feeling irritated with him for not understanding. "I know I'm asking for too much, but if you can't wait for a year, you're free to marry anyone else."

"Mehnaz! What's wrong with you? Why are you doing this? You know how much I care about you," he said softly.

I covered my face with my palms, the tips of my fingers pressing my eyelids. My eyes were burning. I hadn't slept much last night. "Imtiaz, this is very important to me. My brother needs me. I can't abandon him at this point."

He was silent for a while. "It was never about me, right? You never cared for me the way I care for you," he accused me bitterly.

I looked at the hurt look in his eyes and shut mine tightly. "It's not like that!" I protested.

"Then?" he challenged me.

"I-I do care about you. I really like you a lot," I said.

He crossed his arms across his chest and looked at me disdainfully. "But you don't love me, right?"

I bit my underlip not knowing what to say to him then. I wanted to tell him that I loved him, but the words sounded forced. "I... I..."

He waited for me to continue speaking, his arms still crossed across his chest. "What are you going to accomplish in one year?" he asked me suddenly. "I mean, what will you do? And will your parents agree to whatever it is you want to do?"

I had no answer to that. I didn't know if in one year I would have found the direction in life that I was so desperate for. I didn't know if one year would be enough to help Mateen cope with his trauma and let him emerge as a normal boy. But if I got married now, in December, everything would just stop.

He leaned forward, so close that I could see the faint stubble on his cheek. "Have you ever wanted to marry me?"

I nodded, my mouth dry. "Why don't you understand, Imtiaz? I really need time. I want to marry you but what difference will one year make?"

He had no answer to that. I felt that if I pursued the point, he might just relent. "Please, Imtiaz. This means so much to me. I need your support."

When he still didn't answer, I looked down at my coffee, wondering what had gone wrong. Two days ago, my life was apparently going on course. Why wasn't he able to understand that I just couldn't think of marrying and go away to Madras at a time like this when my brother needed me?

"How about six months?" he finally asked. I looked up. This was so strange. I felt I was negotiating my freedom and my desires with him. He was willing to give me six months, and I wanted to grab the other six and hold on to them too. But I knew when to give in, so I nodded my head. I watched relief flit across his features and I felt amazed that this man really, deeply cared for me.

"Okay, I'll speak to my mother about this, Mehnaz," he said.

I realised that there was nothing more to say. It was getting late and Ammi would be wondering why I was taking so long at the library. I got up to leave and he looked surprised. Where are you going?" he asked.

"I have to go home. I told Ammi I was going to the library to get books for Mateen."

"You didn't drink your coffee," he said.

I nodded. "Neither did you," I said and made a move to leave.

"Wait," he said and I stopped. "Can I call you up sometimes?" he asked.

"Imtiaz, isn't that a bit risky?"

He made a face. "Oh please! What's the risk in that? I'll speak up only when I hear your voice."

I nodded and then spoke again, "Yeah, but be careful. Sometimes my mother and I sound rather alike." I left him sitting at the coffee shop looking thoughtful, yet confused.

❖❖❖

47

Mrs Dahlia

I reached home. Ammi and Mateen were watching TV. The library had closed for lunch when I reached there. Feeling nervous I walked in empty-handed. Ammi looked at me and then at the TV. I started moving towards my room when she called out. "Where are the books, Mehnaz? What took you so long?"

Of course, I lied. "I didn't find any books which I thought Mateen would like." I walked inside my room and removed my *burka,* feeling strangely calm. I sat on the bed and replayed the conversation with Imtiaz in my head. He said six months. Maybe I was the one being unreasonable. But why did I feel like I was going to bargain away my freedom after six months? Bargain it for nothing that I really wanted.

What was happening in my life? Would I ever find any direction? The confused nature of my thoughts spun around in my head, weaving and weaving until I felt there was never really any solution. I had to get married like Rehana and have a couple of kids. And then? And then I had to take care of them, and Imtiaz and then my house. And then?

Why did I have to want something more from my life so much? Why couldn't I be like anyone else? Even Farha was better than me. She too had found what she wanted to do, even if it was running away and getting married. I thought about how life would be here after I got married. What would Mateen do? Would he be happy in another school? Soon, this would not be my priority. I would have other things to think and worry about.

I got up from bed feeling a little dizzy. Why couldn't I just accept it as my fate and move on? But my sense of self-esteem wouldn't allow me to accept it. My belief that I was meant for other things. For bigger things in life. If only I knew what they were! Ammi came to my room and suggested we go to Rehana's house after Abbu came. I was tired and I wasn't up to it. "Why don't you people go with Mateen?" I said.

"I asked Mateen. He said he'll come if you come."

I looked at Ammi, surprised. Mateen wanted me to be there with him? I said okay. Anything to make him feel comfortable and better. I wondered if he felt close to me because I had read his diary first hand. I felt little ashamed when I remembered my outburst against Sahana when she had read my diary. A diary was something personal. And yet, without any compunction I had read his. How could I condone it when I had done it myself?

Remembering my diary, I decided to dig it up once more. I sat down, leaning against the pillow and started reading the entries at the beginning. No mention of Imtiaz there. Mrs Dahlia's name leaped up from the page. I shut the diary with a snap. Of course! Mrs Dahlia would tell me what to do.

I went outside and told Ammi that I wanted to go to Mrs Dahlia's house. I knew she would get angry just on hearing her name. She did. "Why?" she asked sharply. "Ammi, it's been so many days since I went there. She wasn't keeping well the last time I saw her. I have to see how she is doing. Shall I take Mateen also? He's bored sitting at home?" I asked her rapidly. I didn't want to let her think too much before answering. But then, she was after all my mother and she knew why I was speaking so fast. When I was small, I used to wonder if she read my thoughts before I even had them.

She switched off the TV and turned away. "Do what you want."

I asked Mateen if he wanted to come with me. He nodded. We both left the house, seeing Ammi fume. The last time I saw her, she had been looking old and wasted. A surge of sympathy rushed through me as I walked through the narrow, tree-lined lane in the November afternoon.

A chill wind swept through us as we neared her house. Mateen was quiet. I didn't speak much to him. I wasn't in the mood for conversation. We took the turning to her house and I stopped. Mateen stopped too, and looked at me surprised and then looked ahead.

Mrs Dahlia's house wasn't there. Instead, there was a monstrosity of a building being constructed, right where her house stood. If the buildings adjacent to her house had seemed huge to me, this building now towered over them. It took me some time to get over the shock and understand what it meant. I walked quickly with Mateen and reached the building. The lawn had been dug up, the turned-over earth looking pathetic against the grey afternoon. I approached a small hut which had been built at the fringes of the lawn. There was a woman there, cooking rice over a smoky stove. She was waving at the smoke with her hand. She looked up when I stood at the door.

"Yenamma?" she asked me. I wished I could speak Kannada well, but with the little knowledge I had, I asked her where Mrs Dahlia was. *"Nan ge gothilla ma,"* she said. She didn't know. Deep inside I knew that something had happened to Mrs Dahlia. I felt despair loom within me, and yet I had to know for sure. I walked towards the horrendous construction. Mateen was standing outside the compound.

The contractor was there, issuing instructions to some of the workers. Once again, I tried my Kannada, asking him what had happened to the old lady who lived here. "She died four months ago," he replied in English. The words burned into my ears. I didn't think I was capable of framing any more questions, in English or in Kannada. I wanted to ask so many things, but words failed me. How had it happened? Had she been sick? Why had they broken down her house so soon? Who was constructing this building?

I dragged myself outside, not willing to accept that not only Mrs Dahlia was gone, but her musty and aged house which had been such a refuge to me was also obliterated. I felt tears pricking my eyelids, but I wanted to go back home and lock myself in a room and cry. Mateen looked at me and didn't ask anything. We walked back in silence. I didn't want to go back home and face Ammi.

Changing direction suddenly, I decided to walk towards the park. If Mateen was surprised, he didn't say anything. He walked with me in silence. I sat on one of the stone benches, slumped forward. We sat together, quiet for a very long time. I didn't want to speak to anyone, and Mateen was anyway used to being quiet. Finally, when I could hold it no longer, I burst out, "She was the only one who ever understood me, Mateen. And she's gone now." The tears started then and I cried hard. I knew there were people in the park who were staring at me, and Mateen was probably embarrassed. But I couldn't stop the tears. I cried loudly, harshly, my eyes now hurting from crying so much. I hadn't cried this way since Fathima Phuppu had died.

Mateen placed his hand on my arm. I looked at him through the tears, through the haze that had filled my mind. His lips were quivering and he too looked ready to cry. "Don't cry here, Api. Let's go home," he said. Nodding, I got up, my crying having given way to an endless flow of tears. I sniffled and felt Mateen press something into my hand. He was giving me his hanky. My heart warmed at that and for a moment I felt better.

We reached home in the same condition though. My tears refused to stop and Mateen held on to my arm tightly. Ammi was shocked to see my appearance when we reached home. But I couldn't bring myself to say the words to her. I felt overwhelmed with anger towards her. She had never let me visit Mrs Dahlia often enough. She had always stopped me from going there. Maybe I would have been able to help her. Maybe I could have done something. "I suppose you'll be happy now that I will never go to Mrs Dahlia's house ever again," I said bitterly. "She died four months ago."

Ammi looked shocked. She opened her mouth to say something, but then she saw my tear-streaked face and my red eyes and she kept quiet.

We didn't go to Rehana's house that evening. I didn't emerge from my room for lunch or dinner. I wanted to see what Mateen was doing too, but for the moment, I wanted to be selfish as I had always been. I wanted to think about myself and the loss it implied.

After crying all day, when I finally came outside, it was evening. Abbu and Ammi were talking about which new school would be better for Mateen. Abbu saw me but he didn't say anything. I was hungry but not in the mood to eat. I poured a glass of water and sipped it, the cool water soaking my raw throat, providing me some relief. By now, most of my grief had been spent. Now, it was only self-recrimination that I hadn't done anything for her when she had been alive.

I was about to walk back to my room when the phone rang. Ammi and Abbu looked at me expectantly. Feeling annoyed that they wanted me to answer the phone, although they were closer to it, I walked up to it and picked up the receiver. "Hello," I said huskily. My throat hurt. I shut my eyes, wishing whoever it was to speak up soon so I could go back to my room.

"Is this Mateen's house?" a woman's voice asked. She identified herself as Nikhit's mother. "You are his sister, right? We spoke this morning... I'm sorry I behaved that way with you." Her voice broke. "You were right. My son has been abused and

I-I... don't know what to do," she cried softly. "My husband isn't here with us right now. If he finds out, I don't know how he will react."

Momentarily, my grief was once again forgotten. I tried to get back into the mode I was in this morning, but it was still difficult.

"We have to do something about this," I said, trying to sound assertive.

"But what?" she whispered. I held the receiver from my ear and motioned Abbu and Ammi to come over. "It's Nikhit's mother." Ammi looked worried and Abbu frowned. "But I thought we decided..." he started. I motioned him to stop. "Abbu, earlier we didn't have anything to prove it. But maybe we can do something to stop those boys now at least."

When they didn't reply, I spoke into the receiver, "We should complain to the school authorities." I thought for a moment and then added, "But before we do that, we have to get a medical check-up for Nikhit."

Shefali, Nikhit's mother, agreed. But she was sobbing as she spoke. "I can't believe something like this happened to my baby. When you came home and told me this morning, I refused to accept it. But when I went to Nikhit and told him that Mateen had come, he started crying and told me everything."

I tried to console her, but what were mere words pitted against unflinching reality? She said that she would get the medical examination done and then contact us, so we could approach the school together. I agreed and hung up. Forgetting Mrs Dahlia for the time being, I sat down with Abbu and Ammi and tried to convince them that complaining to the school was the correct thing to do. They had decided that enrolling Mateen in a new school was the better option, and refused to listen to me.

I hadn't noticed Mateen come up and stand behind me. When Ammi became quiet and looked beyond me, I turned around and saw Mateen standing there with a pained expression on his face. Abbu let out a deep breath. "Mateen, didn't you go to sleep?"

Mateen didn't answer. "I want to help Nikhit," he said. "He is the one who got hurt. Those b-boys shouldn't be in school. If I-I don't do something, then they might hurt others."

Abbu's and Ammi's face fell. They had wanted the easy way out. They still preferred it. But now, faced with Mateen's wavering courage, they looked uncomfortable.

48

Crime and Punishment

At the all boys' school that Mateen went to, all of us walked quietly to the principal's office the following day. Shefali looked ahead, trying to behave normal but she wasn't feeling it inside. She kept twisting the *pallu* of her saree between her fingers. Ammi and Abbu looked uncomfortable. The lady sitting outside the office at a desk looked at us questioningly. "Do you have an appointment?" she asked. I shook my head. She shook her head too. "You can't meet the principal without an appointment."

I gritted my teeth and told her that it was very important that we meet the principal. She was staring at the computer screen and tapping the keyboard every now and then. "Excuse me, but it's very important for us to meet the principal," I said. Without looking up, she said, "Get an appointment, *ma*. Then we'll see."

Feeling angry, I walked on and pushed the door of the office. The woman looked up and protested angrily, "Hey! You can't do that! Come back!"

But I had already walked inside. The others were still outside. I walked inside the cool, air-conditioned office and saw the principal talking on the phone. He was a balding man, probably in his fifties. He sat on the chair comfortably, his paunch touching the desk. He adjusted his collar as he spoke. He looked at me and narrowed his eyes.

"I'm sorry for barging in like this, but it's something very important." The lady had followed me inside and had caught my elbow roughly. She dragged me backwards. The principal's face seemed to relax, before he continued his conversation on the phone.

"Sir, please listen to me. It's very important."

Finally, the principal replaced the receiver. "Please leave. I don't meet people unless they have an appointment." Saying so, he busied himself with a diary in front of him. The lady had dragged me out till the door. I didn't know what I could say that would catch his attention. Then, just as she was finally trying to push me outside, I said, "If you don't listen to me now, you might have to read about it in tomorrow's newspaper. And I don't think they will show your school in a positive light."

By now, I was outside. Ammi was looking at me, shocked and worried. "Why did you do that, Mehnaz? Now they won't even give us an appointment."

Shefali shook her head. "Yes. You should have waited some more time, na?" Nikhit and Mateen were not looking at each other. Abbu spoke. "You should have let me do the speaking, Mehnaz."

I was thoroughly annoyed by now. "Why didn't anyone do anything then?" I said. The principal's assistant looked at all of us and made a face. "Madam, please take your argument outside. You have disturbed all of us already."

As we walked outside the office, Ammi spoke. "You should have let your father do the talking. Why are you always so reckless, Mehnaz? Now they won't give us a chance to speak." I was fuming, but I kept quiet. We stopped at the corridor. Ammi was about to start berating me again when the principal's assistant came through the door and stopped us.

"Principal wants to meet you. He said only five minutes." There was no time to gauge the surprised reactions on anyone's face as the woman grabbed my arm and asked me to come inside. Abbu moved forward and Shefali spoke. "I have to meet the principal too," she said. The woman shrugged. "Principal wants to meet her."

Once again, I stepped inside the air-conditioned office and shivered. It was November, after all. He didn't ask me to sit down so I quickly told him what I knew, trying not to miss anything in the five minutes he had allotted me. His expression remained blank as he heard me relate everything that had happened to Nikhit, Ankit and what Mateen had witnessed.

He spoke with slow deliberation. "What proof do you have about this?" Feeling shaken that even after hearing this, there was no shock on his face, I told him about Nikhit's medical report. His expression changed slightly then. "Can I see it?" he asked.

For only five seconds, I allowed myself to think about what kind of a man he was. He didn't even ask if Nikhit was okay, or how he was coping with the trauma. He wanted to see the proof. I nodded, and told him that it was outside with Shefali. When he got the report in his hands, he scanned it briefly and then stared at me for a whole minute. I don't know what he was trying to observe. The silence in the air-conditioned thickness of the room was overwhelming. I was dying to say many more things, but I knew that it was best to keep quiet and wait for him to speak.

"What do you want me to do?" he asked finally. Curbing my anger, I spoke calmly, "I want you to expel those boys from the school."

He was silent again. His assistant came in then. She looked at me suspiciously and then at the principal with worry. She hovered around until the principal got annoyed and asked her to bring in my parents, Mateen, Nikhit and Shefali. She threw me an angry glance before leaving.

Everyone looked anxious, except for Mateen. He looked at me, trying to catch my eye and when I finally did, he smiled briefly. His smile eased the tension that had coiled itself around me, and I felt slightly relaxed.

The principal made the boys narrate everything. Shefali broke down when Nikhit started speaking. She turned her face away, trying to hide her sobs. Nikhit faltered and then continued. The principal heard the whole story twice, once from Nikhit and once from Mateen. "Do you know who those boys were?" he asked finally. Mateen nodded. "They're in the eleventh standard, sir," he said softly.

There was an uncomfortable silence. I realised that the principal had not asked anyone of us to sit down. What was going through his mind? Could we expect justice from this man who didn't even extend courtesy to his visitors, traumatised visitors especially? Most probably, those eleventh standard boys were the children of some important people who mattered to him.

"Do you know their names?" he asked Mateen. Mateen shook his head. The principal looked thoughtful. I wondered what he was planning to do.

"You will have to identify them. Only then can I think of a future course of action." Yes, only then will he know if he can take action or not, I thought. I looked at Mateen, wondering how he would react if he had to face those boys again. I couldn't fathom the expression on his face.

"How do you know they were eleventh standard boys?" he asked Mateen suddenly. "They could have been from any other class too."

"The eleventh and twelfth standard uniforms are different, sir," Mateen replied quietly. I cheered for him silently. Why was the principal trying to intimidate him? Obviously because this was a serious matter and it could mean a lot of damage to the reputation of the school. "How do you know they were eleventh and not twelfth standard boys? Their uniforms are the same after all."

Mateen shrugged. Finally, the principal hit a few buttons on his telephone and spoke to his assistant. She came in once again, looking eager. He asked her to get the vice principal to the office.

We spent most of the day answering questions asked by the vice principal and then by some other teachers. The principal remained quiet during all this interaction, watching Mateen and Nikhit's face intently. Abbu and Ammi had gone to sit outside the office. The principal had asked Mateen and Nikhit to sit down finally. Nikhit sat down gingerly and a painful expression flitted across his face. I felt bile rise up. Curling my fist into my palm, I stood next to Shefali, who looked drained. I held her hand, wishing I could lend her some support.

When finally they were satisfied with their questioning, the school authorities decided to call the boys from the eleventh and twelfth standards. "You both have to identify them," the principal said before getting up from his seat.

I looked at the horror on their faces. I wished there was some way we could help the identification take place without the boys having to come face to face with them. I spoke up. The principal was discussing something with his assistant and he didn't hear me speak. I spoke again loudly, "Excuse me, sir." The principal looked at me, irritated. "What is it?" He asked.

"Is there anyway we can let Mateen and Nikhit identify the boys without revealing them to the eleventh standard boys?" I asked hopefully. The principal shook his head. "This is a school, not a police station."

"Then I think we should take this matter to the police," I said suddenly. "This is a matter for them too. You can't just decide arbitrarily whether those boys are guilty or not and punish them accordingly. We came here to complain about them. But I think this is a matter for the police."

The principal looked at me silently. "I think it's better you go and stand outside with your parents," he said finally. I stared at him. "I mean now. Please leave." Mateen turned to look at me, scared.

Feeling shaky, I told the principal, "I'm sorry, I'm not leaving here without my brother. I haven't done anything for you to ask me to leave this way."

His face stiffened and I knew that he was angry now. But something inside me urged me on. I couldn't abandon Mateen at the mercy of those boys. I couldn't just walk away simply. He didn't say anything.

There was a knock on the door. The assistant opened it. It was the first eleventh standard boy who had come for identification. He didn't know, of course, the reason why he had been called. He stepped in and stood there quietly. The principal motioned him to leave. I noticed that Mateen looked stricken. Nikhit wasn't even looking at the boys. One by one they came in. After nearly eight boys, a boy stepped in. He walked in with a swagger and stopped short when he saw Nikhit and Mateen. Mateen stiffened and I saw anger on the boy's face. Then he looked at the principal and that anger was replaced with fear. This boy was asked to wait outside. When Mateen had identified all the three boys, the principal asked them to come inside.

I felt hatred surging inside me so deeply that if I had a sharp instrument in my hand, I would have gleefully plunged it into their hearts. The sturdiest of the boys spoke up when he entered. "It's all lies, sir. We didn't do anything."

The principal was quiet. Another boy spoke, "These two are talking rubbish. They don't know what they are saying." The other boy was silent and looked at the two other boys annoyed. He motioned them to be quiet, but the damage had been done.

"What are you two talking about?" the principal asked them. "Can you explain? I didn't accuse you two of anything. So why are you defending yourself?"

"I... we... I... uh..." the first boy mumbled. He looked at the ground. I looked at Mateen and saw the frozen expression on his face. Nikhit had slid down low in his seat. If he had shifted any lower, he would have slipped down under the table. I glanced at Shefali and saw the anger on her face.

The principal turned to us. "Take your son and this other boy and go outside please. I have to speak to these three boys alone." Shefali stood rooted to the spot and didn't move. Mateen got up but Nikhit was still sitting. I shook Shefali's hand. I wanted to hear what the principal would say to those boys, but I didn't think Mateen would be able to bear being in the same room with them. We stepped outside and saw Ammi and Abbu looking at us, questions in their eyes. I watched Mateen and Nikhit find places to sit down.

Both of them should be discussing cricket, or G I Joes, but instead their lives had been marred by a single horrific incident that threatened to take away their childhood. "We need to take these boys to a psychiatrist," Shefali said as fresh tears filled her eyes. I nodded. I didn't know how Abbu and Ammi would take to that suggestion. A psychiatrist for them was just a *paagalon ka doctor*. They would probably be horrified.

She sat down near the two of them. I went up to Ammi and Abbu and told them that Mateen had identified the boys. They looked uncomfortable and Ammi even looked scared. "Have you done the right thing, Mehnaz?" she asked. "What if those boys try and do something to Mateen?"

I shrugged. "Ammi, I don't want Mateen to live in constant fear of something that might happen in the future. Those boys have to be punished. That is what's important."

Ammi didn't look convinced. Half an hour later, the principal's assistant came outside and said that the principal wanted to meet me and Shefali. Feeling nervous, I walked inside with Shefali. She was still looking shaky. The three boys had been sent to another room. I felt thankful that I didn't have to look at their hateful faces.

"These three firmly deny they have done anything like this. The medical report is a proof and if Mateen agrees to bear witness to whatever happened on the spot, maybe we can do something about it," the principal said to us. I looked at Shefali. What could we say?

"Sir, how do you plan to punish them?" I asked him. He looked at me and spoke wearily,

"If they are guilty, which I think they are, then they will be expelled from this school."

"What about the police complaint?" I asked. "Your punishment isn't enough. Their crime should receive a proper punishment, sir."

"I can't take this matter to the police. It will mean bad publicity for the school," he said quietly. I was dissatisfied with his explanation, but I was exhausted. We had been standing for nearly the whole day and my head was aching badly. I hadn't slept well the previous night. I looked at Shefali, wondering if she would protest. But she hadn't said a word.

We left the school that day, a very quiet group. Abbu dropped Shefali at her place and we went on towards our home. In the last two days, life seemed to have changed drastically. Just two days ago, Abbu and Ammi were so happy about the impending marriage. And now, it was the last thing on their mind. I didn't care, really. After all, Imtiaz had given me six months.

Those six months were going to tick away into oblivion so soon that before I knew it, my life would have changed forever. As we passed the lane that led to Mrs Dahlia's house, I felt something grip me. My desire to do something was always so intangible. But today, as I rested my head on the back rest of the seat and closed my eyes, I could see Mrs Dahlia pottering around in her house, bringing me plates of butter cookies or cake. I could see her sitting with me, giving me priceless advice. Advice which actually was most often the practical solution but it would have eluded me totally. In the back seat of Abbu's ageing Maruti, I saw my life's desire with sudden clarity. I wanted to be a writer.

Why? I didn't know, but I could only remember Mrs Dahlia telling me that I should do that which I truly loved doing. Writing was one of the only things that gave me an outlet for my emotions. Writing was the only thing that shifted the focus until the picture was clear enough to touch and leave an impression. Writing was the only thing I could do without anyone objecting and destroying my dreams. Writing it was going to be.

49

Phone Calls

There was no news from Mateen's school. We decided that we would send him to school only when we heard something from the principal. Mateen sat in his room arranging jigsaw puzzles, which Abbu had bought for him, and reading comics.

The first phone call came at 11.30 in the morning. Ammi was in the kitchen and she had turned on the electric chimney. She couldn't hear the phone. Abbu had gone to his shop. The hall was darkened as Ammi had forgotten to pull the curtains. I picked up the receiver and said, "Hello."

There was a pause and then Imtiaz spoke. "Mehnaz!"

"Hey!" I whispered. "What happened?"

"My mother refuses to give me the time till six months," he said. "She says that I should either marry you when she says or to marry whoever she chooses."

"But that's absurd!" I said loudly. Then, lowering my voice, I spoke again. "Why is she in such a hurry? What will happen in six months?"

"Well... I can't really explain it. So I called to tell you that it's got to be December."

"But Imtiaz," I protested, "My parents have to agree to it. They may have a lot of preparations to do. How can they get me married in just two months?"

"How do you know what they are capable of? If they want to, it can happen," he said calmly. I was getting angry. Why were he and his mother such insufferably stubborn people? "But why, Imtiaz? I thought we had decided this and..."

"It's either yes or no, Mehnaz. Answer me, please," he said. I felt cornered and extremely frustrated. "You have to tell me why she wants it in December and not after a few more months. What difference will a few months make?" I said breathing heavily.

"My parents are going for *Hajj* and they want to get me married before they leave," he said finally. I didn't understand. What did that have to do with anything? When I didn't respond, he spoke again urgently. "Mehnaz, hurry up and answer me."

"How can you even ask me like this? You were the one who wanted to marry me in the first place. If you want to marry me, then it's up to you to take it ahead. Anyhow, even if I agree for this December plan of your mother's, my parents won't agree. If this was going to be such a sham from the beginning, your mother shouldn't have come to my place at all," I whispered heatedly.

He didn't answer. I heard a click. That was it. He had hung up without saying anything. I stared at the receiver, not willing to believe that he had just cut the call. What did this imply? That he was no longer interested in marrying me?

I put the receiver back in its place calmly. He would call again. Maybe he was just joking. After all, he was the one who had insisted on all this in the first place. I sat down near the phone and looked at the blank wall ahead me. I watched some TV. When an hour passed, I realised this wasn't a joke. I was so desperately waiting for his call that I had decided to agree to whatever he was going to ask.

I should have taken the number of the place where he was staying in Bangalore. I didn't know how to contact him. As the minutes moved slowly, I realised that I hardly knew him. I didn't know him well enough to predict anything about him. So, if he was serious, I hoped his parents had the courtesy to at least call up my parents and inform them that they were calling it off.

I felt a heavy weight at the pit of my stomach. My throat felt like I had swallowed something greasy. What if his mother told my parents that I had met Imtiaz and had bargained for more time? How much did his mother know about my meetings with him on the terrace? What if she told everything to my mother? There were so many things I wished I knew about him. I got up feeling broken and dismayed. Should I have trusted him so much? I had really thought of him as a friend and I had told him so many things about myself, my family, and even Mateen.

Maybe I should be thankful that I wasn't getting married to Imtiaz. But the disappointment was so acute, I realised that I had taken things for granted. Still, I tried to convince myself that he was too stubborn, too bossy, and even condescending at times. Yet, the pain wouldn't go. All along I had wondered if I was in love with him. Sometimes, I thought the answer was yes, and at other times, there was a wavering no. Now that I wasn't going to get married to him, I think the answer suddenly leaned towards yes.

I had to do something, I thought frantically. Anything. I quickly dialled his Chennai number before I realised what I was doing. When the phone rang, a plan formulated itself in my mind. A man answered. I took a deep breath and asked for Imtiaz. The man said that he was in Bangalore. I asked for his contact number in Bangalore. There was silence on the other end. "Why?" the man asked suspiciously. "It's rather urgent. It's about his new contract. If I don't speak to him now, he may lose it." I had no idea what I was talking about. I don't think hardware businessmen even talked about contracts or such. Still, something in my voice must have convinced the man, for he reeled off a number.

After hanging up, I called the number I had jotted down hurriedly. My hands shook as I held the receiver. I had no idea what I was going to say, but I knew I was going to improvise as I had done with the last call. When a woman answered, my courage collapsed. She was probably his mother.

"May I speak to Imtiaz, please?" I asked in my most polished and refined English. The woman asked, "Who is it? What is your name?" I faltered. Then, continuing with the same story, I told the woman about an important contract for Imtiaz. She, however, wasn't fooled as easily. "What contract?" she asked, her voice rising. What should I say? "It's a business contract, madam. I need to speak to him urgently. I have other calls to make also," I said, hoping that would prevent her from asking more questions.

"Okay," she said gruffly. When I heard Imtiaz's voice over the phone, I felt relief gush through me. "Hi!" I whispered. There was silence. "Who's this?" he asked cautiously. Maybe his mother was standing there too. "It's me," I whispered. There was silence once more. I was afraid he had hung up.

"It's Mehnaz," I whispered once more.

"What is it?" he asked curtly.

Tamping down my irritation, I spoke quickly without realising what I was possibly committing myself to. "I'm willing to marry you whenever you ask me, Imtiaz," I said. I felt foolish saying it. It wasn't like me. I mean, this girl so eager to get married... she wasn't me. Still, this wasn't the time to ponder the question.

When there was silence once more, I started getting angry. "What? Can't you answer?" I asked him.

He sighed loudly. "I'm sorry, but I can't," he said. I couldn't believe it. "Can't?" I asked stupidly. Suddenly he started speaking. Maybe his mother had left the room.

"Look, my mother was never really for this whole proposal. She asked for your hand only and only because I forced her. When I told her that it might be at least six more months before I could marry, she got angry. It seems she was planning on getting me married in December so she and Abba could go for *Hajj.*"

I cut him in the middle. "But I'm willing to na..."

He sighed once more. The sigh sawed through my heart. I knew this was bad news and I sat down. "My mother had set her heart on getting me married to my cousin in Bangalore. We're staying in their house. She had agreed to see you only because I had asked her. When she heard that you wanted to wait for six months, she got angry and said that we had to call it off. She's really angry that I preferred to listen to what you want instead of what she wants, Mehnaz."

I digested this. "Well, what's wrong with that, Imtiaz? Why shouldn't you listen to me?" I asked haltingly. This wasn't the reaction that I had been expecting from him. "How come you never told me about this cousin before? Did you know this all along?" I asked him.

He paused before speaking. "Yes, I have known about this for a long time. Ammi had told me about this when I was fifteen. But still, I couldn't stop myself from meeting you. Each time I met you, I grew more intrigued by you. You were like none of the other girls I had ever known. After our last meeting, I spoke to my mother about you. I told her that I wanted to marry only you. She was shocked and she refused to speak to me for a few days. But Abba was on my side and we somehow convinced her to speak to your mother."

I listened quietly. My ears were humming from holding the receiver so tightly against my ear. "She came to your house and she saw you. She even liked you. But she didn't like the fact that we arranged for it together."

"What do you mean?" I asked him suspiciously.

"We-ell... Ammi wanted to know how I had your phone number and address so conveniently. So I had to tell her about our meeting on the terrace. She wasn't happy to hear about it. Still, she proceeded."

I quailed at the thought of his mother learning everything about our terrace meetings, suddenly feeling ashamed, though I hadn't done anything wrong. What if she told my mother about it? Before I could let that thought take root, he continued.

"Ammi was really angry when she found out that I had spoken with you and that you wanted to wait for six more months. You don't know my mother, Mehnaz. She demanded to know what the reason was. When I told her that you wanted some time for yourself, especially to adjust to the situation that your family is going through, she wanted to know about that too. So I told her about Mateen's incident at school."

"You told her about Mateen? What all do you tell your mother, Imtiaz? Do you tell her everything that happens to you?"

"Shut up, Mehnaz," he growled. I had never heard him speak so rudely before.

"So what did your mother say then? Is that why she refuses to have me as her daughter-in-law?"

He was silent. Meaning, it was true. How ridiculous! I didn't even know why I was trying to reason with him. "Imtiaz, why should that affect anything? Mateen just witnessed the whole incident. Allah forbid, even if he had been the victim, why should that make any difference?"

"Mehnaz, she just can't stand you. She thinks your mother has given you too much freedom and she hates the very qualities that I like about you. I don't think our marriage will be very peaceful or happy. And now, after hearing about your brother... she thinks your family scandal will follow our family too."

Before I could tell him what I thought about his mother's narrow-minded ideas, he continued speaking.

"She's fixed my marriage with Shireen in December. I'm getting engaged to her the day after tomorrow."

I couldn't speak. "Hello? Are you there?" he asked. I still couldn't speak. "Mehnaz, I know I told you that I really loved you. And truthfully speaking, you are the only girl I have ever had such strong feelings for. But if you had just answered yes in the morning, this would have been our engagement. I still can't believe this is happening, but there's nothing more I can do. I did my best to convince Ammi, but she just refuses to listen. Even Abba feels that getting me married to you isn't such a good idea. Without any support from anyone, I have to give in. Anyhow, I don't think we were meant to be together. You need someone who can really understand the dreams you have. I hope you find him."

I dropped the receiver and walked back to my room numbly. I just wanted to collapse on the bed, scream, cry, and bring the roof down.

"If only I had said yes in the morning."

Somewhere inside me I was glad that this had happened. Somewhere inside, a small part of me was able to rationalise the situation and see the good that came out from it. That Imtiaz was not really worthy of me. That I was better off without him. Yet, that small part was unable to outmanoeuvre the bigger part of me that had realised just twenty minutes ago that I was in love with him.

I wanted to run to my mother and cling to her and cry. Just, what had stopped me from doing it? Well, firstly my mother was uncomfortable with physical displays of affection from her own children. And secondly, I would have to explain to her why I was crying so much. Mrs Dahlia's loss cut into me deeply. She would have understood. Who could I go to and pour my heart out? I didn't want to call my friends. Suddenly, this didn't seem like something they would be really interested in. After college, we had drifted apart.

Rehana? Would she understand my pain? I stopped mentally listing the people who I could confide in and entered the bathroom. I opened the tap so water gushed into the bucket and cried loudly. I stood near the mirror and watched myself cry. My misery was deep. Half an hour later, I was able to contain myself. I stepped outside and wiped my face with a towel. I sat at the edge of the bed and let my thoughts wander vacantly, aimlessly. What was going to happen? How would my parents react? Just now they had faced the situation with Mateen. How would they cope up with such a big disappointment? That was what I was turning out to be, to my mother. A huge disappointment.

I pushed the thought away and got up resolutely. I wasn't a disappointment to anyone. Maybe Allah had other plans for me. Maybe I wasn't meant to marry Imtiaz. But marrying a complete stranger made me shiver a bit. I wasn't going to think about marriage at all for now. I sat at my desk and pulled out my diary to pour out my feelings, my anger and my rage.

What sort of person was this Shireen? Probably very pretty, I thought. That's why he didn't sound so disappointed. I shut my eyes as painful memories came back of him jumping across the terraces to meet me. I had felt so special then.

For girls like me, cocooned in the safety of their homes, dealing with heartbreak wasn't something that happened regularly. Yet, when that safety is breached and hurt overtakes all the other feelings, what can one do? I wrote furiously for an hour, not realising what I was writing. I had to let it out or the frustration would simply kill me.

I had no idea what the time was. For all that had happened, I wasn't going to pine over him. Not me. No.

When the phone rang once more, I felt fear lodge itself inside me. It had to be his mother calling to give us the bad news. I got up unsteadily and walked outside slowly. Ammi was at the telephone.

Mateen had come out from his room and I stood beside him. Who was it? Ammi had turned pale. Was she going to take ill because of what Imtiaz's mother had said? I felt like strangling Imtiaz and his mother.

Ammi replaced the receiver. She looked ashen, ready to collapse. "What is it Ammi?" I asked her fearfully, rushing to her and held her icy hands. "Ammi!" I shouted, now fully scared. "What is it? Mateen, call Abbu right now. Something is happening to Ammi!"

Ammi dropped to the floor. I managed to steady her. She swayed before saying only one word, "Zulekha."

50

Once More, the Terrace

Once again, like many years ago when we took the car and rushed to Vellore in the middle of the night, Abbu took the car out. This time, however, there was less urgency in his actions. He calmly checked the oil and water level in the car and then came inside, telling us to get ready.

Ammi had just stopped moving. She sat on the floor while Mateen and I rushed around, packing clothes in an overnight bag. Finally, I dropped down beside Ammi and handed her *burka* to her. She took it from me and put her hands inside it and then her head, looking rather awkward in the process. I helped her get up, and she straightened her burka and looked around.

I decided to think about everything that had happened once we were in the car. Right now, thinking about anything would make me stop in my tracks and I just wanted to sit down somewhere and have a good cry. When the house was locked and all the windows closed, I handed the key to Ammi. She wouldn't take it from me. Her hands were closed into a tight fist. Finally, I gave it to Abbu, who gave it back to me with a small sound of irritation. "Keep it in your handbag," he said gruffly.

Ammi sat in the back seat, with me. That left Mateen to sit in front with Abbu. No one questioned her behaviour. After all, her only sister, her only living relation, had died. And in a most horrific way. The stove had burst, exploding in her face, and with her, her son too had died, trying to save her.

I leaned my head back against the head rest and closed my eyes. What plans we make in life and what plans Allah has in store for us... there was no way to know. Ammi had stood by her decision to ignore her sister stoically, with more pride and righteousness than had been necessary. If she had her way, she would have never entered that house again to see her sister. But now, Allah had proved her wrong. She was going to enter that house and she was going to see her sister. Ammi had regrets. I knew that with certainty as she started crying slowly, words escaping from her tears, mingling into a mumbled litany.

I wanted to comfort her, but she had withdrawn into a cold, tight shell and refused to let any of us reach out and enclose her with the warmth of life. Still, I tried holding her cold hand but she shook me off. Finally, exhausted with my own crying a little while back, I shut my eyes. Two hours ago, Imtiaz's betrayal had seemed almost like the end of the world. I had felt like a martyr and I wanted comfort. Now, I wondered how Khala's daughter was doing. No one knew how she was. Was she injured? If not, how was she coping with the loss of her mother and brother? What was going to happen to her? Would Ammi let her come back with us? What would she do here?

The thoughts whirled around in my head as Abbu sped away on the highway. The towns and cities blurred in front of my eyes, and I wondered how Mateen was doing. What was he feeling now? His situation in school hadn't been fully resolved yet. But we had taken a step in the right direction.

When we entered Vellore, my eyes spotted Sundaram Jewellers and something inside me seemed to squeeze, little by little. Anger at Imtiaz wasn't good enough. I wasn't capable of rational thinking at the moment, but some part of me was relieved also. After all, I had not pursued him so relentlessly and I was spared living my life with a man who couldn't make decisions for himself.

Abbu parked the car at the usual spot. He spotted a rickshaw puller, lounging nearby, smoking a *beedi*. He hailed him and told the address. Ammi and I sat in the rickshaw while Abbu and Mateen walked on ahead. It was so strange. It wasn't like we were going to Ammi's sister's funeral. It was more like we were attending some distant relation's funeral, with polite civility.

When the rickshaw stopped, I got down and held my hand out to Ammi. She ignored my hand and got down blindly. Steadying herself, she walked to the front door. I held my breath instinctively. She looked at the house and then finally walked inside. We followed.

Inside, there were a few people sitting quietly. An overdose of *agarbatti* fumes filled the air, trying to mask another, more putrid smell. I felt like gagging, but controlling myself I walked in with Ammi. Khala and her son were laid out in the centre of the same hall where I had sat last time. All the rituals were over. They were both laid out in wicker coffins, their bodies wrapped completely.

A few women sat nearby and Khala's daughter sat leaning against a wall. Her eyes were puffy and tears rolled down steadily. She didn't react when she saw us. After all, she didn't even know who we were. Ammi walked towards the bodies and I held her hand. She shook it off imperiously and got nearer.

We had reached just in time. They were going to take away the bodies for burial before *Maghrib namaz*. A woman who stood near the coffin saw Ammi and came to her, tears streaming down her eyes. "Shabana! See your sister! What a wretched fate she had! What a way to die!"

Ammi flinched. The woman was dragging her towards the coffins. Some of the men who had been standing there stopped her. They were going to cover the coffin. "You have to see her," the woman moaned, "You have to." Before anyone could stop her, she had uncovered the face of the body nearest to her. I turned away horrified. Ammi stood still, and then reached out and clutched my hand.

When finally both the bodies had been taken away, Ammi cried. Tears seemed to well from her endlessly as she hiccupped and cried. The woman who had dragged her to see Khala was Ammi's cousin. I had never seen her before because Ammi had severed her relations with everyone in her life before marriage. Her marriage had given her a new birth. The relatives who had been a part of her life earlier, had been forgotten. Still, I remember she used to send money and clothes every Ramzan to her poor relatives as *zakath.*

Khala's daughter – I didn't even remember her name – was still sitting against the wall and sobbing. I didn't know what to tell her. What could one say? Losing the only people whom she knew and loved and to be left all alone in the world... I would never understand what she was feeling.

I went to her and laid my hand on her arm. She looked up, but she didn't recognise me. Ammi saw me and then she too came up to her. She sat down beside her and stroked her arm. "Razia?" she said softly. The girl looked up. She seemed to recognise Ammi and fresh tears appeared in her eyes. Still, she was uncertain about what to do, whether to embrace Ammi or not. I felt embarrassed, awkward, caught sitting between them.

Ammi moved closer to her, and Razia finally collapsed in Ammi's arms, crying loudly. "Don't cry. I'm here. You'll live with us." Razia looked up and shook her head. "You can't live here alone," Ammi told her gently, her voice breaking. I sat back and noticed something that had eluded me all this while. The *salwar kameez* that Razia was wearing was one of my old ones. It was a pretty pink georgette *salwar kameez* which I had worn for Eid a few years back but now it was brown and black in places and one corner of the sleeve was torn. Sometimes, I would return from college and see my old favourites missing from my cupboard. Despite fighting with my mother, she would insist that after I had worn them as much as I could, someone else could enjoy them. Here's where some of them came, apparently. I felt no bitterness now. I was happy that despite her anger with her sister, Ammi hadn't forgotten her totally.

Mateen had gone with Abbu to the burial ground. I was tired and I desperately wanted to sleep. When the men returned from the funeral, there were only a handful of people left in the house. The kitchen had been totally destroyed and I didn't have the courage to walk in there.

It was nearly 10.30 when Ammi asked me to wear my burka. I looked up, surprised. All the people had left. Only Abbu, Mateen, Ammi, Razia, and I were there. "Mehnaz, pack some of Razia's clothes in a bag. She's coming with us right now." Razia shook her head vehemently. "No arguments, Razia," Ammi said firmly. I was glad Ammi was back in charge.

I almost wanted to hand over the house keys to her from my handbag, but this wasn't the time. Ammi locked up the old, crumbling house and handed the huge key to Abbu. Mateen looked at the key with wonder. It was bigger than his palm. We slowly walked through the rubbish-infested *gallis,* Abbu leading us, until we reached home.

That night, Abbu and Mateen slept in the hall. Ammabi slept in her room, and the three of us squeezed together in the other room. I closed my eyes and thought back to the events today. Right from the first phone call, it had been only disaster. Would things have been different if I had said 'yes' the first time I spoke to Imtiaz? I turned over and saw Ammi staring at the ceiling. Razia had fallen asleep. Ammi was sleeping between both of us. She saw me turn over and lifted a strand of hair that had fallen on my face. I was surprised at her gentle gesture. I felt angry when I thought of the hurt she was going to face in the days to come because of Imtiaz.

"I didn't hate her totally, you know," she whispered suddenly. I was wide awake. Ammi was talking about Khala. "Yes, I told you that I couldn't stand to see her, and it was true. You don't know how it used to feel seeing her sometimes in that house. That's why I vowed never to go there again. But every month, I sent her money for her expenses. Sometimes, I used to even wish that things were different. There were so many ifs... if her husband hadn't died, if her in-laws had been more supportive, if he hadn't come from Hyderabad... I don't know... I'm saying all this because maybe, she would have had a better life. Sometimes I shudder when I think of the fate she suffered. It could have been me too!"

I turned around in the bed and raised myself on my elbows. "What do you mean?" I asked her. "Well, our lives were different because of destiny. Destiny is responsible for too many things here, Mehnaz. You have to realise that. What I am today is because of destiny."

She laid her hand across her forehead and closed her eyes. I lowered myself on the bed and thought about my life and those of the people close to me. I had to agree. Destiny was everything. No matter how well we had planned, there it was, ready to pull the carpet from under our feet.

One question lingered in my mind, hovering at the edges of my consciousness. Would Ammi have been so benevolent if Khala's son had survived? Would she have promised to look after him and decide something good for his future too? I had no answer to that. It is only when we are faced with the actual situation that we can react and realise the kind of people we are and were meant to be.

****

Life changes and yet it doesn't. Here we were, heading back to Bangalore, this time with Razia. She was going to live with us, and Abbu and Ammi were going to get her married. I heard them talking about it at breakfast. They said that as soon as my marriage was out of the way, they would start preparations for hers. I felt sad at the disappointment they would have to face. And here was Ammabi, still living, still coping. She refused to come with us to Bangalore even now. Maybe the next time we came to Vellore, it would be for her funeral I thought irreverently.

I stood on the terrace, the cool wind blowing against my hair. Here it was that so many things had started. Here, Rehana, Basheer, Imtiaz, and even Aasia... our lives had entwined briefly like kite strings bracing themselves before the big fight. One by one, they had all fallen along the way.

Basheer was the first one to go from our lives. I still harboured the hope that I would meet him one day and I vowed to myself that if that happened, I would treat him better and with more respect.

Aasia, the girl I could have mentored and given her something better in life, the girl who I had hated... I had watched her leave with great satisfaction. But today, an uneasiness gripped my heart. I realised how selfish and mean I had been to her and it was too late to change anything about it.

Rehana, my cousin who had slowly drifted away from me, from being my closest confidante to someone I rarely thought about – I had no clue what went on in her life, what was important to her or why. Sadness at what we had lost was definitely there.

Imtiaz, the boy who had defined the reason why I had loved coming to the terrace in Vellore... there was nothing I could do about him. I looked at his empty terrace, and willed away the pang that gripped my heart.

I looked at the mountains in the distance, at the houses where some women were drying chillies and rice. A flash of colour erupted when a woman dropped the cloth she was holding and all the dried chillies fell on the terrace. I heard another woman berating her, her voice carrying all the way to our terrace.

I felt a hand on my arm. I looked up surprised. It was Mateen. “Come, Api. Let’s go. Abbu is waiting,” he said. I looked at him, and felt like I was seeing him for the first time. All the people I had known on the terrace were gone, each pursuing their own life. But there were others too. Others like Mateen who had been there with me all along, and some like Razia who had entered now. They too would go and life would continue. And yet this didn’t feel like the ending. It was a beginning of sorts.

I took a deep breath and looked at the dusty terrace in the warm afternoon. Maybe I wouldn’t come back to this terrace again. Or maybe I would.

❖❖❖